Yellow Jack

Yellow Jack

JOSH RUSSELL

W. W. NORTON & COMPANY

NEW YORK • LONDON

Title page illustration: Glenalvin J. Goodridge, 1829–1867, unidentified
mortuary portrait—daguerreotype, ca. 1845. From *A History of Black
Photographers,* edited by Deborah Willis.

For information about permission to reproduce selections from
this book, write to Permissions, W. W. Norton & Company, Inc.,
500 Fifth Avenue, New York, NY 10110

The text of this book is composed in Sabon
with the display set in Cezanne and Engravers Roman
Composition by Julia Druskin
Manufacturing by Haddon Craftsmen, Inc.
Book design by Chris Welch

Library of Congress Cataloging-in-Publication Data

Russell, Josh.
    Yellow jack / Josh Russell.
        p.   cm.
    ISBN 0-393-04768-7
    I. Title.
PS3568.U76677Y4   1999
813'.54—dc21   99-21657
                                                        CIP

W. W. Norton & Company, Inc., 500 Fifth Avenue, New York, N.Y. 10110
www.wwnorton.com

W. W. Norton & Company Ltd., 10 Coptic Street, London WC1A 1PU

1 2 3 4 5 6 7 8 9 0

For Kathryn,
for my parents, Linda and Terry Russell,
and for Matt

One-thousand-and-one thank-yous to Kathryn Pratt, Michael Koch, Joanna Scott, Geri Thoma, and Elizabeth Clementson. Many thanks as well to Alane Salierno Mason for her wise advice, encouragement, and patience.

༉

A portion of this novel appeared in *Epoch* and in *New Stories from the South: The Year's Best, 1998.*

Yellow Jack

🔮 🔮 🔮

Plate 1—Louis Jacques Mandé Marchand, *1845. Half-plate daguerreotype.*

IT IS A MYSTERY why those chronicling the history of photography have chosen to ignore Claude Marchand. This assistant of L.J.M. Daguerre (after whom the subject of this portrait was named) was the first American daguerreian. Marchand opened his New Orleans studio in the fall of 1838, and in November of the same year he staged the first public display of daguerreotypes. That these dates precede Daguerre's official announcement of August 19th, 1839, may be explained by the fact that Claude Marchand, a name so common in the Paris records of the day that an accurate biography is impossible, once admitted that he and Daguerre had been working on the invention together, and that after a spat with Daguerre he left the city "with one of the earliest cameras and as many of the silvered brass plates as [his] pockets could hold." Out of fear of prosecution, or out of an odd respect for the European rights to the miracle that would lead Paul Delaroche to declare on the event of its unveiling, "From today, painting is dead!", Marchand made his way via sail to New Orleans. There he and the marvel he called *soliotype* were warmly received by the French community and the city at large.

Of the hubbub that arose when Daguerre presented his camera obscura and its shimmering trapped moments to the Académies des Sciences et des Beaux-Arts, the New Orleans *Bee* opined, "It is no great surprise that the Europeans are aflutter about a miracle we have had for these many months. Once again America stands at the forefront of Science and Art."

Marchand flourished in the '40s as a photographer of varied stripe but he was best known as a portraitist. It was not purely novelty and the vanity of New Orleanians that led to his success. During the yellow fever epidemics that annually plagued the city it was common for doctors to recommend that the very ill be transported to Marchand's studio so that a last portrait could be made. In the middle four months of 1845, one of the worst summers of yellow fever the city ever saw, Marchand estimated photographing over 400 terminally ill and recently deceased fever victims.

(For an example of his landscape work see Pl. 45—*Trees Being Felled Near Lake Pontchartrain to Combat the Yellow Fever*.)

Because of his constant contact with the mercury vapor used to develop daguerreotype images Marchand had lost all of his teeth and was reportedly mad for the final months of his life. A short note in a *Daily Tropic* gossip column written by Felix Moissenet describes the day Marchand closed his studio: "The artist flew into a rage and struck a woman when she, made moronic by grief, claimed the infant in a memorial portrait was not her child. He then sent a long line of portrait sitters away after standing on a chair and explaining to them that they were philistines and fools, none of them worthy of his art." His wife died in childbirth a week later, and Moissenet's column reports that Marchand spent his last hours wandering the streets "crazed by grief." On the morning of September 22nd, 1845, his body was pulled from the turning basin of the Carondelet Canal. He was twenty-five years old.

It is assumed that this portrait of his son is the last daguerreotype he made. It holds the only known image of Claude Marchand, his right hand. The hand rests gently on the infant Louis's head, steadying the child before the camera.

❦

FOURTEEN YEARS AFTER my mother died giving birth to me my father followed her into the dirt because he paid a girl to fellate him in a shop's doorway. Halfway through the act she clenched his balls in her fist and mimicked the whistle of a swallow. He wept while her friends came from their hiding places at the signal and ransacked his dropped pockets. When my father split the girl's lip with his kneecap, one of her comrades stuck a short, rusted kitchen knife into his belly. That night I answered a frantic knocking and found him standing with the knife quivering in his navel, an apron of blood over his lap. He lived just a week after the doctor came and jerked out the stubby blade.

Before he was stabbed my father and I spent our Sundays in the city's gardens and parks admiring the clean lines of paths and the precise curves of flower beds. He was a cobbler, and we dedicated evenings and early mornings to making our already orderly shop even more so. He could not stand clutter and he taught me to hate it. We walked with our eyes on our shoes. When I looked up, I saw the city as he saw it—a mess. He taught me logic, and to him the labyrinth of God and Hell and all the rest was illogical and as much a mess as was the city of Paris.

"Death is no more than a line drawn through a man's name," he told me one day while we watched a gardener pepper a furrow with poppy seeds. His wound changed his views. There were blue flames when he closed his eyes and he was sure his pain would never end. Even full of laudanum he would promise me Hell was waiting for us, we all deserved it and it simmered below. I was still convinced there was nothing inside a man but twists of guts. Death, I assured myself in the kitchen, was a line through a man's name. Above me in his bed my father yelled "A mouthful of nettles!" as if he could hear my thoughts, and suddenly I shared his visions of fiery mazes, meals of thistle, streets paved with red-hot cobbles.

The day he died my father grabbed my wrist. "Vanity of vanities, saith the Preacher; vanity of vanities, all is vanity. What profit hath man of all his labor wherein he laboureth under the sun?" He looked at me as if he wanted an answer. "To spend your life making another man look ten years younger and fifty pounds slimmer is vanity. God wants you to be a cobbler. There is no vanity in a shoe."

A portrait painter had come to my father's shop and noticed, tacked up above the laces and tongues, one of my drawings of trees. I was a prodigy, he swore. I begged my father to let me apprentice myself to the man. In three weeks the artist had me painting still-lifes with a steady hand. He needed only to tell me that the face was five eyes across—a third where the nose hangs, an extra from ear to eye socket—and I became a portraitist of high talent, or so he claimed. I adored brushes and the palette with its thumb-hole; I loved poking an egg's yolk and watching it ooze a slow line of viscous yellow. I adored the way things could be left out in a painting, others made more vivid. It was only when my father died and I could no longer pay for my lessons that the truth came out—I was competent, but no prodigy. My painter had a small army of similar students.

Debts took the shop from me. Sure then that my father had been right and that my true calling was hammering shoes, I found a job with another cobbler, a kind man named Richard, an old rival of my father's. I suffered only a week before he said to me, "I see the way your eyes dim when you speak to customers. You should never do what you hate. What do you love?" I told him about the flush that came over me when my brush replicated the curve of an aubergine's purple skin, about the joy of transforming a bowl of fruit into a single pear. I told him about my father's threats. He closed the shop and took me to a café, bought me sweet rolls and let me cry over my dead father, the first time I'd been allowed such weakness.

Richard made Louis Jacques Mandé Daguerre's boots, and because of his cobbler's recommendation, Daguerre took me in as a houseboy.

In less than one year I graduated from carrying Daguerre's coal and fetching his groceries to serving as his assistant. He introduced me to art in ways my painter never had. My former teacher's was an art of imitation and reverence for what was loved by critics. Daguerre's was art of spite and overthrow. He taught me to see the flaws in paintings others considered perfect. Daguerre was father to the life my true father had cursed on his death bed. He introduced me to poets, sculptors, prostitutes. When he found I knew no Latin he was so upset he paid a tutor to pour the language into me. I read Horace to my new father and we laughed together at the most obscene poems.

I was a split boy, one side God-like, tallying every sinful move, the other paying what may have been the same girl my father had paid to perform the same service on what may have been the same dirty doorstep, my friend Claude, a tailor's apprentice, standing lookout for thieves and waiting his turn. Most days pleasure outweighed my dead father's promised punishments—I was fifteen years old and stronger than threats—but there were times I found myself unable to breathe under the guilt, then Daguerre would offer a party, a glass of wine, an edition of Ovid, the name of a new girl to be found at Madame Sigrid's, and I would be cured.

Daguerre's diorama was loved by all who saw it, but his urge to make sunlight draw a picture was so strong that the praise in the papers and the money he made from diorama shows meant nothing to him. Late into the night he and I toiled like alchemists, boiling quicksilver and iodine, soaking paper in albumen, brushing bromide on squares of plated copper. Faint forms appeared, their edges like smoke. Only because we'd aimed the camera obscura at the apple could we recognize the blurred globe.

One morning the answer came by accident. A silvered plate of copper had been stored in a cabinet in which I'd hidden a broken thermometer. An image resting invisibly on the plate was touched by mercury fumes and appeared as if by magic—a sunflower hung its round head.

We stood amazed by the sight. I saw instantly that a man's faults would be impossible to hide if his portrait was made the same way. A weak chin would be weak, small ears small. I fell in love with that sunflower, with its heart of seeds and its petal-tongues. It was more perfect than a painting. Even the best painting adds something to the subject, either by its flawed attempt at replication or by vanity's demand that nature be expanded, but the picture the sun had drawn had no such flaw.

I wished I could have made my father's portrait in the same way. I began to cry. I suggested we call the miracle *soliotype*. Daguerre ignored me and named the marvel like an explorer would an island—*daguerreotype*.

We did not sleep for days. I arranged fruit and jugs of flowers for dozens and dozens of still-lifes. When the mercury vapor magically filled a blank mirror with a scatter of apples and pears I felt like screaming out my joy. Daguerre laughed and slapped my back each time the process worked. When it failed we mourned. It seldom failed. He was sure to be wealthy beyond measure, but the secret had to be kept.

I suggested he make a portrait of a skull taken from the catacombs one drunken night by my friend Claude. I stacked books and balanced the thing atop them. Daguerre gave me the portrait and I gave it to Claude, who gave it to the young whore he visited the evening we filched the skull. That night Claude waited until she undressed, then demanded the skull share the bed with them. I heard her yell from a bed down the hall. The gift was intended to make up for the fright.

Claude's whore was so proud of the skull's portrait that she ignored Claude's directions to keep it to herself and showed the plate to everyone, including Daguerre, whom she met while he was buying coal in a *café carbon*. I was drinking with Claude, the reason Daguerre was fetching his own fuel. My master hunted me down and beat me with his cane in a barroom full of men.

Claude's tailor dreamt of the day he would be insulted by a gentleman; he kept a brace of fine small-bores in anticipation of the wished-for disgrace. At dawn Claude fetched me one of the pistols and I went to murder Daguerre. His rooms were empty. I stood waving the pistol at a bowl of pears like an idiot. The concierge told me Daguerre had left the city to visit a sick friend, she did not know who, and that he would be gone until the next noon. I went to Claude and had him make me a coat like a chest of drawers. It took him all day to cut and sew the remarkable thing, guilt over giving the portrait to the foolish girl hurrying his shears and needle.

The sun burned an orange trail across the Seine as I filled the coat's many pockets with Daguerre's things. I put a camera in a burlap sack, then took a hammer to the others. I crushed the pears and apples and their bowl, then knocked the skull to bits. I was far from the city when dawn began to tear the clouds.

During my destruction of Daguerre's studio I toppled his prized orchid from its windowsill. Coins pooled on the floorboards when its pot broke. Under the left arm of the miraculous great-coat Claude had installed a pouch which accommodated the take. The money was enough to get me to Calais and across the Channel, but proved too little to transport me further. I owe my escape to New Orleans to the fact that Americans are enchant-ed by shiny objects. In return for passage across the Atlantic, I made a dozen portraits of a sea captain named Sylvester Lune. All I remember of him is the fact that his surname and quarter-moon chin were a perfect joke.

I remember the voyage more precisely. While on the Atlantic I vomited my weight several times over. I emptied myself into the sea so often I soon became convinced I'd gone hollow and I learned why fasting saints witness such wonderful things: Angels mobbed the rigging, some swam alongside the ship like burning fish.

We took on supplies and cargo in Haiti, then crossed the Gulf of Mexico and aimed up the Mississippi. I became ill in a new way—drenching sweats, black vomit, visions even more vivid than those I'd experienced on the open sea.

As soon as we neared a dock in New Orleans, a plank ran from it and a man waving a ledger rushed aboard yelling about landing tariffs and a tax on bananas. The heat was unbearable and his shrieked oration stopped suddenly when he saw me in my huge coat. The look in his eyes made it clear he feared he'd made the bad choice of trying to swindle a ship of fools. The sight of an idiotic but sane sailor hiding bananas under a tarpaulin restored the cheat's voice. He demanded we line up and pay up. I walked down his narrow plank, ignoring his threats.

I counted the bells ring ten times. Stinking smoke cocooned the lamps and I wondered if I'd died and gone to the Hell my father promised. When I finally met another man in the street he was masked. For a moment I was sure he was a bandit, but he crossed the narrow avenue to avoid me. I was watching his back fade into the fog when the cannons began to boom, rattling the boards covering the windows of the shop I stood before. The mask and guns and fire made sudden sense—it was July and I had arrived during America's violent celebration of independence.

I spent my first night in New Orleans hiding in a looted tobacconist's. In the dark I was seized with the belief that I was to be sacrificed as part of the festival, my corpse used to fuel the reeking fires. In the hours before dawn I reminded myself of the coat's contents—the hammer I'd used in Daguerre's studio, squares of copper plated with silver, a snuff box of iodine, mercury shuddering in a vial, a lens plump as a swollen coin. I fingered the talismans, eyes closed so tightly that Paris lit inside my head like a scene inside one of Daguerre's dioramas.

I heard the bells ring five and worked up the courage to light a match. Showcases held broken pipes and a fine dusting of fragrant tobacco. From the corners of one case I scraped enough to fill the cracked bowl of an abandoned meerschaum so small it must have been meant for a baby. Smoking my busted pipe and watching the sun tint the tar smoke I fell into a sleep so deep that the hot plug of tobacco fell from the pipe and burned a moon-shaped scar onto my hand without waking me. I slept for half the day and woke swimming in my coat, the fever broken. The sun had fallen. When I took to the streets I felt a chill and huddled deep into my blessed greatcoat, the camera slung over my shoulder in its sack. People stared as they passed, all but their eyes and brows hidden behind kerchiefs and under hats. I was weak from hunger and thirst. No café presented itself.

I walked and walked, the bells' count climbing to eleven, then twelve, then beginning anew at one. Just after they sounded four o'clock I followed my nose down an alley and found a baker stacking fragrant wands of bread into his cart. Swooning from the brown smell I begged him for a *batard* and he spat at me. I produced the pistol with which I had intended to murder Daguerre. I felt no guilt, the weapon was harmless: I'd fired its only ball at an angel who stuck out her tongue at me. The baker cried out as if shot, then fainted. I took as many loaves as I could carry. Hidden in my tobacco shop, I gorged on bread, the cannons giving cadence to my chewing, and the sun rose dully behind black clouds.

*C*P

I memorized and recited my apology. I identified myself as an artist, holding aloft the camera in its sack as proof. Consider yourselves not victims, but patrons, I said. I learned my English from listening to tourists in Paris and then the sailors during the crossing. It was jagged and filled with curses, so I offered my speech in French. In New Orleans it did not matter if they understood me; when I gestured with the pistol my patrons promptly handed over their money. The pocket under my arm filled and I walked tipped to one side.

I returned to the tobacconist's one morning to find the lock snugly replaced. I took a room near the waterfront. The room's other occupant was a stevedore whose taste for whiskey bankrupted him and he let his bed to me from dawn to dusk in order to afford his habit. Through the night hours I roamed the narrow avenues with my pistol, earning my keep.

The first portrait I made in New Orleans was of the stevedore sprawled across his tattered scrap of carpet. My hands shook as I coated the plate with iodine. I had no tripod, so I balanced the camera on a stool and aimed it at the snoring drunk. I expected the portrait to hold no more than indistinguishable smears, but the pattern of the carpet looked as if it had been drawn with a rule. I tried to call the portrait *soliotype* in an attempt to regain my sovereign claim—it was my hiding of the cracked thermometer that had engendered the marvel—but it was no use. Calling the daguerreotype by another name was as ineffectual as calling New Orleans Paris.

Each night the stevedore shook me awake and made me watch as he carefully inventoried his possessions. He wanted me to know that I could not get away with robbing him of his pornographic etching, his spy glass, or his Chinaman's robe.

⌘

In middle-August, a month after I'd come to the city, the cannons were still firing, the barrels of tar still burning, and those brave enough to walk the streets still wore masks, not props from an independence celebration but futile attempts at fighting the fever that'd rattled in my chest and come forth as coughs of inky syrup. I read in the French editions of the papers that the epidemic was in full fury, all that could save the city was October's cold. Almost half-a-thousand were dead. The papers claimed only the foolish or the mad would be out-of-doors at night, the time, it was agreed, during which the Fever was most likely to be acquired. The English editions, as I understood them, claimed news of an epidemic was a hoax, a lie, an attempt to slander the mayor.

I hid in the gloom and waited for fools, madmen, and subscribers to the English papers. When I caught glimpses of myself—in a shop window, in a pool of stagnant rainwater—I realized people must have feared the camera, which in its bag was the size and heft of a man's head, as much as they did my useless pistol.

One night I spotted a couple on a corner. A man was laughing, his head tipped back, as a woman cursed him. She wore a deep purple gown that lightened her skin. The man was narrow at his hips and had a head of honeyed hair. They were dressed for a ball and I imagined my armpit pocket filled to overflowing.

"Forgive me," I begged, "I am an artist." I aimed the pistol at the man's back. The woman stopped yelling and looked at me impatiently. The man turned. His eyes were glazed and he smiled dreamily, traces of a laugh still at the corners of his mouth. His pants were unbuttoned and he held his cock in his hand. Startled, I tried to begin again. "Forgive me—"

The woman stomped off. The man began to button his pants with slow care.

I shook the pistol below his nose to bring it to his attention. "Forgive—"

"An artist!" He yelled, looking up as if he'd just remembered I was there. His smile was fixed on his face as if painted. "Brother!" He lunged forward and embraced me. My coat creaked as his hug tightened. "Brother artist!" He linked his arm with mine and pulled me along.

⌒

My new brother was a painter of miniatures. Every shelf and sill in his house on Toulouse Street was mobbed with portraits and landscapes all smaller than a child's hand. He pointed to himself and announced "Peter" as if instructing a savage. I borrowed the name of my lost friend the apprentice tailor and claimed Claude Marchand was me. I was afraid Peter would hear the lie in the name, but if he did he did not show it. Instead he nodded and smiled, then asked me if I had anything to drink. "*You* invited *me* to have a drink," I reminded him, glad to converse in comfortable French, even if it was with a madman.

He shrugged and left the room. I picked up a landscape and could find no fault, a miracle in a work that small. Figures so tiny they must have been painted with a single hair were detailed perfectly—noses no bigger than commas boasted exquisite nostrils. It looked as if he had painted over a daguerreotype. "Soliotype," I told myself.

When Peter returned he was carrying a pipe, a spirit lamp, and a carved ivory box.

"This is remarkable," I told him.

He took the painting from my palm and squinted at it. "Yes," he agreed, "it is."

I followed him along a narrow hall to a room appointed with a high bed and stacks of newspapers leaning at dangerous angles. A door opened onto another room no larger than a pantry which held a tin tub and a huge kettle. A final door let us into a small,

roughly paved courtyard. Flowers in uneven rows filled hap-
hazard beds. Peter sat cross-legged on the flags and patted the
stone beside him. The ivory box held little pots of opium beneath
its frieze of elephants. He lit the lamp and we passed the pipe,
orange plumes from burning barrels of tar visible in the distance.

"It looks like giants are smoking pipes over there," I said.

"A giant's pipe!" Peter jumped up to see the fires better. "Yes!
A giant's pipe!"

The bells rang a dozen times and he yelped a dozen times in
response, then yanked me to my feet and dragged me into the
bathing room. Once there he took the coat off me and hung it
on a peg. I stumbled, unsure of my footing when freed of the
weight. Peter jerked my shirt's buttons from their holes. My
pants fell and I assumed he aimed to push me to the floor and
bugger me. The prospect was hazily thrilling. Peter helped me
into the tub and poured cold water from the kettle over my
head. My teeth rattled. I peered at him from behind the opium
as he used a brush on me, then toweled me dry. He led me, stag-
gering like a cripple, into the bedroom, then dressed me in a
clean shirt which felt like wind on my shoulders. He guided my
legs into a pair of trousers, put a jacket on me, then pulled me
down the hall, out the front door, and into the street. "I am a
mixed-up man," he sang as we dashed along. "I am part of
many things and whole of nothing." He stopped suddenly and
grabbed me about the neck, put his mouth to my ear as if he
meant to kiss it. "My father's father was an African." Then he
did kiss me, once on each cheek. "My father's mother was
French." He laughed and took to his heels. I happily followed,
more and more convinced the opium had put me to sleep and I
was enjoying a dream.

To a black dressed like a magus Peter handed an invitation. We were ushered into a room filled with familiar faces. For a moment I thought the door had led me dreaming back to Paris, then I realized I was in a hall peopled by men I'd robbed in New Orleans. I saw one who had cried, one who'd laughed as he paid me, one who had said "That's made of glass" when I aimed the pistol at his eye. Peter began to introduce me. My patrons smiled and shook my hand; none recognized me. They were a jolly gang; an epidemic was not enough to make them sad.

Daguerre once took me to a similar banquet in reward for a second fluke discovery I had made—the plate develops better if tilted at an angle over the mercury vapor. In a rush I remembered the wrongs I had done Daguerre. My lungs tightened, so I read to myself from the long list of wrongs Daguerre had done me.

I followed Peter as he navigated the crowd, leading me to a table piled with food. He popped a radish into his mouth. I picked up a date and saw a wiggling toe. "Is this the opium?" I whispered. Peter laughed and pointed. A naked girl was prone across the table, covered with meats and fruit. She balanced a cake on her navel. I took a chop from her thigh, a few olives from between her breasts. Her skin had a hint of purple. I stood chewing lamb and admiring her face. She looked as if she were adding figures in her head.

Peter called, "Claude, you have already met Millicent," and then buried his face into the cake on her middle. A cheer went up from the room; men rushed forward and began to eat like dogs. Peter wore a mask of custard.

I bent and passed her an olive in a quick kiss, observed her chew, amazed by the hinge of her jaw. Her eyes were light gray, almost white, the pupil dark as ink. Each of them looked like a soliotype of an eye. "Soliotype, soliotype, soliotype," I chanted, the word growing less and less odd in my mouth.

♂

I opened the top louvers and as soon as the light allowed I posed Millicent and made her portrait, then posed Peter and made his. He closely observed the process and demanded I stand so he could make a nude of me, my neck and ears hot with embarrassment.

I heated the mercury in its shallow dish, making myself concentrate on the flame and the wavering vapor so as not to gawk as they sat naked and drank coffee. Millicent never addressed me. She spoke only to Peter, even when we three were in Peter's bed and I was licking sweet custard from her belly. I was removing the plates from the developing box when she spoke her first words to me: "Claude, you turn red when you think of me." Peter laughed when I colored, Millicent stretched like a cat.

I handed Peter the portrait of Millicent and he quit laughing. Millicent looked up from the portrait of Peter and said, "Let me see the one of myself." Peter traded and then paced the room looking at himself, the only man I have ever seen who looked dignified out of his clothes.

"It is two mirrors at once," Millicent said. "Tilt it one way and you see the past, tilt it another and you see the present."

A frown pulled Peter's face. He bit the portrait like a shopkeeper testing a coin. "I brought him to the party solely because I thought we would enjoy him," he confessed to Millicent. Peter gazed at the soliotype, then at me, his eyes sparking. My heart rang.

"I had no idea," he said.

♂

Peter and I went to a battered door on Marais behind which a courtyard lay green as an oasis. Stone walks wound between beds of garish flowers, fish ponds were canopied by palms. A parrot stood on a perch and muttered hello in French, English, Italian, what I guessed was Greek.

Peter had an appointment to paint a woman's portrait. The small ivory lozenges that were his canvases looked like pieces for a game. A servant brought us a tray of tea and cakes and Peter poured. "Madame demands I arrive promptly at ten so I can sit and wait," he told me under his breath.

"Why bother?" I whispered back.

He rubbed the tips of thumb and forefinger together, then used a brush to measure the parrot's height. With rapid strokes he drew the bird's outline. I set up the camera, desperate to further prove myself. His brush made chiding noises while I worried over the light and prayed the parrot would stay still. I removed the lens cover and counted carefully to myself.

Peter looked away from the bird and said, "This soliotype of yours provides a perfect representation of Nature."

Soliotype!—Peter's praise made the marvel mine.

"There are those who believe such perfection is an insult to God." He turned back to his small masterpiece. "Church doors have a botched hinge, rugs have a dropped stitch. There are those who believe only God should make a perfect thing."

The parrot he made of paint was as perfect as the one I had inside my camera.

"But color," I argued, pointing to his handiwork. "The soliotype may render the line perfectly, but it cannot reproduce color."

With a flick of his brush he flawed a wing. "Color is nothing."

Madame Dupin appeared beneath her parasol. Peter kissed her hand and introduced me as the man who would make her portrait. I was startled. She was annoyed. Her smile was forced while she sat in the sunlight and I made her likeness. I hid in a dark pantry and finished the plates of the parrot and Madame.

Her smile flattened when I handed her the portraits. She spoke to them. "In Natchez, a group afraid of the city summer has asked me to send a diversion." She could not look away from the portrait of her parrot. "I had intended to send you alone, Peter, but this marvel must go as well." She gestured to the camera and to me, her eyes still on the likeness of the bird. "What is it called?"

"Claude," Peter said, as if naming an odd style of dog.

"Soliotype," I furthered. The word hung in the air. I wished the parrot would repeat it.

Peter hired me a horse that afternoon, bought me a leather-and-canvas valise that accommodated my camera more elegantly than the flour sack. He had too many things to do in the coming weeks, there was no way he could justify a trip to a den of fools hiding in the woods, but such a trip would be good for me. The fools were members of New Orleans's finest families. They would pay well for portraits and tell everyone they knew about me and my miraculous soliotype. It was the situation I needed to quickly establish myself. I agreed. I would have agreed to anything he suggested.

That night Peter, Millicent, and I smoked our pipe while the giants smoked theirs in the distance. We played a game of cards in which the winner of each hand was allowed to remove some of the losers' clothes. We undressed each other and then tumbled onto a rug which covered the courtyard's flags, the figures on the scattered playing cards our audience.

ↂ ↂ ↂ

Plate 2—Nude Female on Couch, *c. 1838. Sixteenth-plate daguerreotype.*

Plate 3—"Peter" (Nude Male before Shuttered Window), *c. 1838. Sixteenth-plate daguerreotype.*

Plate 4—Nude Male Holding Goblet, *c. 1838. Sixteenth-plate daguerreotype.*

THE DATING OF these three plates (as well as of Pls. 5 and 6) is based on their size and the fact that they appear never to have been cased. A sixteenth-plate daguerreotype barely fills the palm. Marchand may have brought these small 3.5 x 4.2 cm plates with him from Paris, where the size was popular for miniature oil portraits. He never again uses the sixteenth-plate; the 7 x 8.3 cm sixth-plate, also know as the medium plate, was the smallest available in his studio.

In January of 1839 Marchand began placing his daguerreotypes in the same kinds of cases in which miniaturist painters placed their portraits and landscapes. (For a more complete discussion on cases see Pl. 7—*Still Life of Daguerreian's Tools.*) These silver-coated copper plates have aged considerably because they were not protected; all are spotted from dust and moisture and faded by the sun; Pl. 3 bears teeth marks on its upper-right-hand edge.

The decision to date these portraits circa 1838 can also be justified by an examination of their subjects and style. Marchand was yet to experience the rigid confines of expression and prudish morals of commercial art, and the unfiltered light and unembarrassed camera angles he utilizes are inspired and free.

In Pl. 2 the slightly plump female reclines on a couch, the plate's deterioration oddly selective. While her face, feet, and the couch have faded to little more than outline, her body from the chin down and ankles up is unflawed. Time has also left a bowl of papayas and grapes unblemished. The fruit looks ripe even in the gray spectrum of the daguerreotype.

The regal pose and unabashed nudity of the man lit by stripes of sun sneaking in through louvered shutters in Pl. 3 is remarkable, even more remarkable when one considers the extent of the daguerreotype's damage. Aside from the teeth marks, Pl. 3 has incurred many scuffs and scratches. The effect once given by the highly polished surface is lost because of this damage; the man seems slightly out of focus. The name "Peter" is scraped onto the verso of the plate, but a survey of the gossip columns and other social records turns up no Peter in connection with Marchand, leaving the labeling a mystery.

Pl. 4's subject is sheepish, his wine cup held before his crotch. Again, similar settings can be distinguished. The fruit bowl seen in Pl. 2 is discernible in the background of this portrait, and the stripes of light from Pl. 3 are on the floor before Pl. 4's young man.

NEW ORLEANS WAS like a shrunken Paris and for weeks I was able to pretend little had changed in my life, but now mile after mile of Mississippi loudly announced I was no longer in Paris. My eye was used to a city's colors—brick and paint and the shimmer of window glass. The jungle held too many different greens, too many different trees and weeds.

I arrived exhausted in Natchez as the sun was falling and paid a child to lead me to the Leone plantation. The boy delivered me into the front hall of a house filled with running children. I followed a servant to a library where a dozen men sat stupefied by the heat. I was led through a fog of cigar smoke to the stoutest in the room—Leone. He accepted Madame Dupin's letter and after careful consideration spoke to me in French. We discussed Paris for a few sentences, then Leone rose unsteadily and led me to a room peopled by a dozen lethargic women. A child played a piano.

"Julia has sent you a portrait painter," Leone announced.

The women looked up, the girl stopped playing. "Hello," she said. Her lump of a mother cut her a reproachful look and the girl covered her mouth with her hands as if she'd said something obscene. It was my first glimpse of Vivian Marmu, aged ten years.

The next morning I set up my camera in a room with tall windows and a convenient closet. There were jugglers on the lawn, their Indian clubs chopping the air. The children of a dozen families ran across the turf like dynamos, pausing only to agree on new games and fight over the rules. Adults knocked croquet balls through wickets.

With so many diversions, the first to come for portraits were the truly vain—the three youngest mothers and a foppish boy of thirteen pretending to be my age. They had expected the smell of paint; my camera confused them. As soon as their portraits were in their hands they ran to tell the others what I was about and a line quickly formed, husbands and children irritable in their hot clothes. They brought books and parasols and swords and keepsakes which I made them put aside. I allowed them to hold only a pinecone.

The last man to have his likeness rendered was Leone's brother, a lout with a red face and midlife belly. "How do you mint the face onto the silver?" he demanded. He stomped off in a huff when I laughed at his boorish visions of himself as Caesar, profile illustrating a coin.

The light was almost gone when Mrs. Marmu entered leading Vivian like a pet dog. Mother and child looked equally grim. "We have come for a solo-tip of Vivian," Mrs. Marmu informed. The child nodded solemn agreement. I explained to Vivian that she would have to sit perfectly still until I told her it was safe to move. She agreed and I removed the lens cover. A devilish smile took hold of her mouth and she stuck out her tongue.

I swallowed a laugh while I counted. "I've botched this one," I lied to her mother. "I'll need to make another."

Mrs. Marmu sat across the room watching her daughter's back as silently and stiffly as if she were the portrait's subject. Vivian imitated her mother's somber face.

That night the children put on a Punch and Judy show on a stage haphazardly rigged up in a gazebo. The plot was improvised and made less and less sense as more puppets—rag dolls bound to sticks—made their entrance. Mothers and fathers yelled huzzahs. I held the portrait of Vivian and her tongue and I peeked at it and at her. She sat beside her mother, the only child in the audience, and watched the silly show, her body pulling toward the stage.

I took portraits all the next day, the sitters waiting even before the sun crested the trees. Most came because they were tired of jugglers and croquet, not because they were truly amazed by the soliotype. The rich quickly overcome amazement. Portraits littered side tables and made reflections of chandeliers dance on the walls when the lamps were lit. There was a new player in the Punch and Judy show—a soliotype lashed to a willow switch.

My makeshift studio was almost empty the third day. The

young fop came early and retreated to a corner of the lawn to admire himself. I sat and enjoyed the solitude. My pockets were plump with money. On the lawn the jugglers had regained favor and were tossing apples. The children were demolishing the stage in the gazebo.

Stephanie Leone, one of the youngest wives, came for a portrait. Her husband, the plantation owner's younger brother, was the ape who dreamed of his fat head on a coin's tiny plate. "I wonder," she stuttered when I came from the closet with her likeness. Her cheeks were red. She worried the prop pinecone until it shed a spine. "I wonder," she said again, then checked over her shoulder. "Would you make a nude study of me?"

I was startled. Stephanie was barely older than I was, and I had judged her prim. "There is no privacy," I reminded her.

"I know a place in the woods," she whispered.

♂

She held her skirts high as she tromped through the underbrush. I followed in her thorny wake lugging tripod and camera, trying to avoid tripping over roots. We emerged in a small clearing carpeted by wildflowers, the trunks of trees on all sides so close to one another it seemed we stood enclosed by walls.

Peter's shoulders were broader than mine and in his borrowed shirt I suddenly felt dressed in my father's clothes. Stephanie bent and picked flowers as if that was what we'd come for, her hair metallic in the light, her skirts flaring from her hornet's waist—a prim wife on a picnic. I took my time balancing the camera on the tripod; I was sure she would change her mind and I did not want her to do so at the last minute, naked and ashamed before me. The ground glass showed her empty dress hanging from a limb, moving slightly in the breeze. I looked up from the camera and a new Stephanie, prim wife no longer, held a crown of flowers against one breast and smiled coyly. "Shall I stand?" she asked.

"Recline on the flowers?" I said, my tongue dry in my mouth, my stare fixed on the nipple floating amid blossoms. She did, opening her legs slightly, and the sun painted the glossy triangle of hair gold.

Stephanie did not rise and dress while I packed up the camera. She swatted a mosquito on her belly and scratched the bite, her nails leaving red trails. "My husband is twice my age." Her voice wavered nervously. "How old are you?"

I added two years to the truth.

"You're not much older than my brother, but you look stronger." She took a deep breath. "Come and try and lift me," she invited.

Twigs and leaves tangled in our hair. Her hip bones were sharp and prominent and she pressed them into mine so roughly that two blue circles reminded me for weeks how she laughed while I slid into and out of her. She capped me with the flower crown as we finished, both of us laughing and shuddering, and kissed me for the first time, a chaste kiss on the cheek.

"I have never done that before." She was beaming while she combed grass from her hair with her hands. "Never cuckolded my husband," she clarified, then laughed again. She stood and took her dress from the tree, stepped carefully into it, gave a short wave, and walked into the woods giggling.

I lay back and basked in the sunshine, the sockets of my hips stinging but not yet colored with the greens and blues of bruise. Stephanie's smell was strong on me, mixed with that of smashed vegetation and dirt—a stripe of the last ran jaggedly across my belly. I looked up into the trees and saw Vivian Marmu above, a little girl hugging a limb.

"How long have you been up there, monkey?" I asked.

"A bit."

I covered myself with my hands. "And what did you see?"

She grinned her grin. "A bit."

✐

Vivian demanded I make a portrait of her sprawled across the flowers upon which Stephanie and I had coupled. If I did not, she threatened, she would tell everyone what she'd witnessed. I envisioned a duel with Stephanie's twice-as-old-as-I husband in which I would surely be killed, so I agreed, relieved the girl's blackmail was so cheap.

Vivian walked to the spot and dropped her frock. I had expected a playful recreation, a child's version of the pose. Instead she mimicked Stephanie to the letter, parted legs and all. I removed the lens cover, fearing a husband and now a father.

I locked my eyes with hers to avoid the urge to look at her child's nipples, her hairless pubis. She fiercely returned my stare while I counted. Her eyes were the color of amber, flecks of gold trapped in them. When the count was done, Vivian picked up her dress and darted into the woods, the fabric trailing, her skin flashing.

✐

Stephanie and I were seated side by side at the evening meal. Every brushed elbow made her giggle, every giggle turned me red. Vivian sat across from us, between her mother and father, and watched me eat, her stare as sharp as it had been in the woods. I made myself look away when I realized I was judging her mouth the same way I had judged Stephanie's before I crossed the flowers and tried to pick her up.

"Looks like you have an admirer," Francis Marmu gaily observed.

I choked on a piece of bread, blushed, and stammered, "She's a little beauty." Her father nodded and smiled, her mother glared, Stephanie ran her hand up my thigh and pinched.

Moments before I quit the house, Vivian changed her mind and demanded I give her the portrait of Stephanie as payment for her silence. Coward, I gave it and ran.

✺

27 August 1838
Told Peter I was tired of the silly thirds he forced on me and this tramp who held a pistol in my face was the last insult I would suffer. Peter woke the boy—Claude—who brought out a wood box from the sack he carried and claimed he would make our portraits with the box. The boy lit a lamp and poured liquids from bottles over polished squares of silver. The squares of silver were our portraits and they knocked us silent. They are two mirrors at once—Tilted one way the past is reflected and tilted another the present is seen. I am thrilled and confused by the things. It does not seem right that a hungry boy dressed in Peter's pants can stop time, but he can.

2 September 1838
As soon as Claude was gone to Natchez Peter hit me and claimed I favored the boy. Fled to the kitchen pantry and locked myself in. Peter kicked the door and told me I was lying when I promised I loved him more than I loved the boy, I was lying when I swore I loved his little paintings more than the boy's mirror pictures, I was lying when I complained about the thirds he brought home—He yelled I know you favor any strange man to me. Peter gave the door a vicious

kick and it splintered and swung open and he stood startled on the jamb. Threw a spoon and it hit him in the face and told him it was true I preferred a stranger in bed, true there was no poorer a lover than he. Told him the pocket full of gewgaws stolen from the parlor of the rare fool who hired him to paint a portrait was proof he was void of talent else he would not have to steal to eat. Told him Claude's mirror pictures caused my heart to skip in a way his paintings never made my heart skip. He suffered my yelling until I said the last and he heard the truth in it and the truth infuriated him. He slapped my ear and I fell. He kicked me three times and the third time I caught his foot and jerked him down. His head tore a shelf from the wall and I crawled out of the pantry while he called me Whore from the floor. Ran to the back of the house planning to escape through the rotten courtyard fence but in the tubroom Claude's coat hung on a nail and the butt of his pistol stuck from a pocket. Peter was coming down the hall yelling Whore again and again, his head bloody. Held the pistol in his face and said This is the pistol Claude pointed at you and now I am pointing it at you. Cocked the hammer and Peter swallowed and tried to smile and I said Put on Claude's coat and get out of here. He took the coat from the nail and said If you make me leave like this I will not come back. Wanted to cry but smiled and shook the pistol like Claude had shaken it and Peter put on the coat and said Goodbye forever, Whore, then turned and walked down the hall. Pulled the trigger but the pistol did not fire. Silence so wonderful after the yelling it took me a bit to realize Peter was truly gone. Gathered his paintings and burned them in the stove then realized I had done so hoping he would come back and find them gone. His mirror portrait sneered at me. Cut a map of the world from an atlas and tore it into strips and wrote his name on the back of the mirror then wound the strips around him and put the wrapped portrait in a box. It is a hex I was told would keep men away, any picture of any man sufficient as long as the specific man's name is written on the picture, a bit of wisdom passed to me by my aunt when I was a little girl in her kitchen. Claude came back and is upset Peter took his coat. I am not—The coat was a skin he shed and Peter took up. Led him to bed and he was grateful. Took some jollying to get him talking about himself but once he started he could not stop. He explained how the mirror pictures are made and it is no less a marvel when one knows, the same way a cake is still marvelous when one finds it is no more than flour, sugar, eggs, and soda. He sleeps and I look at myself in the picture's mirror and know I did the right thing when I made Peter take the coat and leave.

ᑯ ᑯ ᑯ

Plate 5—Nude Female Adult Out-of-Doors, *c. 1838. Sixteenth-plate daguerreotype.*

Plate 6—Nude Female Child Out-of-Doors, *c. 1838. Sixteenth-plate daguerreotype.*

PL. 5 SHOWS HOW the elements can destroy a daguerreotype. Sunlight has harshly faded much of the image and humidity has added a patina of tarnish. Only the subject's left breast, left shoulder and head, and a swatch of the flowers upon which she lies retain their original clarity. The adult model's flowing hair, her crown of black-eyed susans, and the carpet of flowers on which she poses hint at what must have been an amazing portrait. Pl. 6 provides the second half of an almost-diptych. The plate has faded to little more than a mirror, but careful scrutiny finds a child similarly posed in the same flower patch, the flower crown of Pl. 5's subject looped around the little girl's right ankle.

The nude disappears from Marchand's work until 1845, nearly a decade marked by brilliant art managed within the narrow bounds of making a living. His wife, ironically, provides the return. (See Pl. 38—*Vivian Marchand Before a Potted Tree*.)

♊

𝓘 MADE NEW ORLEANS at daybreak, the tar smoke lifting with dawn. When I slammed into the house, eager for a homecoming, Millicent stood in the middle of the room draped in a bed sheet made luminous by the new light.

"Close the door," she said, and I did. "Peter says that all that was his is yours." She handed me a document which seemed to explain that Peter had given me his house. His miniatures were gone, the tables and shelves and sideboard bare. The portrait I'd made of Millicent was propped prominently on the mantle. "All that was his." She dropped the sheet and the sun outlined her. "And all that was yours is his. A trade."

"All that was mine?" I held my empty hands in front of me.

"He took your coat."

I had not thought of my Paris treasure chest since Peter lifted it from my shoulders the night I attempted to rob him. I felt a sudden slash of homesickness when I remembered its weight.

Millicent set a hand on each of my shoulders and reminded me of my consolation: "But you have me."

She took me to bed. There is no solace like that of a woman's body. By dusk my heartbreak had churned to rage and I hated Peter for stealing my beloved greatcoat, loved Millicent for staying behind. She wanted me to explain the soliotype, so we sat up late into the night and I explained, glad to share my secret. It was the only secret I knew.

♂

The noise of a workman hanging a sign woke me. I was rubbing sleep from my eyes when Millicent handed me a newspaper open to a page with the sign printed in miniature:

Claude Marchand—Magic Portraits Drawn by the Sun

"I've had twenty inquiries already," she told me.

I was confused. "There is no magic; the sun doesn't draw them. I explained this last night: A plate of silvered brass is made light-sensitive—"

She stopped me by handing me an apple. "Telling someone there is no magic is a quick route to poverty. A friend told me she heard Samuel Leone speak of you and the magic way you made the sun draw his picture. When a rich man says you're a magician who can make the sun draw pictures, you are a magician who can make the sun draw pictures."

We went to balls where she introduced me to men of wealth. She flashed the nude I had made of her like a calling card, then pressed the real card, buff paper and black ink, into their sweaty palms. She snickered at their lustful backs when they staggered away. "You men," she informed me after charming a fat one with a peek at the portrait, "are marionettes pulled by a single string."

The puppets whose strings she jerked came to the house, wives and brats accompanying. Soon my appointment book was filled weeks in advance. A line formed down the block on the special days I accepted customers without appointments, another of Millicent's ideas. When the residence became too cramped to accommodate all the business, I transformed a maisonette at the back of the courtyard into a true studio—skylights, a developing room, a couch for waiting customers. It was tiny, barely twenty feet square, but customers could sit in the courtyard's shade on benches Millicent hired a boy to install, or, if the line was very long, they could stand along the path of crushed shell which appeared one morning, a white stripe from the street to the studio's door.

Months passed and I did not think of Peter or of Paris, but then I would see a man wearing a cape the burned-chocolate color of my lost greatcoat, or come across a tattered book of inaccurate accounts of Parisian landmarks, and then would fall into a melancholy cured only by Millicent.

She was not my first love. There had been a few others before her who elicited the small loyalties of hands or feet or arms and commanded small nooks of memory—small loyalties which always suffered rebellions. Not so my allegiance to Millicent. I turned toward her like a compass needle when she passed. Meals went cold while we tumbled under the table; invitations to tea were snubbed when the promise contained in the curve of her elbow drove me to kiss her neck and beg. She held more than my body's simple loyalty, the loyalty of the young and the foolish. I thought of her always, delighted in the tiny notes she snuck into my pockets. I ignored others when she was in the room, a habit she tried to break me of for fear I'd offend a portrait sitter. A rotten poet, I composed sonnets and odes to her, troubling for hours over rhymes. When at night she threw a leg over me and pinned me to the bed in her sleep I was more than sure I had no wants in the world.

⌒P

1 January 1839
*Went to a party at the home of a man who admires Claude's
soliotypes and drank so much I was sick in the street—Poor
omen for the New Year. Claude in his cups prone to cruelty—
As I gagged up my liquor he reminded me it was illegal for us
to marry then carried me home and spent a long time kissing
my feet and ears. In bed he is prone to patterns, afraid of
looking like a fool or fraud and sometimes I wish for Peter's
hand at my throat when I have Claude's mouth on my toes
but then I remember the sting of that hand. Claude worries
over his work and fears the soliotype lacks painting's art and
this fear makes me sure he is more an artist than Peter who
had no doubt of his own brilliance. Claude listens when I talk
and does as I tell him when I tell him gently. There are lines of
people at the door each day waiting for him to make their
portraits. How many weeks did I watch Peter sleep all day to
avoid the truth that no one wanted him to paint a portrait?
No dinner is small, I want for nothing. Why should I want
Peter? Each time I see myself in a soliotype I forget for a
moment that it is a portrait and when I move my mouth I
expect the mouth in the mirror to move. Peter never made my
portrait. Each portrait Claude makes of me makes my heart
tug at my side. The feeling is somewhat like fear, somewhat
like lust—though I feel neither when I look at myself in the
glass—and somewhat like the wonder conjurers' tricks made
me feel when I was a girl.*

⌒P

𝓜ARDI GRAS CAME, with it balls and binges. Late in February Millicent and I went to a quadroon ball to drum up business. I watched wealthy men dance, dandy as bachelors, their wives forgotten while they whispered promises into the ears of lovely Creoles. After each dance a few couples adjourned to corners to strike their deals—houses and promises of acknowledged bloodlines—still-pretty mothers joining the negotiations. Millicent told me some contracts were so complex that even the Continental education of offspring and the color of the house's rooms were agreed upon in writing. The music was sublime, the room shook with light, the women were beautiful; it was easy to imagine a man losing his head and promising anything. A boy circled the crowd with a secretary under his arm, ink pot and quill in his hand.

Seeing the faces of men I'd once robbed over the shoulders of their mistresses caused not even a flinch this time—many paid to sit for portraits, ignorant they'd paid before—but my breath caught when I saw Francis Marmu crossing the room. At best I feared he'd found the nude of Stephanie Leone and wanted to know why I'd given it to his child, at worst I feared he thought I'd raped his daughter. I was trapped in a corner by a pair of twin brothers Millicent had sent to ask me about pornographic soliotypes. Marmu reached between them and pressed an invitation into my hand. He wished me to attend a salon. A poet from London was to read and Marmu's wife felt a painter was needed to complete the guest list. "But you are better than a painter," he told me. Flattered, I forgot my fears and agreed.

Millicent was furious: On the other side of the room she had told the mayor I would attend his fête, scheduled for the same day. We argued so loudly we were shooed into the street. Millicent announced she would bed the first willing man she could find if I did not cancel the Marmu engagement.

"There is more money to be made at Marmu's," I reasoned.

"I will look like a fool." She cooled herself with a paper fan.

I was unwilling to let her boss me about. "You *are* a fool," I told her. "Only a fool would make appointments without asking the permission of her . . ."

She waited, the fan a blur in her hand. "What are you to me, Claude?" she asked. "Not my husband; that would be illegal, as you like to remind me." She snapped her fan against her knee. "Perhaps I should go back inside and dance."

"So find a banker and haggle," I invited. "Don't forget to agree on the firstborn's name. I've always liked *Claude*."

I wish I could claim I apologized and we reconciled there in the street, but I cannot. As soon as she went back into the dance I hurried toward a brothel recommended by the twins, a place they claimed held many willing models for lewd portraits.

It was on a street I did not know in a quarter with which I was unfamiliar and I was soon lost. I gave a rag picker all of my coins and he led me down an alleyway so dark and foul I was sure he planned to kill me. A girl in a huge hat answered the beggar's knock. "I've been waiting for you," she told him, then winked. His smile was missing teeth. He pointed to me. "I've been waiting for you," she assured me, then offered the same wink.

I arrived (sour luck) during a burlesque of some sort and was made to go and watch. On a small platform in the courtyard three women were acting out a morality play. All were nude. They wore absurd wigs and read from one book which they passed back and forth. A velvet cord divided the audience from the actors as if the men sitting on long benches could not be trusted. The girl in the hat pulled me along by my elbow. There was no place to sit but she would not let me stand at the back and watch. A fat man in a cutaway was screaming laughter and kicking the velvet rope as if testing its strength. The girl jerked me over to where he sat and he angrily made room for me on a bench. He yelled, "One hopes you're better in bed than on stage," as the morality players exited to light applause. His breath was rotten with beer. An Irish girl with chalky skin and huge breasts with dark, large nipples followed the actors and sang in a flat soprano; a quadroon with a surgical scar's dark line across her belly accompanied her on a tinny piano. My benchmate hiccuped laughter the entire time.

"Quiet!" someone called at him.

The fat man elbowed me in the ribs and said loudly, "These men know good singing." The girl missed a word and came in late on the chorus. Someone behind us hissed.

"The critics are beguiled by her voice," the man beside me said. He pronounced the last word while fondling a pair of phantom breasts.

The girl broke off her song in the middle of a verse and hurried from the stage.

The fat man turned to me. "Did you read my thoughts on the pathetic exhibit of water landscapes by Pfeffer?"

I was baffled. I had come for a woman, not some fool's lessons. "Who are you?"

"Who am I? I? Am? Who?" He looked around for witnesses. All eyes were on a harpist tuning her strings. He giggled, then turned and told the hissing man, "The magic portrait maker does not know me!" The harpist plucked a string. The fat man turned and watched her press a thigh against the harp, cleared his throat over and over.

"Beguiled by her voice?" I snapped.

He bellowed laughter and clapped me on the back. "You're

ignorant, but you learn quickly," he judged, then pulled me to my feet. He paid for my night with the flat-voiced Irish girl, adding bills when told she'd already been claimed.

The girl was weeping into her pillow when I reached her small room.

"Are you new to this?" I asked, standing with my fly half unbuttoned.

"No one is new to this." She bawled on the narrow bed. "Felix Moissenet does not like my singing," she stammered between sobs.

That was my introduction to Felix, the man who could break a prostitute's dream of being a singer with a few sharp words, the fat man with foul breath and foul manners to whom New Orleans looked for judgments on all things beautiful—in fact, I remembered in a bitter rush, I *had* read his savaging of Pfeffer's pondscapes.

She reached out and hooked a finger in my belt, pulled me closer to the bed. "I might not be able to sing as well as he likes, but I know how to fuck. You can tell him that." She tugged down my pants. "You'll have plenty of good things to tell him about me, sweet."

"I liked your singing," I fibbed.

"Liar," she said, then took me in her mouth.

❧ ❧ ❧

Plate 7—Still Life of Daguerreian's Tools, *c. 1839–40.*
Quarter-plate daguerreotype.

CLAUDE MARCHAND REMAINED the premier daguerreo-type portraitist in New Orleans despite the leporine proliferation of other studios and daguerreians. He was a zealot with regard to his work, so it is little wonder that he made this still life of his tools: the box camera, a dozen slim-necked bottles, and a trio of shallow dishes.

The daguerreotype is a one-of-a-kind photograph. There is no negative, making it more akin to painting than to print photography. The daguerreotype process is arduous and extremely involved. The silvered copper or brass plates are prone to tarnish, especially in humid New Orleans, so Marchand's first step was painstaking polishing, a chore usually done with a spinning buckskin-headed apparatus. Next the shiny plate was suspended over iodine, the vapors uniting with the silver to produce a light-sensitive silver-iodine coating. The prepared plate was transferred to the camera in a plate holder, exposed to catch the image of the subject, removed while still in the holder, and then placed above a dish of heated mercury in a developing box. The mercury vapors reacted with the exposed silver to produce an image in an amalgam of silver-mercury. Finally, the image was fixed by immersion in a solution of salt or hyposulfite of soda.

After it was fixed, the plate was covered with a sheet of glass and the two were sealed together with tape and mounted in a book-like case with a hinged cover. These cases are to be thanked for many of the dates assigned the plates in this study. Marchand's case supplier was W. Lauren Wilson & Co. of Boston, an art and photography supply house still in business and in possession of records over a century old. They provided Marchand with cases of morocco and also with "Union cases" made of thermoplastic (pressed sawdust and resin). All of the cases can be dated by color. Marchand ordered black, oxblood, and brown from 1839 to 1840, and replaced brown with red in 1841. Pl. 7's possible dating is based on its chocolate goat-leather cover.

The daguerreotype is delicate; New Orleans's climate is perhaps the worst for such photographs. Mildew, palmetto bugs, and mice destroy the cases and the sealing tape, exposing the daguerreotype to humidity which pocks faces with tarnish and breaks down the silver-and-mercury images; sunlight makes figures fade as if the past is tugging at them. That the plates in this study have survived is a wonder. Many of the daguerreotypes discussed here were discovered in the attic of Marchand's former residence on Toulouse Street by workmen renovating the house. The trunk they were placed in was watertight, intended to hold papers on ocean voyages, and thus many of these photographs are exquisitely preserved.

⌘

At BREAKFAST MILLICENT and I were glaring at each other across the kitchen table, the tick of forks and knives the only noise, when someone knocked at the door. We both continued to eat. The knock came again. I motioned with my head for her to answer it. She threw her plate into my lap, dumped her coffee after it, then walked down the hall to the bedroom opening and slamming every door she could.

There were four urgent raps.

Food fell from me as I walked. I jerked open the door, ready to yell curses into the street, and was greeted by two men, one young, one old, both wearing worn suits and hats. They held opposite ends of a pine coffin.

"We have come for a memorial portrait," the older man at the rear of the box announced. The younger looked at the mess painted across the front of my pants, then past me into the room. I followed his eyes and saw footprints of egg and jam.

The older man adjusted his grip on the coffin. "Your advertisement states you make memorial portraits?"

I nodded. It was true, the advertisement claimed it, but no one had yet come for such. The older man moved forward and the younger was pushed over the threshold. They stopped in the center of the room and looked at me.

"Two chairs," the younger man said. "One for the head, one for the feet."

"The studio is back behind the house," I told him.

"So you're not Marchand," the younger congratulated himself.

"I am, but these are my living quarters."

"They're quite nice," the older man judged sweetly. He nearly dropped the box when he tried to get a better hold on it. "Now let's go get this done with."

I felt my meal rising when the coffin was opened in the studio. The woman was no more than bones and papery skin, a skeleton wrapped in tissue and dressed in a yellowed bridal gown. I covered my mouth.

"He's never done this before," the younger man said, his voice sharp with disgust.

"He'll do it fine," the older assured. "And he's on the way."

"He may be an idiot, but he's convenient. Mother would approve."

They were ignorant about the soliotype. They figured a living likeness could be made while she lay in her coffin, her fingers twined about a spray of limp violets. When I explained that the coffin would be a part of the portrait—this was not painting, I could not leave out what I chose—they decided to pull the woman out of her box and prop her on the sofa.

The dress had been split along the back, and a wide stripe of skin showed when her son lifted her. My hands shook while I prepared the camera. I held my breath when I removed the lens cover, the husband wandering the room humming an obscene song I heard when I went to barrooms. While I finished the plate in the developing room, I listened to father and son discuss the weather while they replaced the woman in her coffin. I put the soliotype in a mourning case, the first one I had used, and was amazed by the beauty of the silvery image next to the black kidskin. I walked out gazing at it. The son yanked it from my hands, then passed it to his father who pocketed it without inspection. The son handed me half of what I told him he owed. I mentioned the short and he answered by driving a knee into my groin. His father laughed while I curled on the floor. Tears of joy were streaming down his face when he and his son picked up the box. My stomach cramped and the vomit I had been holding back poured forth until I was heaving only air.

I did not know Millicent was beside me until she nudged me with her toe. "Go clean yourself," she said softly. "You have the Marmu engagement in less than an hour."

♎

The salon was a travesty. Mrs. Marmu was dressed like a duchess from a fairy book, her homely face topped by a powdered cone of hair a hundred years out of style. I was brought into a library filled with ladies dressed in similar attire who'd arrived early and without husbands. The true party was to begin after dark, but my contribution required daylight. I wished I had taken Millicent's advice and reneged. One after another they sat stiffly holding fans and bouquets of wilted daisies, their faces tight with smiles uncannily similar to the one the dead woman had worn. The lot of them responded with a quick intake of breath when I handed over the first portrait. The gasps grew less audible with each following. They deserted the room en masse after the last lady had covered her heart with an edition of Virgil dusted off for the occasion.

I was exhausted. The mercury vapors made my head spin. Reflexively I loaded another plate holder into the camera, then realized I was alone. The sun came through the windows in a column. Louisiana sunlight is heavy and golden and warm, like Armagnac. The room was quiet as a church and smelled sweetly of leather and paper. The Marmu cat, fat and gray, hopped into the chair and curled in the magnificent sun. I removed the lens cover, happy to have a sitter who did not remind me of the dead bride. After I developed and finished the portrait I lifted the limp cat and sat with her in my lap. I chucked her under the chin and she rumbled as if coming to boil. I showed her the soliotype. She touched her nose to it, judged it no good to eat, and went back to having her chin chucked. I did not blame her.

The vision of the dead woman's sawtooth spine faded. I opened the slim volume of Virgil and happily made my way through a dozen lines. A pair of small hands covered my eyes and I dropped the book, startling the poor cat. I heard her cross the floor.

"Who is it?" I asked, my heart stupidly racing.

"Guess," Vivian said, her voice poorly disguised.

"Is it the King?"

That got a giggle. "No." She removed her hands. "Make my portrait."

I stood and she curtsied demurely.

"I do not like the one you made before," she told me.

For a sudden moment I thought she was talking about the nude. "The one in which you look like your mother?" I hoped.

She pursed her face in perfect mimicry. "I think she is very, very ugly. I do not want to look anything like her. Make *my* portrait."

"And what will you give me?"

She pondered. "A kiss."

"I would rather have back that portrait of Stephanie Leone." With alarming regularity the soliotype appeared in my dreams, an omen of angry husbands, pistols, and the field of valor, I feared.

"I would rather give you a kiss and keep it."

I shrugged, then packed up the camera. The cat had not gone far. I patted it for a moment. Vivian frowned, her brow furrowing.

"You look like your mother when you do that," I told her.

The girl stomped out, her small shoes making so much noise that the cat ran behind a chair. She thundered back into the room holding the plate of Stephanie wrapped in a scrap of velvet drapery and thrust it into my hands. I pulled the camera from its valise so that I could keep my side of the bargain.

"Stephanie Leone is with child and fat as a mule." Vivian caught the cat and waltzed with her.

I stared at the tiny nude in my hand, then at the little girl dancing with the cat. Vivian's smile was not the smile of a child. It was the mistress's when the bride proves a pale substitute. I pocketed the plate and set the camera atop its tripod. "Sit," I commanded.

Vivian dropped the cat and slowly walked to the chair. She smoothed her skirts across her knees. The sun was fading and I feared I would lose the light. She fiddled with her hair, then her skirts again.

"Stay still or you will be erased," I barked.

The portrait was botched. Only a ghost of Vivian in a ghost of the chair appeared. While I cursed, she stood on the couch and appraised my eyes.

"When she has the baby I want to see if I can recognize the color." She hopped at me, her mouth colliding with mine. "Now you owe me two portraits." She strolled from the room, cat in tow.

I escaped the house, begging off the rest of the party with complaints of a bad stomach. In the street I stood and looked at Stephanie and the flowers. Desire made my heart stutter. I went to a café and quickly drank an absinthe, then another, my heart slowly finding an even rhythm.

Stephanie died giving birth to a boy her husband named Stephan. There was a wake and I offered to make a likeness of the child to explain my attendance. An aunt held the baby for his portrait, then passed him to a wet nurse and headed for gossip in the room's corners. Every chair was filled by a woman in black shaking her head at the coffin in the middle of the room. I rushed to the studio, developed the plate, and hurried back with it.

Samuel Leone was nowhere to be seen. A servant pointed down a hall when I asked; I opened the door when my knock was not answered. I had the new portrait of his son in my hand, the one of Stephanie among the flowers in a pocket. The widower was sitting on a stool before a caged parrot and did not hear me enter. His hands were full of fruit scraps and his shirt looked as if he'd not changed it since his wife died. He tempted the bird with a bit of banana. "Say it," he begged.

"Oh, Lolly, what mishmash," the bird sighed, its voice a harsh imitation of Stephanie's. "Oh, Lolly, what mishmash," it said again. Leone rewarded it.

I set the baby's portrait on a side table and slipped out.

I found the nurse in the kitchen pantry suckling Stephan. She turned her face down when I came in, tugging her shirt closed. The child fussed.

I touched a thumb to his forehead. "His eyes," I said, "what color?"

"Blue," she said, and I closed my brown ones in relief.

I told myself I wanted a daughter, a son. My heartbreak over Stephanie Leone was fueled by a young man's desire for a family. It was covetousness of another man's wife and still another's child that made me so melancholy. I began to appraise prospective mothers, note wrists and noses, imagine combinations of my forehead and their ears. Every young woman who kept an appointment before the camera was a possibility. Then it occurred to me that I despised each infant held in its mother's lap, that my head hurt when families—mother, father, sundry brats—showed up on a Wednesday afternoon dressed for Sunday morning complaining about the heat, the light, the whatever. I did not want a child—I hated children. What I wanted was Vivian. Leda and the Swan, Temperance League evils-of-opium propaganda, descriptions of the body's miraculous elasticity—all seemed addressed to my perversion. I lashed myself to the mast of morality, flimsy as it was. I pulled myself raw while looking at the portraits of Vivian I'd made in Natchez, her stuck-out tongue, her ankle shackled in a flower hoop.

I turned my bedsport into play acting: In the dark, Millicent became Vivian.

Millicent admitted she'd felt neglected. "When will you stop looking at women as if they are cows?" she asked one night as we lay spent, me carving juicy chunks from a papaya for us to suck. "It makes me feel I need solid hips and udders to interest you." I slid a sliver of golden papaya flesh across her ribs, followed its trail with my tongue into her sharp armpit.

ℒ

Felix Moissenet sent a boy to fetch me one noon when summer was at full boil. Millicent's nervous attention to my jacket, my shoes, and my hair infected me. I quizzed the boy about the reason I'd been summoned while we walked to Moissenet's home café. "There are only two reasons Monsieur Felix buys a man a drink, to praise him or to mock him," he explained through a smile.

Moissenet sat behind a bottle and a plate of oysters. His face was crossed by a huge grin. I knew it was mockery that would pay for my drink. "I have received a letter from a friend in Paris," he told me, then daintily unfolded the epistle. "I won't tire you with news of good weather, a murder in his quarter, and the health of our mutual friends, but this bit should interest you: 'There is to be a new invention displayed next week, and many of us are sleepless with anticipation. The diorama-maker Daguerre, we have been told, has overcome the destruction of his workshop by a faithless apprentice and has deduced a method of fixing onto a metal plate the image floating inside a camera obscura. These images have been viewed by Madame Lamont, and she tells me that they mirror nature perfectly.'" Felix peeked over the top of the note. "Interesting news, *oui?*"

I could not answer. I thought of Daguerre, his hand tucked inside the breast of his coat like Napoleon, his hair a mess of wild curls.

"We are two frauds, Claude. I did not like the daguerreotype from the first."

"Soliotype," I unthinkingly corrected.

Felix rattled the letter. "*Daguerreotype*. Two frauds, Claude, you and I. A faithless apprentice and a critic—two failures. Every failure is driven by jealousy of those who have not failed, but I no longer hate you now that I know you're a fake like me." He dismissed me by turning his attention to the letter.

ℐ

29 August 1839

Felix Moissenet this morning told Claude he planned to expose him as a thief of Daguerre's secrets and Claude paced the room for hours holding his head with both hands telling me he would be ruined. Told Claude I needed to fetch bread and went to Moissenet and made a bargain. He sat by an open window and laughed and waved and called hullo to neighbors while I worked him out-of-sight. In the street after I thought of my father, the first time in a long while I have thought of him. He was a man haunted by the guilt of killing my mother by filling her with me and when he saw his guilt walking and playing with dolls he hoped teaching me would save me from my mother's fate. Pure delusion to believe the girl child of his quadroon mistress could avoid the bed if she could read, write, and talk like a boy of no color. Pure delusion to believe any woman can avoid the bed. God rest him, the only useful thing he taught me was snobbery. Felix's praise of the soliotype and of Claude in the evening paper tells the story of my mouth on him if you know how to read it. Claude is gay and cannot understand why I am not jolly. He kept putting the paper under my nose to show me the good news until I tore it from his hands. He asked Are you jealous of me? and I told him You are the one who should be jealous and left him to puzzle out my meaning.

⌒P

*I*NSTEAD OF ANNOUNCING me as a fraud, Moissenet labeled Daguerre a parvenu and hailed me as the true pioneer: *The Man Who Brought New Orleans the Soliotype!* his headline read. I was stunned, but I did not argue.

As soon as Daguerre outlined the process in Paris, pamphlets explaining every step were published and distributed. To many I was still the wizard Millicent made me out to be, but now there were others who knew my tricks, a magician on every street. I pulled a hat down over my ears, turned up my collar, and went from studio to studio. The clutter was disgusting. The modest called their portraits Daguerreotypes, Soliotypes, or Heliotypes; the not-so-modest invented a language of knock-offs: Frederikotype, Haeganotype, Etcetera-o-type. No matter what they were called, every portrait was filled with gangs of fools in silly costumes. Each studio seemed to have agreed to ape the other's collection of garish prints of flat-faced nobles of unidentifiable pedigree. In waiting rooms babies yelled, wives snapped at husbands, the aged broke wind.

A studio opened directly across Toulouse. Its windows were painted with numbers, prices lower than mine. The owner was a ruffian named Billings, an Irishman with red hair and a missing finger. He stood in front of his crudely lettered windows and called to my customers, waved them over with his three fingers and thumb. Business fell off a bit, but I had a steady group who were not lured by saved pennies; in fact, higher cost was important for the people to whom my portraits mattered most.

The Marmus showed up often in order to placate Vivian. Following her eleventh birthday she wanted a portrait a month, a demand her father was more than willing to meet—anything his pet wanted she got. I made portraits of her riding a rocking horse, sipping drinks, reading books written in languages she did not understand, gazing out windows, touching a brush to a canvas turned so that the camera would not give away the little artist's scam—there was no paint on her palette.

I once asked Mr. Marmu what happened to all of the portraits. I imagined a room like a shrine. "She gives them away," he admitted. "She handed one to a boy she did not know a few weeks ago. Saw this dirty boy in the street and handed it to him."

One sunny Saturday father and daughter arrived to keep their appointment. Francis Marmu worked numbers with a pencil stub and a square of paper. Vivian was to have two portraits, one in which she held a paper lily sent from an English aunt, another in which she was dressed in an Indian maiden costume she'd worn in a play. After the lily portrait had been made, Vivian went in to the developing room to change into her costume.

Mr. Marmu pulled me aside. "My wife has forbidden me to make money on Saturday," he confided. "I aim to make a deal with a man from Havana, but I need to make it today, not when the woman feels business should be conducted. Watch the girl."

A moment after her father slammed the door behind himself Vivian entered naked. She'd stuck a feather in her hair and she held a wooden scalping knife. Between her legs her few hairs appeared to have been carefully combed. I looked at the floor. My heart beat as if my head were being held under water.

"My father went to buy the Cuban ship?"

I nodded to the rug.

"Look at me," she said. I raised my eyes. She smiled, then let loose a war whoop and skipped about the room thrusting her knife at cushions and drapes.

I watched, fascinated, until she jumped from a chair and landed before me, the play knife held at my throat. I should have scolded her, sent her to dress. Instead I pushed eleven-year-old Vivian Marmu onto the couch. I kissed the rise of her belly, then ran my tongue up her ribs, over the button of a nipple, into and out of the valley of an armpit. I nipped her neck and the child saved her virtue by returning the favor with too much vigor—she bit my ear with such force that the lobe was nearly severed. I yelped and she looked baffled until she saw the blood on my shirt. She laughed and darted into the developing room, dressing with amazing speed.

Vivian plastered my ear and played nurse. In her dress she was a child and my stomach turned when I realized the taste in my mouth was perfumed powder I'd licked from her.

"There was an accident!" she exclaimed when her father returned, then proceeded to invent a story involving an explosion and an act of heroism on my part. The child could lie fabulously. Marmu paid me double, eyes happy with business. Vivian pulled the feather from her braid and stuck it in my hair. "Be careful," she warned.

When Millicent came to the studio looking for me I dragged her to the floor, damaged ear forgotten until she touched it and I squawked. Apples from her parcel rolled off into the corners of the room.

ℐ ℐ ℐ

Plate 8—Girl on a Rocking Horse, c. 1839–43. Quarter-plate daguerreotype.

Plate 9—Man with Sideburns, *c. 1839–43. Quarter-plate daguerreotype.*

Plate 10—Masked Couple, *c. 1839–43. Quarter-plate daguerreotype.*

Plate 11—Butch Billys Dog June '42, *1842. Quarter-plate daguerreotype.*

THE DAGUERREOTYPE MADE posing for a likeness more democratic than ever, the price of a portrait even cheaper than that which was charged by an inept painter. In 1841 a New Orleanian could make an appointment for a Marchand sitting and obtain a cased quarter-plate portrait for as little as two dollars.

These inexpensively attained portraits made many happy, but this bargain also put art into the hands of people who did not think of it as such. Oil paintings hang above fireplaces for generations while daguerreotypes, even memorials, are seen as part of the effluvium of a life lived in the 1800s—like stereo card viewers and worm-tunneled croquet mallets—little more than rubbish to be discarded when cleaning out attics. These plates of four unknown human subjects and one identified pet are an excellent example of this egregious tendency. They were found in an antique store in the French Quarter, a flea market in Arabi, and a junk shop in Grosse Tete.

The dates given Pls. 8, 9, 10, and 11 are based on the backdrop which appears in them. The woodland landscape behind the pigtailed girl in Pl. 8, the man with the full sideburns and the top hat in Pl. 9, and the masked sitters in Pl. 10 does not appear in Marchand's work before 1839 or after 1843. An inked caption barely discernible on the verso of Pl. 11's battered case—*Butch Billys Dog June '42*—provides an even more specific date.

All four portraits are marvelous examples of Marchand's artistry. Pl. 8's child looks unposed on her hobby horse even though she would have had to remain still for the photograph's long exposure. Pl. 9 has the formal stiffness many wanted in their portraits, but Marchand has inserted a unique twist—the man sports a fat magnolia blossom tucked in his top hat's band. Pls. 10 and 11 are lively novelties, even for Marchand. The couple in Pl. 10 wear bawdy masks with long, penis-shaped noses, a sure sign that this portrait was made during Mardi Gras. Now common in snapshots, animals were rarely the subjects of early photographs. When they do appear it is rare that they are as well-focused as is Pl. 11's Butch.

The most saddening thought occasioned by the lucky discovery of these Marchand masterpieces is that the works which remain may be far inferior to those produced during the genius's lifetime. Who can say that Marchand's greatest art was not stupidly lost or destroyed by those unable to recognize its wonder?

Soon Millicent took up with Billings from across the street, Daguerre getting twofold revenge: The cut-rate studio was beginning to steal a noticeable bit of my business. I could see Millicent and the orange-haired ape laugh at me behind the painted glass of his windows. He gave her an ugly pin, a tarnished bug she wore like a trophy. His grin was nasty when I saw him in the street. I watched her like she'd become a new creature and she treated me as if nothing was awry.

A week after their affair began I sat in the courtyard and smoked opium until the breeze ignored me and flowed through my bones. A boat was afire on the river and the column of smoke and flame rose above the rooftops like a monstrous mimic of the tar barrels. Down the slim alley paved with luminous crushed shell I could see children and dogs running to witness the disaster. I was content to observe, the opium making the fire, the children, and the dogs flat as soliotypes. I watched Millicent cross to Billings's door. I blinked, and when I opened my eyes the boat had burned out, dawn was flaming on a different horizon, and Millicent hurried across the street.

She went in the front door, I the back. In the bedroom I slipped down on my belly and I moved along the hall like a snake. I found her in the kitchen and hid under the table. In the middle of the pantry floor she'd planted a candle in a pool of its own wax. Millicent stripped off her dress. From a shelf she fetched a piece of paper cut to the crude shape of a man, kissed it, then drew from her mouth a long copper hair. Her body was trembling; her smile showed all of her teeth, her tongue. She pierced the paper doll's forehead with the point of the insect pin and threaded the hair through the holes.

"Hello," she greeted the doll, then reached between her legs and put her fingers inside herself. She smeared the doll, then snapped its head with a finger. "So clumsy," she chided. "So stupid." She touched the doll's foot to the candle flame and the paper curled and blackened. She flipped the doll, now no more than fire, out the open window.

"So clumsy," she said again. The sun painted the sky green and she stood before the window, her head tipped back and her eyes closed, then turned and left the kitchen, her feet inches from my face as she passed. I listened to her walk down the hall. In a moment I heard bath water ring in the tub.

℘

I woke when a tympanic roll of thunder announced the coming of afternoon rain. I looked up at the table's secret underside, its pegs and screws and hinges. I felt like I had not eaten in ages. Knees and neck popping, I crawled out from under the table and hurried to the pantry to hunt for food. I found a cracker box on a high shelf, but instead of crackers it held a salad of torn maps, and atop that salad lay the portrait I'd made of Peter. Upset there were no crackers, and puzzled by the nude, I combed the confetti with my fingers. One of Peter's tiny landscapes surfaced.

Hideous screaming came from the street. I rushed to the window in time to see Billings stagger from his studio, his sleeve a flag of fire. Millicent came and stood beside me. Women pressed against storefronts like broadsides, their faces twisted with fright. Millicent's eyes were filled with amazement while she watched Billings hop and yell and wave his burning arm. Her mouth opened slightly in wonder and she gently shook her head when a brave boy snuck behind the Irishman and shoved him into a horse trough. A cheer went up, there was applause. A group of men hauled Billings howling from the water.

"I'm starving," I told her.

Millicent took the portrait of Peter from my hand, filled my palm with coins, and sent me off to eat.

Billings was gone, but a mob had congregated around a sot in a soiled bowler hat who was explaining what had happened. "His sleeve touched the flame and—." He waved his arms and staggered in imitation. A knife of lightning cut the sky.

Night was coming but the air was still oppressive, the day's heat not yet absorbed by the dark or cooled by the light rain which fell with a whispering noise. In the oyster house I found

Peter's landscape in my pocket. A tendril of Scotland trailed it. On a tiny hill a tiny man looked over a tiny sea, a tiny sail on the short line of horizon. I looked up from my beer and thought I saw Peter, the coat Claude had made for me hanging from the bony rack of his shoulders. When the figure standing in the bright square of the doorway stepped in from the glare I saw he was not Peter and the coat was not mine. A tramp in a battered jacket, a length of hemp for a belt, hair a bird's nest above wild eyes.

I shook my head and drank. For a moment I'd been sure Millicent had hexed Billings by burning a paper doll even though my own cuffs were notched by the spirit lamp's flame, sure she'd exiled Peter by packing his portrait in torn maps even though I knew what wildness and wandering we men are prone to.

When I ran out of Millicent's coins the day was gone, and in the cool street I was filled with love for her. I crossed the threshold guilty for fearing her and set to doing small favors. She laughed as I drunkenly tried to fold shirts. The two of us crowded the tub and I scrubbed her back. We were wrestling below whitecaps of soap bubbles when someone began pounding on the door. Furious, I left the water, stomped naked through the rooms, and yanked open the door.

A servant girl covered her eyes with her hands. "Mr. Marmu asks that you hurry." She pulled her apron over her entire head. "His child Vivian is dead, or nearly."

℘

I went knowing I could not make her portrait; I needed the sun. The child's bedchamber was crowded and dank as a barroom. Vivian looked like a model of Vivian made from candle wax. Francis Marmu stood declaiming the Lord's Prayer to the room as if he were giving a schoolboy's recitation; Charlotte Marmu held her daughter and wept. I kept to a corner, my stomach pierced with pains. I heard a nurse hiss, "The child will surely die within the hour," into the ear of another nurse. As if cued, Vivian coughed black vomit across her mother's shoulder. "Her heart!" Charlotte called out. Francis Marmu and I collided when we both lurched toward the bed, then I shot out of the room and ran into the street.

On Bacchus Street a man and a woman hurried past, arms hooked, and the simple fact that they were the same height brought me to tears. I wandered until the lamplighter began snuffing the lights. The cannons were silent and the first bits of dawn burned the edge of the sky—two days in a row I'd seen the sun rise.

Millicent was at my desk with a newspaper. Her lips formed slow words and I knew she was reading the French *Bee*. She had not heard me open the door. I looked at her profile, her skin's tinge of purple just beneath its surface, the brass sheen of her black hair announcing some towhead's stray from his wife and into his quadroon sweetheart's arms. I knocked her down when she came near. She looked up, confused, a line of blood running from her nose, over her lips, and onto the upsweep of her chin. I moved my mouth, apologies canceling out accusations, silence the end result. I covered my eyes with my hands, peeking through parted fingers at her, then ran to the pantry.

The cracker box with the plate of Peter inside it was on a lower shelf than it had been before, its cover now fastened with a score of brads. There was a second box, its cover held down by a knotted strip of calico I recognized from one of Millicent's dresses. I untied the knot and found wrapped in a map of New Orleans the plate Peter had made of me. Millicent was well aware of the fickle and inaccurate compass that is a man's heart;

she knew her hexes were in vain. I tied the calico in a strong knot I'd learned from a sailor.

The blood followed the curve of her neck and stained a red brooch on her collar. I reached down to touch her and she slapped my hand. I fetched a cloth and she let me kneel and clean the blood from her throat.

♄

Unable to sleep, I left Millicent in bed and wandered the streets. I went to the Marmu house to offer my sorrow. There was no answer when I knocked. I was looking into a window when someone spoke behind me: "They're gone to Boston." It was the nurse who'd predicted Vivian's death.

"To Boston? What about the girl?"

"The child recovered."

"Recovered?"

"Some recover." The nurse put a finger to my lips. Her breath was sharp with wine. There had been a celebration. "You've got a good-looking mouth," she judged, then turned away.

I walked along St. Peter and on the corner of the Public Square I watched barrels burning the last of their tar like snuffed candles trailing long twists of weak smoke. The truth of Vivian's death slowly replaced the truth of her survival. I decided I would forget Vivian by remembering her as I'd last seen her—yellow and still. I vowed that no lack of obituary or news of her alive and well in Boston would convince me otherwise. The first trickles of daybreak lit a coin between my feet. It was cold from absorbed night and I hid it in my fist until it warmed. I found a goldsmith and had him make two rings from it, a pair of heavy bands. "Pretty little shackles," he joked when he dropped them into my palm.

Millicent was sewing, the jalousies half-closed against the

morning heat, a ladder of sun and shadow climbing her shoulders and neck. I took the needle from her hand and slipped the ring onto her finger. Her smile twitched to a frown, then back to a smile, then went flat. I held out my fist.

"It is not legal," she reminded me.

I silenced her with a kiss.

My ring was too big. It wobbled beneath my knuckle, a constant reminder. I smiled when it rang against bottles and the handles of forks. I had to walk with my hand fisted so as not to lose it. I put on weight, the happy man's calling card, and my hand fattened to fit the ring.

Billings disappeared and his shop stood vacant. When the summer heat began to fade I hired a set of twelve-year-old orphans from the Ursulines, a boy named Remy and his sister Madeleine, he to be my assistant, she to cook and clean. They had the bad luck to be twins, the good looks intended for one child split between two: Remy was muscled like a statue, but his left arm was no bigger than an infant's, a tiny hand on its end. Madeleine's face was so beautiful it pained me to see it hang from her twisted neck.

The girl cooked so well we seldom left the house for a meal. She doted on Millicent and Millicent doted back. They brushed each other's hair and giggled over jokes told in whispers. The boy was a quick study. Soon I no longer prepared my own plates or worried over their developing. They lived in the studio, slept on mats they rolled and stored in the developing room.

Francis Marmu did not bring his family back to the city when summer ended. Rumor had it he'd made a deal involving a slaver with a man on his deathbed—the Havana captain, I assumed— figuring to inherit the partnership's joint luck, and the crew

muti-nied and left the ship adrift, leaving Marmu with the debts
of his dead partner. Felix Moissenet told me Marmu's plan was
to retreat to a city where his creditors would not publicly hound
him. "A man like Marmu does not like his friends to know his
purse echoes when he calls into it," Felix explained. Vivian's illness supplied him a legitimate reason to flee New Orleans. Thorn
entirely pulled from my paw, I slipped into a comfortable domes-
ticity.

⤢

17 November 1839
*I woke alone in the dark and had to hunt for Claude. Found
him crying in the kitchen—Vivian Marmu has died. Put my
hands on his shoulders and agreed It is always sad when a
child dies. His eyes were strange when he looked up as if he
had not considered this truth. I told him I would light a candle for her after Mass.*

25 November 1839
*Claude's only anodyne is opium—Only when stumbling is
he nearly happy and when the opium's happiness wears off
he yells angry questions at the ceiling. I went to the Sisters
this morning and begged to adopt a girl. Told them my
daughter had died and my husband was insane from grief.
Held my left hand over my breast so my ring was there for
the nuns to see and came home with two children, twins,
twelve years old, a girl named Maddie and a boy named
Remy. A husband, a daughter, a son—One I want, two I
will suffer.*

*

WEARY OF SEEKING out French barbers and grocers, I became the pupil of Mrs. Smithe, a British widow. Mr. Smithe had been at Oxford. When he died, her son, a rum importer, had imported her. Through the mild winter months she trained me in vocabulary and in grammar. To practice elocution she had me read aloud from Suckling.

I brought home a volume of Shakespeare and one night after dinner Millicent and I and the twins acted out the first bits of *The Tempest*, passing the play back and forth. I spoke Caliban's lines slowly, Millicent played Ariel. Remy took Prospero and Madeleine did Miranda. When I managed "You taught me language; and my profit on't is I know how to curse," they applauded.

I told Felix about our play acting.

"Who do you do?" he asked.

"Caliban," I told him proudly.

"So Millicent does Stephano? *Kiss the book*."

"We haven't gotten that far."

"Yes you have," he said, then hurried off laughing.

When Christmas came Millicent and I snuck through the courtyard in the dark and left packages wrapped in bright paper just inside Remy and Madeleine's door. When the sun rose we hid below their window and listened to them laughing and opening the boxes, then ran back to our bed and lay with our arms around each other.

There was a surprise on New Year's Eve: Millicent and Madeleine sewed costumes, Remy hammered together a seashore of painted wood. I returned from my English lesson to find them waiting for me to don my costume and say my lines. We played at being what we were not: Millicent a spirit, Madeleine a queen-to-be, Remy a duke, I his slave. We handed the book around, and 1839 became 1840.

We acted our roles, playing family. Days passed smoothly. Business picked up in the winter months, waned in the summer save for the boom in memorials. I spent my days in the studio making portrait after portrait, my twilights in the courtyard reading aloud to Millicent, my nights beside her in bed. My English became more and more fluid, the twist of my French no longer garbling words. The nuns had taught the children to sing, Remy to play the violin, Madeleine the flute. When Millicent admitted she could play the piano I had one shoehorned into the small front room. The three musicians would perform and I would turn the pages of Millicent's score.

Each morning I sent Remy for the newspapers, and while Millicent and Madeleine had their breakfast, I fetched the Natchez portraits from a hiding spot in a small chest I kept filled with papers and receipts and gazed upon Vivian on her bed of flowers. I noted the two perfect rows of toes, the narrow feet with their high, white arches, the slim stalks of her ankles. Her ghost's form was luminous against the green jungle floor translated to black by the soliotype. When I closed my eyes she burned on the backs of my lids for a moment, then I blinked her away.

I was content and when a man is content he lives inside a faceted gem; even the ugliest things are refracted into bright beauty—the pretty little caramel-haired girl dumping a chamber pot into the street, the round bellies of rotting dogs dead from the poisoned sausages set out to kill rats.

ᘒ ᘒ ᘒ

Plate 12—Memorial Portrait of a Young Boy, *c. 1844.*
Half-plate daguerreotype.
 Plate 13—Memorial Portrait of a Mother and Child, *c.*
1844. Quarter-plate daguerreotype.

PORTRAITS OF THE dead seem odd and macabre to the
contemporary viewer, but during the mid-nineteenth century
they were common and often considered necessary as a means
of keeping the deceased in mind. Even the extremely poor
scraped and borrowed to afford a memorial portrait of a
loved one. For many, the memorial photograph was the first
and only in which they would appear. Hundreds of memorial daguerreotypes are affixed to the doors of crypts in New
Orleans's many cemeteries. Time and sunlight have turned
many to tarnished squares. A very few portraits hold faint
images of the crypts' occupants, but most are dim mirrors
that show only the visages of the living.

 An advertisement Marchand placed during the summer
months promises to provide "Keepsake portraits so carefully
prepared the deceased appear only asleep." Such claims may
have helped business, but Pls. 12 and 13 both point out the
troubles even a master like Marchand would have had keeping this promise. In Pl. 12 a young boy is amid what one
assumes were his favorite toys, his arms akimbo, the blanket
tossed aside, a glass of water on a side table. The pose sug-
gests the boy had been in bed playing with his ball and pin-
wheel and had become tired, but the child's drawn face and
stiffened fingers point out the fiction of the setting and the
props.

Pl. 13 is an even more extreme example of memorial daguerreotype make-believe. In this keepsake the deceased is posed seated upright, holding her newborn. Careful observation reveals a thin cord binding the wrists of the mother so that she embraces the dead infant.

⌒♉

*T*HE SUMMER OF '44 came early. The first acknowledged Fever death was not reported in the papers until late July, but even in April there were rumors that a shipload of Germans with the Fever had been allowed to disembark before someone recognized the sickness in their yellow eyes, in the chorus of their grinding coughs. They were loaded back aboard and sent down the river and out into the Gulf to die at a safe remove, or so the rumor claimed.

A version popular in barrooms promised that the fool who'd allowed them to step ashore (it was agreed his name was Jones) had died within hours, falling—the original teller had surely remarked, and then each new Homer repeated—like the first in a row of dominos. Some claimed hundreds were dying every day, their bodies burned at night by the mayor's henchmen to hide the epidemic. Others claimed only immigrants, poor and dirty, were susceptible. Twice-a-day bathing became a fad; stevedores and chimney sweeps were sweet with perfumed soap.

Every chemist set to making jumbo batches of his own cure— iodine tablets with crosses pressed onto their surfaces, gold dust and pickled apple peel suspended in laudanum. Millicent fed the twins and me shavings of High John the Conqueror root.

I witnessed dozens of victims in my studio before the *Tropic,* the *Picayune*, or the *Bee* confessed. Remy could not bear it—he was reminded of his parent's deaths from the Fever every time he glimpsed a dead face, the skin tightened over the skull. He prepared plates in the developing room and handed them out through the barely open door. Millicent and Madeleine took over the rest of his job out of pity. Women know death more intimately than do men. Being reminded it exists does not affect them with the same force. Remy hid, Madeleine helped a mother straighten an infant's shroud, Millicent gently pulled a little girl's lip down over bared teeth.

The first dozen-odd memorials made me feel as poor as Remy felt, but soon I was numbed by the sheer number of dead I helped pose for the camera. I could no longer recall my father's voice; the threats he'd screamed became quiet as words on a page. Even the memory of him standing with a knife in his gut and blood puddling at his feet faded like a cheap print until all I could see was an outline of a man with a peg where his top trouser button should have been. New Orleanians were just as numb as I. They looked at portraits of relations living and dead with the same emotion.

Large numbers of the population left the city in the summertime to escape both death and the weather, but a few remained to enjoy hedonistic freedom—burglars looted houses, men sent their wives and children away for safety's sake and then strolled the streets with their mistresses. There were summer parties with young women dressed in cakes and puddings, men stripped and sliding naked along floors slicked with spilt wine. Temperate, home at dark, I heard about them from Felix Moissenet when he'd call me to come and share a plate of oysters, or when he would notice me breakfasting in a café and bully me into buying him coffee and rolls. Felix named names in a loud voice and mocked my temperance. "What kind of artist does not need to fuck a variety of young women for inspiration?" I laughed at his abuse and he kept praising me in print.

One hellishly hot morning he peeked over the rim of his coffee cup and provided the news that the Marmus were back in New Orleans after their four-year vacation. I left him and made my way to the Marmu house on St. Anne. Standing in a candy shop across the street I watched trunks being carried into the house, Francis Marmu supervising the effort with a smile on his face. A gang of blacks repaired various bits of the neglected house. Wet paint glistened in the sun and hammers beat a happy tattoo. I was so sure that Vivian was dead, that I was right and others were mistaken, that I thought I was seeing an older sister or a cousin when a curtain was drawn and Vivian leaned out, her elbows on the sill.

When she faded back into the house I hurried home. I sent Remy to buy a box of chocolates from the shop and take them across the street to Vivian and her mother.

"She said 'Thank you,'" he reported upon his return.

"The mother or the daughter?"

"The mother was not around. But the girl—"

"Vivian?"

Remy nodded. "She said to give you this." He gently kissed my cheek. The message tightened my lungs.

<p>

The July day when Francis and Vivian Marmu came to revive Vivian's monthly portrait sitting, Felix and the other café gossips were aflutter about a rumored slave rebellion. Masters away from the city, trusted blacks had supposedly joined with conspiring freemen and were raising an army to take over New Orleans. It was said the mayor had fled during the previous night and at dusk the blacks would march. Like most summer rumors the revolt was hardly believed and much discussed.

Marmu was skeptical. "Our kitchen niggers can't bake a cake without being told how to three times—how could a bunch of them take over the city?" He paced the studio and fiddled with a new mustache with upturned points. It took all my strength to pay him enough attention that my nods and smiles were appropriate.

Vivian had gained nearly a foot of height. Her shoulders had widened, her neck had grown long and graceful, her brows were thick and dark. She wore a velvet jacket the color of tobacco, and her hair was braided into a long rope that hung down her back.

"They come back from the market with half of what they were sent for, amazed there are coins left over. We've got nothing to fear," her father assured himself.

Vivian had bitten her lips to redden them, slapped her cheeks to raise a flush. Pearls of sweat quivered on her forehead—it was far too hot for the velvet jacket.

Marmu yelled, "Niggers running the city!" like it was the backbone of a joke.

I removed the lens cover and used the moment as an excuse to stare. Her forehead was high, her nose had a slight tilt to the left. One ear hung a tiny bit higher than the other. She stared back at me until her lower lip began to tremble. I knew her mouth would be a blur when the plate was fixed. I lost count of the exposure, hating myself. I could only offer what's seen in a mirror viewed in half-darkness, shapes and shadows, but not color.

"Why not tie hats to the heads of dogs and have them run the city?" Francis Marmu wanted to know.

"Stop it!" Vivian yelled at him. She jumped from the chair and ran out the studio's door. Marmu stood for a moment with his mustache tip gripped between thumb and forefinger, then set out after her.

I took the spoiled portrait into the developing room. The small window covered with yellow tissue lit the room with thin light. I heated mercury below the plate, then washed and treated it. Vivian's mouth was a pale smear. Above it her eyes were completely round. Her flight from the chair was recorded as a streak. Her ears burned red in the weak yellow light like a miracle. I blinked, and when I opened my eyes I held a crude silhouette. I touched her face, my thumb covering her head and leaving behind its swirled mark.

There were footsteps outside the developing room's flimsy door. Francis Marmu called my name, then knocked timidly. I hid the plate in my pants pocket. When I opened the door his cheeks were red and I felt mine hurry to mimic. We stood licking our lips, two blushing men unable to say anything.

"Vivian—," he of course finally said.

I had to force myself not to twitch.

"—has told me I was terribly rude."

"Rude?" I could not understand how Vivian's confession would trigger her father's apology.

He blushed a shade darker and I thought of his daughter's face. "Your . . . Millicent . . . my . . . about the niggers. . . ." He looked at his boot tops. "I meant no insult to you or to her."

"I was not insulted," I promised him. I put my hand in my pocket and touched the portrait of Vivian.

Marmu used his silly mustache to pull his mouth into a smile. "She is a prize," he confided, and I wasn't sure if he meant Vivian or Millicent. He pushed a single theater ticket into my palm. "Shakespeare," he told me. "I'm told by Mrs. Smithe you fancy him."

From the courtyard Millicent saw Marmu force the ticket on me, and when I claimed he wanted to discuss a business venture between acts she slipped a good luck charm into my jacket pocket—a plait of gold and green string. I did not want to see *Hamlet*, but I could not suffer a night of cards and recitations with Millicent and the children while the portrait of Vivian hid hot in my pocket.

The air smelled of a coming storm. Small gangs of young men roamed the streets carrying staves and looking both angry and frightened—the rebellion to be put down. A tine of lightning dropped toward the ground, then fish-hooked back into the clouds as if unable to bring itself to touch the city. I kept to well-lit streets. Yellow placards were nailed to doors behind which someone had succumbed to the Fever or was in the process of succumbing.

A lone black child I recognized as my baker's helper darted from an alley with a basket over-full of rolls. He tripped and dropped his cargo when he saw me, the *petits pains* pattering into the street. He stood frozen like an animal sure its lack of movement makes it invisible. I acted as if his camouflage worked and stepped around dropped rolls. As soon as I passed I heard his departing feet crack puddles.

At the end of the block one of the gangs of idiot boys stopped me. "Seen a nigger carrying bread?" I pointed in the opposite direction the boy had run and the brigade of fools charged off.

The theater's lobby was nearly empty, summer heat and the twin scares of pestilence and slave rebellion ruining everyone's fun. I tipped my hat to a young lady and she stuck out her tongue and so violently grabbed the arm of her young man he was almost knocked down. An usher led me laughing to the Marmu box and closed the small door behind me with a bang. Velvet curtains were drawn and I stood in red shadows. When I raised my hand to part them someone touched my elbow.

I spun and found Vivian behind me. She put her hand over my mouth. I bent and kissed her through the mesh of fingers, first her forehead, then her mouth, then her neck. She pushed her dress to her waist and hid her breasts with her hands. I kissed her knuckles, her fingernails. I fell to my knees before her and she tipped my head, covered my mouth with her hand and kissed its back. Her tongue snaked between parted fingers.

"I've missed you," she admitted, then took my finger into her mouth and with her teeth pulled my ring over the knuckle, then swallowed. Stunned, I flexed my fingers, felt the smooth band of skin where the ring had been. Vivian smiled, then lifted her dress to show me her ankles. I ducked my head up under her skirts.

She made me stand, then lit a candle and clumsily stripped me. When I was bare she stepped back and shoved her dress down over her slim hips. A wine-colored birthmark dotted her thigh as if tattooed by one of my kisses. She stood in her stockings, a pair of opera glasses hanging from her wrist on a braided cord, and tilted her head coyly, a pose surely stolen from an illustration she'd seen in a salacious book.

The failure I felt in the studio was nothing compared to what I felt in the theater box. With the soliotype I could never capture the color her skin took from the reddish light. Like a pencil drawing could, the soliotype could manage her pubis's sparse wires, but her nipples would look like old coins, her birthmark like an ink spot, and the map of veins I could see below the skin of the wrist from which her opera glasses hung would disappear.

"I have been with a man," she announced as she led me to the couch. "I am a libertine."

It was a lie. She groaned and covered her mouth with both hands, shoved me away and got to her feet. Vivian walked a circle with her hands over her mouth, her eyes screwed shut and leaking tears. One stocking fell and bunched around her ankle. Blood ran down her bare leg and curled over her kneecap. She swayed unsteadily, the weight of her opera glasses threatening to pull her down. I stepped toward her and realized with a start I wore only my shirt collar; I felt more guilty than I would have felt if I had been completely naked. The curtains dyed the light. My pulse beat in my ears and for a moment I hallucinated I was within a giant heart.

Vivian put her hand between her legs, looked at the red on her fingers, and let out a moan smothered by an actor's lines. I held her while she cried and jabbed me with her sharp elbows. When she calmed she admitted the other man had been Remy. She'd come to the studio alone to thank me for the chocolates and I had been out. Remy took credit for the sweets and the two of them set to kissing and fondling in the developing room. Unsure how the puzzle fit together, he'd rubbed himself between her legs while she sat in his lap.

Vivian removed her fallen stocking and wiped her knee and thigh, then took off the other and pressed it between her legs. "My mother will be here soon," she stammered. She held out the bloody stockings. "Take these and go."

⌘

I went to a door on Rampart Street and prayed the secret knock had not been changed. "Rule Britannia" was still the key.

Cannons were booming and the smokers scattered on the dirty flags would have looked like battle-wounded were it not for their beatific smiles. The open-air den was cooler than the street and musky with the smell of sweat and opium smoke.

The freedman who ran the place took my money and smiled. "Welcome back," he said. For a long while I'd kept my sins to myself and avoided this place; Millicent brought home a small jar of opium in the same satchel in which she carried a bottle of wine and a cake. I filled my head with acrid smoke. Near a fountain whose carved fish spat a silver tube of water I saw Felix spying as a woman so dark her edges lacked definition fellated a man white as chalk, his prick flashing and disappearing as she nodded. Felix's wrist was moving in time with her nods.

The opium took quick effect and pictures began to flash behind my eyelids—Vivian with her bloody stocking clamped between her thighs, Millicent with her face buried in the pillows. I shook my head and heard my eyes rattle in their sockets. Smoke curled from pipes in gauzy question marks and my mind added questions before them.

I escaped to the street, hugging a lamppost to keep on my feet. There were whoops and yells and when I looked over my shoulder the slave rebellion rushed toward me. I ran. A rock rang a hitching post, another cracked the back of my head. I turned a corner and dove for the darkest corner of a dark nook between two storefronts, hiding myself in a ragged patch of weeds.

The rebels stopped just paces away and laughed. When one lit a match to start a cheroot I saw he was not African. More matches popped and I saw faces blackened with burnt cork. The boys, unable to find a slave rebellion, staged their own. Another poor unfortunate appeared down the way and they set off after him, screaming.

Opium and the chase completely disoriented me. A block I expected to end at my door instead ended at the gates of Saint Louis Cemetery Number 1. I passed a priest with a scribble of dirt on his cheek where he'd scratched an itch. He crossed himself, stepped to the lip of a shallow grave, offered a Latin mumble, then tossed a handful of dirt he drew from a pocket, no time to bend and fetch. The dirt came from his hand in a fan and drummed on the coffin's lid. Flambeaux illuminated rows of crypts and luminous boxes. So many had died that the interments were going on late into the night. Gravediggers leaned on shovels and impatiently watched weeping mourners and priests with dirt-filled pockets.

"I can't," a woman's voice said from the dark behind me.

"Can't what?" a man's voice wanted to know.

"Can't bury him."

"He's *dead*, the boy's *dead*."

"No, look, his mouth's moving."

"Shut up," the man's voice sobbed. "Oh please *shut up*."

A rope of smoke hung like a ghost above each flambeau. Black columns flecked with orange embers rose from burning tar barrels and brindled the sky. I felt fingers closing around my throat and ran from the graveyard.

In every shop window I was sure I saw reflections wielding flashing blades. The sound of my own boots convinced me I was being chased. My eyes were flooded with sweat and tears. I hunted for a handkerchief in my pockets. I mopped my face before I realized I held Vivian's stockings. A mirror in a shop window showed my cheeks painted with her blood.

The house was empty so I went along the white stripe of the shell path looking for Millicent. Vivian lay dead on the studio's couch, Francis Marmu spoke to Millicent in a low voice. I stumbled over the threshold and screamed. Marmu turned with a jerk and was not Marmu—he was clean-shaven and ten years younger. Millicent came toward me. The girl on the couch wore a velvet jacket identical to Vivian's but when her father stepped to the side I saw a flash of blond hair. Millicent put her hand on my elbow and I fell as if relieved of my bones.

℘

18 July 1844
When I ask what happened to his ring he lists the same confessions—Nights with whores and kissing and touching another boy named Claude. Found a stocking in his pocket stiff with blood. Sure he is faking this illness and have taken to feeding him cures to turn his stomach—Made him drink his urine.

25 July 1844
This morning he quit his joke and sat at the table and ate with the children. I considered buying him a new ring each time his naked hand lifted the fork. He ate nearly half a pie then grabbed Remy by his little arm and pulled him from his chair yelling that the boy had robbed him. Claude cuffed him and kicked him and threw him into the street and Remy begged to know what Claude thought he had stolen but Claude would not tell him. A lady chided him for his cruelty to the boy and Claude cursed her so obscenely a man nearly struck him. I pulled Claude into the house while Remy called to Maddie and she ran and hid in the kitchen. Asked him what had been stolen and he refused to tell me, all the while Remy pounded on the door and begged to be let in. I said Remy would not steal from you and when Claude answered You believe him

and disbelieve me? I heard Peter's voice, not Claude's. When
he went to the studio I gave Maddie ten dollars to give to
Remy. She asked What am I to say to him? and I said Tell him
you are allowed loyalty to only one man at a time. She nodded
and went out into the street. From the window I could not
hear their words, only two voices arguing then agreeing, and
she could not stop crying when she came back into the house.
Claude sat at his desk writing all day, whistling to cover the
girl's noise. He says he will not make memorials even though
the only people in the city in need of portraits are the dead. I
fear for our stomachs.

⌁

$\mathcal{F}$OR DAYS I was good for nothing but fouling the bed, then
my head began to kaleidoscope dully with colorless visions of
soliotypes never made—Vivian with blood black as India ink
snaking 'round her legs; twisted death masks of smoke barely
darker than the plates' shimmering surfaces, masks of Vivian,
Stephanie, my father, Peter, the priest with the comma of dirt
written on his cheek. I held my piss. It took me a dozen more
days to recognize my name.

I took warm broths and regained my strength. When I had
graduated to a full meal at the table, I threw Remy into the
street. Millicent and Madeleine wailed when I dragged the whelp
out by his shrunken arm.

"He's *stolen* from me," I explained to them and the few
passers-by who stopped to watch the commotion. "Stolen from
me while I was too sick to keep track of him."

I shoved him and he staggered and fell into a stagnant puddle. His sister begged me to forgive him. Millicent took a dif-

ferent route. "You're not well," she judged. "Remy loves you, he would never rob you."

Remy was on his knees in the water, harlequined by mud. "Please," he begged.

"I will not have a thief in my home," I told onlookers, then turned away.

☞

I placed an advertisement in the *Bee* and one in the *Daily Picayune*. Both announced I would no longer make portraits of the dying or the dead. Any dolt can make a soliotype if he has the tools. The artist's job is to choose, to allow only that deserving replication to be replicated: Death is ugly and ugliness does not merit replication.

In anticipation of the questioning I knew I would have to endure, I included in the advertisement three small paragraphs. One was written by a German critic of art named Oscar Zucker, a man who stated in strong words that the practice of making portraits of the dead and soon-to-be was insulting and ugly. This was followed by the opinions of Father Samuel Rodgers, a Philadelphia priest who questioned the practice on the grounds that it could be seen as idolatry, possibly even necromancy. The final paragraph was extracted from a report made by a London surgeon named Redgrave. A rumor had spread through England that looking into a mirror that had recently held a Fever sufferer's image would transmit Yellow Jack, and Redgrave cautioned that this was almost surely true—he had witnessed at least three cases of Fever transmitted via looking glass. Mirrors in London were being turned to reflect the walls upon which they hung. He went on to note that the reflective possibilities of the soliotype must be considered equally as dangerous as those of mirrors, and thus portraits of Fever sufferers could hold doses of Fever.

Who was I to question a respected critic, a man of the cloth, and a physician? My evidence was strong, my evidence was fake. I invented it all while Millicent tried to comfort Madeleine in the kitchen. The girl had not stopped crying since I threw her brother into the street.

"She hasn't slept for three nights," Millicent announced, interrupting Zucker's rant on Objective Beauty and the Golden Purity of Life. "Yet she still cooks your meals and cleans your shirts."

"She's not a slave," I reminded Millicent. "I pay her to cook my meals and clean my shirts. I paid her brother too, and yet he saw fit to steal from me."

My actions sounded more and more justified each time I was asked for an explanation. The supreme trick of language is to say exactly and fully what you mean and have others hear only the bits you wish them to hear.

"I don't believe this theft even occurred. There is the question of loyalty—."

"You're right, and the question is whether yours is to me or to the thief who stole from me."

Simple as that, the argument was over. Madeleine brought in the meal, her face slick with tears. Millicent touched her shoulder. "Mr. Marchand will let you stay on as long as you wish," she promised.

℘

Back on my feet, my rival homeless and muddy, I prepared to face the ghost which had haunted my fever: I sent word to the Marmus that I was well and would be happy to see them for Vivian's monthly appointment. It took me a solid hour to write three short lines, my hand shaking as if a Paris winter had fallen into the middle of a New Orleans summer. I sent the note. Noon passed. They did not come. No note of explanation arrived in response. She had told her mother, her father—someone—and they had kept her from the sitting. Rumors were growing, I could feel them—seducer, rapist. My ruin was in the hands of the one I had ruined, but it was all a mistake—she had sent me away before I could make clear my feelings and intentions. I had to face her, show her and her parents that they were wrong about me: I was an honest man.

I found Vivian and her mother at home enjoying tea. I was invited in and given a cup. I stood with it rattling in its saucer, ready to be accused, ready to offer to marry the girl sitting on the green couch. "Do you fancy marzipan?" her mother inquired. I nodded too excitedly. With her eyes Vivian motioned to a spot beside her and I sat, a safe distance of pillow between us. Mother Marmu passed Vivian a plate of marzipan roses to pass to me. I popped a small one into my mouth and let its petals melt on my tongue. "Have you heard about poor Samuel Leone and his bird?" Charlotte Marmu wanted to know.

Vivian turned for my answer. Her face had been in right profile to her mother, left to me. Like a clown with an *S* painted for a mouth the smile and happy eye I had been given was only half her face. The half she'd shown her mother was frowning, the eye looked ready to give a tear.

"No," I said in a harsh whisper, then cleared my throat. "A bird?" I put another flower on my tongue.

Vivian crossed her legs, her ankles flashing.

Her father entered yelling over his shoulder at a servant who was not bringing him sweets at an acceptable rate. He joined the conversation as if he'd been listening outside the door. "The thing spoke like his wife," Francis Marmu called from across the room. "A parrot. You remember Stephanie Leone?

"*Cake!*" he yelled down a hallway.

"It grew to forget her words," Vivian told me. "When she was no longer there for it to hear it slowly lost her words and took on her husband's. It is a wonder it managed to remember for so long, isn't it Monsieur Marchand?"

I swallowed the little rose and its sugar thorns scraped my throat.

"He feared it would happen, and he kept the bird locked away in his study. No one was allowed to speak in its presence," Vivian's mother furthered. "It could only say 'Say it, please' and 'Wife, wife, *wife!*' after all the time had passed."

Francis Marmu ended the story. "He killed it when it was no longer the conduit for her voice from beyond the grave, smashed it with a Bible." The room was silent. "Bring it, please: Cake, cake, *cake!*" Marmu cried, then fell to laughing at his own poor joke.

Vivian and her mother shot him identical looks of displeasure.

"He neglected his son," Vivian said. "The boy is little more than an orphan. Before he killed it, Leone spent all his time conversing with the bird. I've heard the child thought the parrot was his mother. Isn't that alarming?" she asked.

I nodded solemnly at her smirk.

I'd made a point of avoiding the Leone household, refusing as politely as I could invitations sent by the spinster sister who'd moved in to care for father and son. I feared looking into a miniature of Stephanie's face and having my eyes look back.

A servant finally arrived with the cake, the morning *Bee*, and my note. Charlotte Marmu opened my letter, amused I'd preceded it to the house. Francis Marmu spread the newspaper across the table like a cloth and scanned its pages, finger tracking across words.

"Look here!" he called.

Vivian gave me a pinch when her mother turned to see what the matter was.

"Marchand, look." He pointed to the print. I rose.

My advertisement, complete with its testimonials against the memorial portrait, covered half the page. The other half was topped with a jaunty caricature of Remy's head and filled with an attack upon me. I was a charlatan, a fake, a thief, a man who did not even create the art for which I was praised. It was he who should receive the notice and respect. He was the one who prepared and finished the plates, and often, he lied, I was so stupefied by opium that he had to do *all* of the labor, working me like a puppet. I pounded my fist down on his cartoon face. The cake jumped, its platter rang.

There was more: I insulted the dead when I refused their business. I was heartless to loved ones who wanted no more than a fond memory of their dear departed.

"Is a picture of a corpse a fond memory?" I demanded. Vivian and her mother shook their heads in answer.

Remy, soft of heart and abused by Marchand, was in opposition to Zucker, to Redgrave, to Father Rodgers. For those who desired, he was prepared to make memorial *Remotypes*. Little curtains of black velvet would be placed inside the memorial case if there was still some doubt. The bastard had found a backer and opened a studio of his own. A map labeled with arrows and landmarks guided customers along Canal to Barone, and X marked the spot.

"Lies!" Marmu judged. "Who but a fool would discount a priest and a surgeon?"

"He stole from me. I took an orphan boy in, fed him, treated him like he was my own son, and he robbed me when I was ill."

"There is no explanation for ingratitude," Charlotte Marmu agreed. "The coarse have it in their blood and there is no amount of kindness that can cleanse them of it."

"Will you duel him?" Vivian asked.

I pictured Remy bleeding and a duel sounded like a marvelous plan, but before I could answer Francis Marmu said, "The bullet would be wasted in his skull." He wadded the paper into a globe and tossed it into the corner of the room. "The scamp must be answered, however." He took his daughter's hand. "There is a ball tomorrow. Escort Vivian."

Mother Marmu started to object, but she managed only a single syllable—a drawn-out *N*—before her husband raised his hand and hushed her.

"It will show everyone he's trusted if he's seen with her. It'll show them that this Remy moron is a liar."

"And a thief," Vivian added.

I loved Francis Marmu for his plan, Vivian for the suddenly symmetrical happy curling of her mouth.

ⵢ

I turned the knob and from the other side Millicent yanked open the door. Startled, I brushed a cake crumb from my shirt-front.

"Now she is gone and we have truly been robbed."

Remy had fetched his sister while Millicent was out. He'd also fetched my cashbox, a camera, and a few gross of plates—he'd become what I'd claimed he was. I was touched by an absurd tickle of fear that he'd passed me in the street on his way to Vivian. Millicent's breath caught as if she meant to cry, and I put my hand on her elbow. A chip of marzipan stuck to my cuff. I jerked away as if burned, shaking loose the pink fleck. Millicent barely noticed.

"Maddie took my ring. She knows I prize it above all my other things." She picked up a fork and flung it out the open window. We stood silent and listened. There was a dim chime and she said, "I'm sorry I did not believe you when you told me he was a thief."

I spent the next day yelling at children to keep still before the camera, at Millicent to stay out of my way. Guilt over trusting Remy and Madeleine drove her to try and have whatever I would need in her hand and ready to pass to me, but like every overzealous assistant she was always anticipating that which did not happen. The sun finally gave up after hours of brats and Millicent's good intentions. Its heat still filled the room while I dressed for the ball.

"Why does he want you to escort her?" Millicent asked again as I buttoned my shirt.

"He thinks that people will take it as a mark of my innocence. What father would let a cad take his daughter from his home?"

"Do you fancy her?" Millicent's voice, usually even and strong, bowed with what sounded like fear.

"I fancy having Remy shown to be the liar he is."

Millicent put her fingers to her forehead.

I kissed her neck.

Vivian was wearing a dress more appropriate for a wedding than a ball. Beadwork terraced satin. The sound of the hem against the floor was like a sigh. Her hair had been piled and pinned into a high mass of curls. Her opera glasses hung from her wrist even though the night's plans included no opera.

"Have you heard about the boy?" she asked.

She may as well have been speaking gibberish. "Which boy?"

"Remy," Vivian said. "He and his sister are dead."

Mr. Marmu pointed to Vivian's head. "Something's come undone. Have your mother fix it."

When she left the room, he told me what had become of Remy and Madeleine. "There was a fire and they could not escape. Some at first thought you might have set it."

"Me? Set a fire?"

He put a hand on my shoulder. "They have the one who did it, a crazy nigger who thought the two of them were devils."

"Devils?"

"Her neck, his odd little arm."

Vivian was back before I could fully understand. Her father smiled and laughed and I followed his example. The news of the twins flew from my brain when Vivian hooked her arm through mine.

In the coach she kissed me, then squirmed away when I tried to return the favor. She dangled a key in front of my eyes. "My French tutor has gone to Savannah to buy books for a gentleman who wishes to amass a library and he's asked me to mind his tortoise." She aimed her eyes at her satin slippers. "I've been negligent; the thing is starving. Can we leave the ball a bit early to go and feed it?"

⁂

We made several circuits of the room, brows raising, hands shooting up to cup neighbors' ears and trumpet the news. Felix raised a toast to me from a corner, his smirk making his wink look like a squint. Vivian danced with a boy half her age, then a man four times it, then came and rescued me from the conversation of a lady who fancied herself a poetess and wondered would I be interested in preserving her verses for future generations by making portraits of them?

Vivian and I danced a dozen waltzes and I suffered as many fools, all of them offering testimonials of disbelief of Remy's slander.

"The tortoise," she finally reminded me. "I'll be in trouble if he dies."

$\wp$

The French teacher's rooms were musty and filled with books. His table was a plank balanced atop legs of mismatched volumes, the tortoise in a large flat bowl. He pulled his head in when we peeked at him, no concern for the four stubby legs he left exposed.

"His name is Mercury," Vivian informed. "The god of thieves." She fetched a tin of dried fish and held a bit in her gloved hand. Mercury's wizened head slid out and clipped the fish from between her fingers. I watched her feed the thing, flinching each time it snapped up a bit of salted cod, fearful it would bite her.

"Be careful," I told her.

She set down the fish and walked around the stacked books. Beside the bed, an island in a sea of pages and bindings, she pulled a glove off one luminous hand. "Claude, if I were careful I would not be alone with you, would I?" She raised her opera glasses to her eyes and in their lenses I watched two of myself grow larger and distort as I navigated the maze of books.

$\wp$

Under clouds that made the sky look as if it had been torn and scattered, Millicent and I sat in the courtyard and sipped tea. Fall loomed and there was enough chill to raise steam from our cups. A chimney divided the falling sun into two half-suns. I was out of sorts, my body remembering Vivian's each time I shifted in my chair. My thumb felt her spine when I lifted the pot to pour more tea.

Millicent had not said a word since I had returned at an hour early enough to be above suspicion. I followed quiet suit, fearful the first thing out of my mouth would be *Vivian*. We ate our breakfast dumb, read the newspapers without comment. Such verbal silence was not extraordinary, but the complete lack of sound was unnerving. Like every man and wife we had languages of our own, alphabets of tongue clicks, rolled eyes, finger snaps. Four ascending hummed notes *Eureka!*, four descending *You lose!* Millicent's silence encompassed all languages and the void filled with Vivian and the flash of pages turning as we tumbled. I stood to escape, so full of the unsaid I was sure I would burst.

"How was your evening?" Millicent asked as I got to my feet.

"I thought of you," I told her.

She rolled her eyes, clicked her tongue.

It was not a lie, but what I did not say was that I had thought of Stephanie Leone, of a girl in Paris named Gerti who had been my first lover, of the whores Claude and I had known. Sublime lovemaking has two parts which gloriously join. The first is the sublimity of the specific—the specific lover, the specific place, the specific time. My obsession had its base in Vivian, in New Orleans in the last days of my twenty-second summer, in a room lit by the white light of open books. The specific lover is enough, but like a plague of blessings there is more. The second part is the way in which memories of other lovers are brought to the fore of the mind. Just like the teapot brought back the base of Vivian's spine, Vivian's ankle recalled Gerti's ankle. Vivian's hip reminded me of the hip of Andrea, a prostitute who liked to forgo the bed and stand for the act. The grip of Vivian's legs about my waist transported me to the Mississippi clearing where she'd watched me couple with Stephanie Leone, then took me back to the bed in which Peter sang silly songs while Millicent moved beneath me. It is not infidelity that causes the brain to make such connections, not desire for the remembered; rather, it is the way in which the ideal partner fills the mind with both glee and remembered glee.

Millicent made to stand, the empty teapot in her hand. I took it from her. "I may not be much of a cook, but I can bring water to boil," I joked.

The tea tin was empty. I'd fetched a box of tea from the studio a few days before, part of Remy and Madeleine's abandoned store. Two soliotypes floated in the leaves. I opened their cases and Madeleine and Remy gazed up at me. Both were nude. Remy was posed in half-profile, his shrunken arm invisible to the camera. Madeleine's head was raised and tilted, her pose careful enough to disguise the twist of her bones. I imagined the two of them in the studio, each wise to the faults of the other's body and able to suggest how those faults could be hidden from the camera's eye, and for a moment I was happy that they were beautiful in their memorials, then the sorrow of their poses came to me, the sadness of realizing all that remained was the trick.

⌐ ⌐ ⌐

Plate 14—Emily Hulbert, *1844. Mammoth-plate daguerreotype.*

IT WAS CUSTOMARY in the social set to have one's portrait made in the spring and a coming-out of both young person and portrait would often occur if the subject was a prominent bachelor or a marriageable young woman. As Marchand's fame grew his daguerreotypes quickly became part of this ritual.

In her memoir *Life in New Orleans in the Glory Days* (New Orleans: Smith & Herbet, 1870) Emily Moissenet (née Hulbert) offers an amusing note on this unusually large (33 x 43.2 cm) portrait and the party at which it and she debuted. She says the daguerreotype "accentuates each and every imperfection of my countenance. My nose is that of a monster, my chin a chisel, my eyes dots. When I complained to Mister Marchand, telling him that my face when rendered in pastel was much kinder, he merely smiled and told me, *My dear, the camera does not lie.*"

The cocktail of art and science the daguerreotype represented was enticing near mid-century, and even if it did point out strong noses and beady eyes, socially prominent young people soon found it the preferred medium for the yearly portrait. The loss of revenue was disastrous and many portraitists made slapdash attempts at embracing the new technology. It was obtainable via mail order and from traveling salesmen who offered their services as portraitists, teachers of the new art, and suppliers of the cameras, plates, and other necessities needed to make a living as a daguerreian. An oft-seen advertisement offered "[a] complete daguerreotype, with plates and appendages, perfect for a man of leisure, or a wise investor in search of a situation." There was money to be made and by 1844 over two dozen daguerreotype studios were listed in the city registry, an impressive number for a small metropolis whose population barely topped 100,000. Many of these studios were operated by artists who had once worked with brush and palette.

Marchand's was the city's most respected photographic studio, yet he was not content to allow inferior daguerreians to go about their business unmolested. He denounced them in farcical newspaper advertisements in which they were given silly nicknames. Exhibitions were held at which their work was paired with Marchand's superior renderings of the same subjects. Rumors circulated that more dastardly forms of sabotage were employed if these means did not drive a competitor out of New Orleans. When a studio operated by an openly disgruntled former Marchand assistant burned to the ground, a short string of letters to the editor of the *Bee* called for Marchand's arrest. The capture and lynching of the alleged arsonist, a free man of color named Antoine Felipe, ended the calls.

Plate 15—Vivian Marmu on Her 16th Birthday, December 19th, 1844, *1844. Half-plate daguerreotype.*

IT IS LIKELY that Vivian attended Emily's debut earlier in the year and witnessed the unveiling of Emily's portrait—W. O. Hulbert, Emily's father, was New Orleans's most successful sugar broker, and Francis Marmu, Vivian's father, was also involved in the sugar trade. Emily offers a list of the sixteen couples she claims her party brought together, but she makes no mention of Claude and Vivian. Perhaps Marchand met his wife when she came to his studio to have this portrait made.

Vivian holds a book with a ribbon tied about it. With the help of a magnifying glass the gift can be identified as the second volume of *The Pictorial Bible*, an illustrated version of the Old and New Testaments published in individual fascicles between 1843 and 1844 and as a two-volume complete edition in 1844. Vivian's head is tilted toward the Bible and her eyes are closed as if she is offering a prayer.

Felix Moissenet's December 20th column reports that at a lavish combination debut and birthday party held in the Cabildo the night of the 19th, Marchand was so "crazed by waltzing with Vivian" that he "tried to make a girl of a bearded man" by comically leading him onto the floor after Vivian had moved on to another dancing partner. The same column offers the news that Vivian had been betrothed to William Spats, a Boston textile merchant visiting the city, who had proposed the match at a dinner before the party. Spats returned to the East Coast to attend to business and arrange for the wedding, and when he came back to New Orleans in 1845 to fetch his fiancée he contracted yellow fever and died.

Pl. 15 is from the collection of Jessica Sayer, great-granddaughter of Joseph Sayer, a kitchen servant who grew up with Vivian and to whom she gave the portrait as a gift. Unsure of his true birthday, the two celebrated on the same date.

꒰ꀿ꒱

VIVIAN MADE IT a point to become trusted with the lives of tamed monkeys, myna birds, sparkling fish in bowls, orange trees in pots. Her pockets rattled with tarnished keys, gilded keys, keys on velvet cords, keys as massy as pistols. We left balls and parties early and made love on couches, chairs, rugs, bare floors in pantries, stairs and stair landings, once brazenly on a balcony from which we could observe two old men matching dominoes as easily as they could have seen us if they'd bothered to gaze out the window.

Guilt grew in me. I felt failure each time Vivian sent a note alerting me of the good news that a finch needed seed, an orchid water.

I convinced Millicent that Francis Marmu and I were finalizing our deal—a new studio in which he wished to invest generously. I returned from Vivian and invented tales of the click of abacus beads and visits to possible street addresses. I embroidered menus of make-believe meals I shared with my lover's father. My lies became so complex and complete that I started to believe them, and when I was nearly convinced of their authority I saw the spark of worry and distrust leave Millicent's eye. She and I debated the merits of the different colors of velvet, choosing couches and chairs and draperies for the studio.

I do not know what Vivian told her father and mother. We met in cafés, shops, a zoological park which charged a penny to see the menagerie. She always carried her opera glasses. She walked with them raised to her eyes, what lay blocks ahead clearer in them than what was below her feet.

Unable to bear another embrace under the watchful glare of a bubble-eyed fish in a jar, I took a small room above a coffee importer's and outfitted an apartment—a high bed with a feather mattress, a case of books, a writing desk. A spiral stair like a giant spring led up to the door and made it look as if the room had popped from a jack-in-the-box.

The warehouse was on the fringe of the district fronting the river. In daylight it was alive with stevedores and blacks loading and unloading cotton, sugar cane, and bunches of bananas. After dark only whores and drunken sailors were in the streets. From the one round window high on the wall above the head of the bed Vivian and I could hear them yell to one another. The window had no glass and the iron mesh which kept the birds out cut the moonlight into squares. While we were supposed to be dancing, Vivian posed in the segmented beam, cubes of light now on her belly, now on her face, now on her feet.

The smell of roasting coffee beans was overwhelming. It saturated the bed linen, the bread we brought to eat, the wine we drank, our clothes. I told Millicent that Marmu fancied coffee houses for our discussions. Once I brought a book home from the room. Sitting with Millicent the next day I opened it and the smell of coffee rose from its pages. I pulled Millicent from her chair and onto the floor. "What on earth were you reading?" she said as we lay panting among knotted shirts and torn skirts.

11 December 1844
Felix sent me a note telling me if I wanted a surprise I should follow Claude when he went to lunch with Marmu. I knew what the surprise would be and spent the morning watching Claude and wondering who she was. I was a fool to believe a man who could not bear the sound of children's voices wept for a girl he loved like a daughter—They held hands in a penny zoo. Followed them to a warehouse and asked a man eating his lunch under the warehouse's sign if he knew them and the man smiled and told me they were lovers who hid away in a secret room. Claude he knew to be an exiled Duke and the girl he had been told was the daughter of an

Ambassador whose family has feuded with the Duke's for generations—Lies upon lies upon lies. The smell of coffee Claude
carries home on him hung on the man and I felt sick smelling
it when I knew what it meant. At home again I broke all the
saucers on the floor—They cannot be replaced. Few come for
soliotypes. So many are dead and he hurts himself deeply by
refusing to make memorials. Those living think he is unkind
for refusing and many believe he paid Antoine Felipe to kill the
children. There is no money. I must be sensible. My father tired
of his wife before a year of marriage was finished and like my
mother was to him I will be to Claude—lover, true friend—and
like my father's wife was to my mother Claude's will be to
me—ignorant provider of rent and food and &ct. I found a
portrait of the girl among the dozens he keeps in a box of
examples and bound it in a red rag and sealed the knots with
wax. Cut two fingers picking up the porcelain. Boiled coffee
and waited. The smell turned my stomach. Claude came in
telling a lie about a sign painter and went dumb when he
smelled the coffee. Poured him a cup of it and asked him to
finish his thought and he said Marmu paid a man to paint a
sign and the man did not paint it and left the city with the
money. When I put the cup in front of him and asked him to
tell me about his meeting with Marmu he smiled and described
the soup he had not eaten and the cheese he had not tasted and
a pastry he may have seen in a baker's window. I listened and
questioned him. He needs the practice if he is to be a decent
fraud as a husband. He paused from praising the wine he had
not swallowed to sip his coffee and I said You should contrive
to marry the girl. He choked and sputtered and began to hic-
cup and stammer about Marmu and I said Marry her so that
we can live better than beggars and I left him to his coffee.

♏

*V*IVIAN'S SIXTEENTH BIRTHDAY fell in the middle of a freak cold snap the likes of which had never been recorded in New Orleans. Ice scummed the river, horse troughs froze solid. Mr. and Mrs. Marmu planned a huge party for Vivian's debut, an affair that marked those who received an invitation, the seal glossy purple and stamped by a heavy signet. Felix told me that a number of lifelong friendships ended when one friend was snubbed, one was lucky.

Mine came directly from the hand of Marmu. He passed it to me after Vivian and I endured her monthly sitting. The sky was curtained by clouds that absorbed daylight; it seemed the sun would never burn through. Marmu smiled at his daughter, three days away from her birthday. Vivian forced a grin so as to not betray us. I kept my eyes on the skylights. Finally the wind blew the clouds away. Exhausted from holding her mouth happy for so long, Vivian relaxed, unaware I'd removed the lens cover until I inhaled deeply, a noise she later told me I always made at that moment. Knowing any twitch would ruin the likeness, she could not change her relaxed pose.

In the developing room I coaxed her face into focus with mercury vapor. Her eyes were aimed at a book an uncle had sent as an early gift, her mouth unevenly set. Unposed she was revealed, nothing was hidden. That moment of nakedness was more breath-stopping than any of the many other seconds of her nudity I'd witnessed.

It pained me to give the portrait to her; I feared she'd hand it to the first urchin she came across in the street. "Do not lose this," I told her. She nodded and held the thing with both hands.

Marmu passed the heavy cream-colored invitation to me in lieu of payment. "You will of course be there."

"Of course," I agreed.

He smiled like a sovereign. "Bring your lady friend."

Vivian looked up from her portrait with a start. A fist closed around my heart as if my wife had been reminded of my mistress, not my mistress my wife.

⌀

Millicent's hands trembled when she held the invitation; she almost sang her joy. If she could have made a shirt of the thing she would have worn it in order to inspire jealousy in friends and shopkeepers. Vivian's debut was the single topic of all conversations. The exotic winter got nary a word, but the list of guests and rumors regarding the decorations spilled from many mouths and hung visible in the cold air.

Millicent was granted an audience with the dressmaker who was assembling the frocks for the list of lucky women. She returned to describe velvet and lace and fringe and satin and beadwork. The bill was stunning. I consulted the haberdasher who had the good fortune to be recommended by Mr. Marmu and established my own outlandish debt.

I did not want to go the ball. My love for Vivian was intensely private, a direct reaction to the restraint required when I was in her company in public. I managed that seemingly loveless control—she walking beside me with her opera glasses to her eyes while I pretended to look into shop windows so as to watch her reflection—because we were on our way to privacy.

The prospect of enduring an evening of handpicked suitors sizing her up was painful. I told Felix I was not going to attend when he summoned me to administer his monthly dose of abuse.

He covered his mouth as if shocked. "Not attend? But you're a favorite servant of the girl, if rumors are true."

Dunce, I stood and said "Servant?" before I could control myself.

Felix grinned, happy he'd trapped me. "Don't want to see her dance with a legion of men and boys, all of them after her . . ."— he fanned his fingers as if grasping at a word floating in the air, then made a fist—"hand?"

"Vivian is a kind young woman and I hope she marries a kind man."

Felix grinned again. "Oh, we all hope for that, Claude."

I did not see her for a week. Wise girl that she was, as explanation for her absence she sent a note that was no more than a list of things to be done for the ball: *Dressmaker, Comfort Mother, &tc.* No one would have known it was a lover's dispatch if it had been intercepted. I added cunning to my growing list of Vivian's qualities.

When Millicent asked why my meetings with Marmu had abruptly stopped, I told her he, like everyone else, was obsessed with his daughter's debut. There could be no business when a man was fixated on cakes and suitors.

I filled my days with work. I was glad to have yelling infants in the studio, overjoyed to greet quarreling young couples. Even a portrait I made of a dog moved me. I posed bottles and fruit when desperate. Millicent found my vigor humorous. Whenever she could she brought home what she considered absurd subjects. I made a number of portraits of sailors, their chests bared to display tattoos of ships and anchors bannered with the names of their mothers, lovers, and homelands. Once Millicent

returned leading a tiny man by the hand. He was no taller than
the chair upon which she had him stand while I made his portrait and she laughed herself blue in the face.

I still refused to make portraits of the dead and dying.

⌘

Millicent decided she wanted a party of her own, one even more
exclusive than the Marmus'. Her ideal guest list included only a
trio of couples. She spent hours writing down and then crossing
out six names. One day we met Felix in front of a fruit seller's
stall. They greeted each other before I could introduce them.
She invited him to dinner while he smelled an apple, and I was
stunned when he accepted without hesitation.

Felix was a block away, his bag of apples swinging with each
step, when I asked, "How do you know him?"

"Felix was young, I was young. . . ." She bit into a pear and
gazed off, a smile moving her face.

"You're young now," I observed.

"You're right." She spat a seed. "I am."

He was our party's only guest. Millicent brought out silver
and china I had never seen, the pantry yielding up treasures of
which I'd been ignorant for years. The butcher made money, the
baker too. Felix arrived with a spray of violets and a small red
glass bottle of scent for Millicent. I received a hearty handshake.
We three ate and then sat dulled by the food.

"Have you heard the news about Vivian Marmu?" Felix
asked as he raised his coffee cup to his lips. "She has been in the
company of a man named Spats as of late. He's from New
England."

"Spats?" I was lucky I didn't say more.

Felix smiled at me and nodded. "This debut may be a sham.
Rumor has it she's carrying Spats's child, and that the famous

fête is a way to trick wags and tell-alls off the scent." He grinned.
"I am not so easily distracted by the red herring."

"Could it be true?" Millicent wanted to know.

Felix spoke while he chewed a pastry. "Truth is not important, my dear. When the truth arrives come summer, be it baby
Spats or virgin Vivian, we'll all see it and the mystery will be
moot. The thrill is in the wondering, in the attempt to sort lies
from honesty. What is important is this: Have you heard some
are saying Vivian Marmu is ripe with the child of a man named
Spats?" He swallowed and rose, bade us good evening, and
made his exit.

"A success," Millicent judged. "I think he enjoyed the soup."
She stuck a finger in a cold bowl and tasted, her eyes closed. I
saw Vivian's mouth, Spats's finger.

"I need to take some air," I told her.

I studied Vivian's note in the warehouse room. I ran my fingers over the words, smelled the ink, bit off a corner of the
paper and let it melt on my tongue.

I had another she'd written, a single line on a strip of paper I
used to mark my place in whichever book I was reading. In
careful letters Vivian had recorded what she'd announced to me
one day: *From this high window, the river looks like a ribbon
for a gift package.*

⌒

So many were on their way to the ball that a carriage could not
be found. The wise engaged them weeks in advance; only the
lucky did not plan and still managed rides. Millicent and I
walked, both of us tortured by new shoes.

The cold had not lessened, but it made the ugliest aspects of
the streets beautiful—dishwater thrown from doorways froze
into mirrors, smoke spun from chimneys in twists that looked

as if children had drawn them onto the bright, late-afternoon sky. A stiff breeze threatened our hats. It smelled of turned earth and cooking carrots, then shifted and smelled of baking bread.

A crowd stood in a long queue before the Cabildo. A tall blond boy made a show of finding my name in his lucky book. Just beyond him there were pewter mugs of hot cider to sip and warm our hands with. Once we had chased off the chill, Millicent and I swam into the ballroom. Vivian was nowhere to be seen. The room was full of ladies stiff with the good posture of tight corsets and men with their thumbs tucked in their vest pockets. I saw Felix and Francis Marmu conversing. Felix winked when Millicent and I whirled past. I became dizzy trying to focus on faces in the crowd while I danced in large circles, then smaller ones. The music stopped but my head kept spinning. Vivian was nowhere.

A dozen dances later she appeared on the arm of a man I knew must be Spats. His forehead was high and shining, his eyes beady and the color of shit, the nose between them narrow and long—British blood. Vivian's dress was a marvel of satin almost the exact color of her skin. From even a short distance it was hard to tell where it ended and she began. Spats smirked the half-hearted smirk of a man who's too easily won a prize. My heart pushed against the keyboard of my ribs.

"Bit of a fop," Millicent judged.

"Francis Marmu tells me his family is quite wealthy," Felix said behind me.

"It's a pity the rich judge by the bulge of the wallet, not the more important bulge," Millicent told him.

Felix went off snickering. I heard him repeating what Millicent had said, heard the wake of mirth the crack left behind.

Another time I would have been proud of her joke, happy for the pinch she gave me when she told it—What poor man does not want to hear that his breechclout is more important than a fortune?—but my attentions were elsewhere. It was all I could do not to crash through the crowd and slap the smirk from Spats's face.

"Go and have your dance with the girl," Millicent said.

I caught myself wringing my hands. "What?"

"My dear, I've forgotten that this is your first debut. All the gentlemen will have one dance with our dear young lady, one last chance to confess their love before the untouched bud weds the shallowpate. It is, sir, a tradition."

I looked into her happy face and it was clear she was making jolly conversation, not taunting me with my infidelity. Fool, I did not realize it truly was a tradition.

Two queues of men formed on opposite sides of the room. The band began a sarabande. Vivian and Spats danced a single full circuit, then he handed her off to the first man in the line in which I stood, and that man took her across the floor and passed her along to the gent at the top of the other. Halfway back in my line I watched her smile while she was handed back and forth, each man obviously saying what Millicent claimed tradition demanded.

I heard the end of a proposal from her partner when he stepped away and let me take her hand. Her fingers were warm and moist. She would not meet my eye.

"Who is this Spats?"

"Tell me you love me," she said bitterly. "What you have to offer are kind words and what God gave you to make you different from me. Every man I've danced with tonight has offered the same or more, and there are hours of men and offers to come."

She jerked her hand from mine. We'd crossed the floor and another man took up where I had left off. He and Vivian stepped away, leaving me with my arms open and empty.

"Go back to your lady and stop making a fool of yourself over the girl," a woman's voice advised.

"You had yours," the man now at the front of the line told me from behind the curtain of a massive beard.

I covered my embarrassment by taking his hand and dancing him away. Stunned, he let me lead him for a few steps, then convulsed with laughter. He was so amused he seemed not to mind I'd cost him his turn. Laughing with his head tipped back, he took a place offered him midway in line.

I did not want to stay and watch Vivian move from one man to the next, then spend the evening on Spats's arm, but I couldn't leave: I was sure all of Felix's rumors would come true if I let her out of my sight.

I found Millicent drinking punch with Felix. "Do you favor that man more than me?" Millicent asked in a chipped voice. She pressed her arms against her sides and her breasts rose toward me.

Felix giggled. "These artists are prone to perversion," he joked to Millicent. "Men with whiskers," he looked at me and flattened his smile, "children," he turned to Millicent and grinned, "high yellows." The two of them laughed and I forced myself to join.

The lines of men were shrinking. My bearded dance partner gracefully took Vivian across the floor and gave her small hand to a red-headed boy with freckles bright as blood. I entered into conversations only if I could see Vivian over a shoulder or out of the corner of my eye, each transfer from man to man a needle in my side. I shadowed her from afar, ending jokes quickly and walking away from half-posed questions when she moved out of sight. Soon no one wished to talk to me. I marked her genuine smile, the way Spats's hand rested casually on the base of her spine as they danced. The Marmus left early. The party raged on.

In the street Millicent tossed her hat to the wind and sang after it as it shot off into the night. She danced down the hall and into the bedroom, an invisible partner in her arms. "I regret I was never given such a party," she lamented. "I would have loved such attention." She leaned to remove her slipper, its coppery satin scuffed, and I saw Vivian in the angles of Millicent's shoulders, heard her in the exhalation of Millicent's breath when she bent. I snuffed the lamp and felt Vivian when I took hold of Millicent in the dark.

Next door to us a family with a young son ran a shop which sold keys and locks. Millicent had hired the boy to fetch us a pan of sweet rolls and the English and French editions of the morning papers.

The *Tropic*'s headline yelled *William Spats to Wed Vivian Marmu* in tall type. The brief paragraph below was little more than the histories of the Spats and Marmu families and their businesses, but I read it again and again hoping to find the clue that exposed the joke. I learned about the Spats and their flax and silk and cotton, about the Marmus and their sugar cane. There was no joke. The food from the party was mentioned briefly and with much admiration; my dance with the bearded fellow got a sentence. Only Felix could have written the thing.

Millicent was still asleep, her deep, even breathing audible through the bedroom's open door. I tore the notice from the

paper and dipped my pen. *Is it true?* I wrote in the margin above
the headline, then folded the swatch of news lengthwise. I threw
a coat over my nightshirt and rushed barefoot from the house
into the frozen streets. The Marmu home was only a few icy
blocks away, and I passed no one. I gave the note to a maid I
found letting in the cat, paying her a dollar to ensure the epistle
was given only to Vivian, and then only when she was alone.

The maid earned her dollar: A black boy I recognized from
the Marmu's kitchen beat me home. He was raising his fist to
knock when I turned the corner onto Toulouse. He handed me
the same bit of news I had left for Vivian.

With a crayon Vivian had drawn an X across the article. *Shall
we drink coffee at seven?* she proposed in neat script along the
lower margin.

I pulled out all the money I had in my coat pockets and gave
it to the boy. It was so much he tried to give it back, sure I had
made some mistake. I insisted I knew what I had given him and
that he take it all. He stood wild-eyed. "I could buy . . . " he
realized aloud.

"Spend it on something that will give you long pleasure," I
told him.

Millicent was still asleep. I crawled under the blankets and
pressed against her. She woke with a shriek. "How did you
manage to get your feet that cold?"

ℰ

Vivian stroked my cheek with her big toe and peered out the
window through her opera glasses. The flicker from the stove
colored her shoulders and the backs of her legs reddish and the
moon through the grated window masked her with lace. I lay at
her feet admiring her painted angles.

"Spats is odious. My mother thinks he would make a good

match because he mangles his vowels and speaks in the same doltish manner as her moron father did. There is a ship flying both the French and, I think, the Italian flag. How can that be?"

I took her toe into my mouth and bit it. Vivian turned the glasses and looked at me through the wrong end.

"When do you intend to break off this sham engagement?" I asked.

Vivian frowned, then turned back to the window, the fire and the moon coloring the quilt.

I wrapped my fingers around her ankle. "When—" I started to ask again.

"Snow," she said, puzzled.

I rose and stood beside her on the bed and watched it salt the rooftops.

"Snow is for Boston," she corrected the sky.

Vivian dressed and charged down the stairs. It took me a moment to find both boots. Her eyelashes sparked with snowflakes when I joined her.

Across the street a young whore stood catching flakes on her tongue. "The stars have come loose," she called to us.

cf cf cf

Plate 16—Eighth of January Parade on Canal Street, *c. 1844–45. Full-plate daguerreotype.*

WHAT WAS IT about photography that so delighted people in the mid-1800s? Never before had a moment been so perfectly trapped. Painters were encouraged to work from daguerreotypes, not fussy paid models or subjects too busy to sit again and again for a portrait. Architects were promised benefits from images of great buildings with details unattainable from even the best lithographs—every gargoyle's smile visible, the mortar between each brick discernible. Photography advanced armchair travel beyond written accounts and imperfect sketches to accurate views of the Great Pyramids and the Parthenon.

America was in love with technology, but it was most in love with itself. Like Narcissus's still water, the mirror of the daguerreotype was irresistible. Local scenes, like Pl. 16's celebration of either the twenty-ninth or thirtieth anniversary of the Battle of New Orleans, were more revered than those of other cities or distant lands. Marchand's gallery was well known for its wide range of New Orleanian subject matter—persons of distinction, buildings under construction, the bustling port, major thoroughfares at noon. The city had suffered a devastating economic crisis in 1837, and each new year of recovered prosperity made its citizens love it more. This image was winner of the First Premium Award at the 1845 Agricultural and Mechanics' Association Fair. Because of the long exposure the horses pulling floats and the floats themselves appear cloaked in clouds, but because the crowds have paused to watch the parade pass, much of the image is remarkably unblurred—the dark Xs of workmen's suspenders, the domes of gentlemen's bowlers, and the cupolas of ladies' parasols.

The *Bee* said of the photograph, "From a rooftop overlooking Canal Street, Claude Marchand has caught in an eye-blink what New Orleans has again become: A Metropolis alive with work and trade and celebration, a port where the World brings its goods and leaves with cotton, sugar, and the knowledge that the Crescent City is the Venice of the Americas. We consider Marchand's Soliotype the *ne plus ultra* of excellence in the amazing art which he has brought to us."

᠊ᡒ

*D*AWN'S SKY WAS blue as a bird's egg and its light was sharp. What snow remained glazed hitching posts and puddles and made small monuments of piles of horse excrement. Each frozen breath I took felt like a drink of schnapps, both cold and burning, and my exhalations smoked in front of me. I went to a *café carbon* to get my morning coffee and buy coal for the studio's stove and found a long queue in the street, all of us holding our buckets and waiting for the tardy shopkeeper to arrive. Unprepared for sudden winter, men and women stood wrapped in blankets. Some wore three or four coats, one over the other, their elbows locked straight inside the layered sleeves. One boy's head was covered in a turban that appeared to be twisted from a pair of long johns. He stood on his bucket and sang "Good King Wenceslas" to us. When the shop opened he was pushed to the front of the line and treated to a mug of chocolate.

When I made it home, hot coffee in my belly, hand and wrist stinging from the pail's weight, I found Vivian and William Spats standing in the courtyard shivering. Spats spoke while Vivian nodded: "We wish to have our portraits made so we can exchange them." Vivian's breath blossomed in the cold. Over her shoulder I saw Millicent watching through a frosted window.

The small stove quickly filled the studio with heat. Spats stood beside it warming his hands. "I seem to have brought Boston with me in my pockets," he joked.

"How do you mean, Willy?" Vivian asked him.

"The cold," Spats explained, annoyed. "It is cold in Boston. Surely you remember how cold the winter months are in Boston?"

"Of course, the cold, how silly of me." She nervously smoothed her skirts across her knees.

There are ways the camera can be tilted and a man can be posed to thin him if he is fat, to shorten his brow if it is high with baldness, to add character to his face if his face is without character. Such processes can also be reversed, and I did my best to make much of Spats's ugliness. Vivian took the portrait from him, trading hers for it, and looked up at me. "This is very nice," she told me. "Thank you Mr. Marchand."

Midday sun burned away every trace of winter and I ate my lunch in the courtyard with Millicent, both of us bare-headed as if it were spring. The note came as we drank our tea: *M. Marchand, Thank you for the fine portrait you made of William. I will treasure it always.* I imagined Vivian writing the brief message, Spats looking over her shoulder, the pen shaking in her hand—the script was jerky and hurried. In her scrawl I could see a message, as if she'd written in a code only we two knew.

"The girl's going to marry Spats," Millicent said, and I acted as if it was a question.

"I'm not sure that's been decided."

She noisily gathered cups and dishes and left me alone in the sun. I put the card in the small wallet in which I kept Vivian's notes: the inventory of tasks she'd sent before her debut, the record of her vision of the Mississippi as a ribbon on a box, the newspaper notice with her X negating Felix's lie.

⁂

I went looking for Moissenet. In each café I was told that he'd moved on to another, and so I searched for hours, leaving the brick and mud of the French Quarter, crossing Canal, and heading into the almost rural fringe of the American quarter. A stinging wind came with dusk and yanked open my coat. I stuck my hands deep in my pockets and shouldered into the cold. I found Felix in a coffeehouse near the Jewish cemetery. He was happy to see me: He wanted another cup and the shop's owner would not extend him credit. I ordered brandy and hot coffee for us both.

"I'm told you made an attractive likeness of Spats this morning," he said.

Brandy burning in my gut, bowl of *au lait* warming my hands, I felt for the first time the fear that the engagement was real, then felt foolish for not feeling that fear before.

"Is she really going to marry him?" I stupidly asked.

Felix shrugged. "Why shouldn't she?" He sipped his coffee and smirked. "There are no other adequate prospects."

I drank so I would not speak.

"Marchand, I'm no fool. You want to be the daddy in a paper-doll family, Vivian your paper bride, a little paper baby connecting your two paper hands."

I nodded reflexively, charmed by the image, then caught myself when I saw Felix's smile. He shook his head indulgently.

"If you were another man maybe you could be that paper daddy, a man more successful in business, a man who did not have a black woman in his bed." He drained his bowl and gestured toward the cemetery. "Do you wish to walk with me among the graves?"

Millicent was on her knees scrubbing the kitchen floor when I returned.

"I have reached an agreement with Marmu," I told her. The lie came easily; I had rehearsed it again and again while walking, and it spilled from my mouth in the smooth, slow gait of recited verse. "Vivian's engagement to Spats is a sham. Marmu intends to swindle the man, then break off the engagement. I am now secretly, truly engaged to Vivian, and we shall marry as soon as Marmu has completed his fleecing of the Yankee."

Millicent slowly circled her brush over an obstinate spot. "And when will that be?"

"Marmu's estimate is middle-June."

She dipped the brush into the pail and set on another spot.

"I have agreed that you will leave the house."

She looked up sharply.

"Mrs. Marmu would object if she knew you were here."

Millicent's eyes were red from the soap.

"Shortly before we marry he intends to finance a studio," I blurted, surprising myself.

Millicent turned her attention back to the floor.

☞ ☞ ☞

Plate 17—Francis Marmu, his wife Charlotte, and his daughter Vivian, *1845. Half-plate daguerreotype.*

The Marmu family was well known. Mr. Marmu was a city councilman as well as a businessman, and his antics were famous. Felix Moissenet relates in his series of pamphlets *Prose Sketches of Notable New Orleanians* that "Francis Marmu was a man of great valor. When a black cat one day found its way into the City Building and then breached the defenses of the Council Room, Councilman Marmu was unafraid. He launched a fusillade of inkstands at the invading feline, chasing and cursing it as it attempted to circle and attack his flank. When other councilmen were struck and splattered by the missiles, and thus awoke from dreams of law and commerce, Mr. Marmu was so wise and quick as to be unharmed by the fusillade they launched in revenge. He dispatched the cat and made motions that the session be ended. Motion was seconded quickly and the brave man was carried away to a fine meal in commemoration of his thrilling victory."

At first glance, Pl. 17 is odd due to the positioning of the subjects, Charlotte and Vivian segregated from Francis Marmu by a column with an almost indistinguishable daguerreotype set atop it. A Moissenet pamphlet offers an explanation: The portrait on the pillar is of William Spats, and the ribbons both mother and daughter wear pinned to their breasts are in remembrance of the dead fiancé. Moissenet tells us, "Vivian wore the grosgrain *in memoriam* of William until she replaced it with one for her father, then replaced that with one for her beloved mother."

<p>

ℳILLICENT TOOK AN apartment on Royal between Bienville and Conti directly after the turn of the year. She refused to even look at the room above the coffee warehouse. "I would feel like stored merchandise," she told me when I offered. It took her three days to find rooms, another two to become comfortable. I was glad to see her narrow, careful script when she sent an invitation to tea on that fifth day.

Millicent's balcony looked over Royal. A pastry shop was two doors away, and while we sat and ate bread and cheese the smell of chocolate and butter was so strong that my cheese began to taste like a sweet. The cold had broken and the streets were filled with strollers gawking into shop windows. I had the playful urge to spit down onto their hats. Happy with the sun on my hands and my face, I turned to Millicent and smiled.

"Don't ever come here again," she said.

I thought she was joking. "I'll be here every day."

She slapped me so hard I dropped my cup. "How will old Mrs. Marmu feel if someone mentions seeing you on my gallery? Won't that expose the counterfeit of your newfound purity?"

"Millicent, please."

"Please what?"

"Please understand."

"I understand, I understand quite well. You must think I'm a fool if you truly believe I don't understand. Either that or you're a fool."

She pointed to the cracked cup at my feet. "Oh! My! Look what you've done! I now have only one cup, and so I can no longer be expected to ask you to tea."

<p>

I stood in the street and people flowed around me. Suddenly the black boy from the Marmu kitchen was before me, arms full of groceries. I sent him home with a note asking Vivian to meet me above the coffee warehouse as soon as she was able.

The sun fell while I waited in the small room, the half-moon rising behind a cloud. Bells rang away the hours. Just as I was ready to give up hope and leave, cursing the black boy for not delivering my note, a key turned in the lock. I jumped up and pulled the door open. The boy stood on the landing silently appraising me, then explained "Miss Marmu gave me the key." He held out an envelope. The note inside was folded many times. I pulled the accordion of pleats flat and read the single line of unsteady letters: *I think of you often and hope you are well.* Again I thought of her at her desk, Spats across the room reading to her from the newspaper, her mother and father watching him and smiling while he mispronounced words. I could feel the fear that tightened her shoulders while she dipped her pen, a fear that someone would ask what she was writing and she would be unable to hold back a confession.

The boy said, "My name is Joseph." He studied me for a moment more, then dug in his pocket and held out his hand. A watch gleamed in his palm. "I bought it with the money you gave me." He gave a short bow and left.

I had brought two oranges to give to Vivian. I skinned and ate both. I pinched the peels over the fire and watched the small, bright flashes of blue flame. There was no reason to stay in the room, but I did not want to return to a place I knew I would find empty and dark. I loitered and touched things I remembered her touching.

The house was indeed dark. I lit every lamp and candle I could find. Once I had the place ablaze, I filled my pipe and lit a spirit lamp and concentrated on the opium. Soon I was floating in warm, dark water. Boats hung with lanterns passed and their oarsmen bade me climb aboard, but I refused, content to bob in the river, or lake, or ocean. The moon was replicated many times by the reflections of the boats' lanterns on the water's surface.

2 January 1845
Claude has made his deal with Marmu and part of that deal has me put out of my house. Broke plates and cups so none were left in even numbers then put the nude Claude made of me in with the linens so she will find it. Took rooms a week ago and have been filling them with Claude's credit—Bought three chairs and three rugs and three small tables and three

elephants made of wood, each the size of a dog. I have given them names and I tell them what a bastard Claude is and what a fool I am.

8 January 1845
Claude found the nude among the pillowslips and brought it to me and first I thought he was apologizing then I realized he was trying to rid the house of my every mark. Sent him away and spent the morning in the bath tipping the soliotype from mirror to portrait trying to see what changes have transformed me from beloved—Same teeth, same breasts, same nose.

$\mathcal{P}$

$\mathcal{A}$ KNUCKLE AGAINST my door stopped a dream in which Vivian became a paper doll. We wed and I folded her into a small shape and carried her in my pocket. I started to slip back into the dream and the knock came again. A large candle spilled skeletal wax trails onto the table at my elbow. Uneasy on my feet, I made my way to the door and found a dapper gent on the top stair, his face masked by a dark beard.

He tipped his hat. "Millicent has sent me." He offered me an open hand which I almost shook—I was opium-stunned and a friend of hers was a friend of mine—then I saw in his palm he held the nude in which she lay on the couch from which I had just risen.

Behind a beard which resembled a disguise made of wool, Millicent's new lover was my fetch. Our eyes—his light, mine dark, our only difference—met when we looked straight ahead. The narrowness of his shoulders was such that we could have traded jackets and been comfortable. He pocketed the nude and spoke: "My name is Victor Benton and I am in dire need of a portrait."

"A moment and I'll meet you," I told him.

I poured a pitcher of water over my head while he waited in the courtyard, his posture a mirror of mine—head tipped to the right, body hinged back a few degrees too far from the waist, right heel touching left toe. The beard tickled his chest. I felt the wires of new whiskers on my chin and yearned to shave. I started when I recognized him as the man I'd danced with at Vivian's debut.

He needed a portrait to send to a fiancée in Boston, a fact that did nothing to soothe me. He was pleased by the likeness I managed. The sun had been kind and the portrait was indeed a good one. "Do you have views of New Orleans?" he asked after he finished his praise of it. "My Susana is convinced I aim to bring her to a city of mud where everyone must live in boats to avoid sinking into the muck."

"I've never made a view of the city," I admitted proudly.

He nodded seriously. "Is the human countenance the only worthy subject?"

I thought of my portraits of dogs and fruit. "No, I've made still-lifes."

"But never a view of a street, or a workman?"

"There is purity in a portrait," I explained. "The subject is removed from the hustle of his life. Attempting to record a workman at work would show only the blur of labor. The only people who would appear as they truly are would be loafers wasting their lives. Why would I want to record loafers wasting their lives?"

"A realistic history would be created."

"Art is not realistic history."

He pulled a cane from the umbrella stand filled with sabers and parasol and tapped a book on top of a trunk filled with hats and jackets and gloves. "A cobbler dressed as a banker holding a law book he cannot read is art?"

I winced at his mention of a cobbler, imagining my father standing for a portrait, his face distorted by an angry frown.

The doctor cut the air with the cane. "I know your kind. You hate it that men are not made of canvas and paint," he accused. "Art to you is canvas and paint, not men. I'm of the opposite opinion. I love the fact that man is beyond canvas and paint. Man is art, art is fake." He held up the portrait and I looked into two versions of his light eyes. "This is why I admire your soliotype."

He opened his wallet and spoke before I could argue. "I need to convince Susana that New Orleans is as much a city as Boston—there's a challenge worthy of your goal to build a high wall between art and reality." He handed me a stack of notes.

I counted the money—two hundred dollars. "I don't understand what you're asking for."

"Her family and friends may be able to get her to negate our engagement if they can convince her that New Orleans is no more than an outpost in the wilderness. I need ten views that will convince her otherwise. I'll pay twenty dollars each. Millicent told me you could do this, in fact that *only* you could do this. Was she wrong?"

I creased his bills in my fist. "Ten views," I agreed.

↶

I aimed to make ten soliotypes that would convince Benton's Susana that New Orleans was in fact a city while at the same time making it clear that images of shop windows and milk wagons are not and can never be art.

I set up my camera on a corner and indiscriminately made a dozen views of fat men dickering with butchers over the price of hams, dirty children torturing dogs, nannies nicking gewgaws. I assumed each soliotype would show only ghosts walking the streets, motion pushing the living into the spirit world, but I did not care. I drank a beer sold to me from an alleyway window, made a plate of the alleyway and the empty glass, and packed up my camera at noon—two hundred dollars for an hour's work and Millicent's lover made a fool.

My happiness over such good fortune did not last long. Business was slow. My credit was thin and I was surviving on shopkeepers' memories of my former ability to pay my debts. A dozen people an hour sat for portraits at the peak of my prosperity; I was lucky if I saw a dozen a week by the time Millicent moved out. I had to sell the piano and most of the furniture from the house. Only the studio's movables were spared in the name of appearance. I spent the afternoon spending Benton's money. At dusk I held only a handful of coins, but I was restored with the grocer, the baker, the butcher, the haberdasher, and the wine seller. I carried home a bottle, a chop, and a loaf of bread, and I wore a new shirt.

I'd tacked a note and a pencil on a string to the studio door inviting those wanting portraits to leave their names so that I could arrange sittings. The pencil dangling on its twine moved in a breeze and made small tally hatches on the blank paper, reminding me of debts soon due—I owed my supplier of plates and chemicals a large sum.

I cooked my mutton and drank my cognac, adding figures again and again on the paper from which the chop had come. No matter how I tried to fool the numbers they always managed to announce I was soon to be penniless. I stared at the map

of blood and calculations until I was nearly insane; I had to
burn the paper in the stove.

⌐P

9 March 1845
*I came home from walking with Benton and Claude was
behind the door waiting. He knocked Benton down and I am
sorry Benton was injured but thrilled by the violence of
Claude's jealousy. I knew I could not seem pleased so I
frowned when he pushed Benton out the door and when he
fell to his knees to beg me to forgive him I slapped him so
hard I split his lip. He followed on his knees when I went into
the bedroom and I taunted him by undressing as if he was not
there while he kept begging me to forgive him and to see that
he knew he had been wrong. Shut your mouth and get into the
bed I told him in a man's voice. Took my pleasure then pulled
free of his arms and got up from the bed before he could take
his. I stood with my back to him while he tugged at himself
and tried to cajole me back into bed with sweet words and
apologies. I acted deaf and stood with a smile he could not see
while he grunted and soiled the sheet. He said I want to show
you a surprise and I thought it was a joke so I put on an
angry face before I turned. Claude was pale as the sheet and
thin as a sick man. He told me Marmu and I have made our
deal and I want to show you where we will open the studio.
On Canal Street I saw in his eyes that he was lying about the
studio. I knew what he was about and when I saw a To Let
sign and asked Is this the place? he smiled and nodded and
assured me it was indeed. He began a long fib and I told him I*

was leaving the city to see my mother. I told him When I come back I will look for you here.

⌀

Z COULD NOT sleep and I had no opium. I stood at the window drinking what remained of the cognac hoping each shadow on the street was Millicent. None were. Soon I could no longer bear the sight of one more pickpocket or prostitute looking for marks.

Unable to find two matching shoes, I wore a boot and one of the dancing slippers I'd worn to Vivian's debut. Cognac made me stupid and I lost my way. I had to convince a whore to lead me—I told her we were headed to my room. When we reached Millicent's address I paid her for what I did not want and she was perfectly willing to take my money and leave me. Millicent did not answer when I called out. I lost my slipper climbing from the street to the second-floor balcony. I took off my boot when I noticed how handy the toes were for climbing. Barefoot, it was easy to get to Millicent's gallery.

I pressed my face to a window. Millicent was not in her bed. I tried to force the sash and could not, then tried others. The parlor's window was not latched. In the dark I reeled from room to room, knocking into chairs. The sharp edge of a table nearly gelded me and in the middle of the table the nude of Millicent flashed moonlight. I put it in my pocket, determined no one else would show up at my door brandishing the thing. One hand over my groin, the other out in front, I felt my way to the bedroom. I turned down the covers and put my face to the linens.

Boots on the landing woke me. A door opened and I heard Millicent's voice, then a man's. A lamp was lit and a band of light came under the bedroom's door. Panic shook me—if I was mistaken for a burglar I might be killed—then I heard Millicent laugh. When I put my eye to the keyhole I saw Millicent and Victor Benton on the couch, her breasts bare and his hands on them. I threw open the door and the doctor jumped to his feet. His pants had been unbuttoned and they fell to his ankles. When I hit him he took one step backward, tripped in the shackles of his fallen trousers, and fell to the rug so hard that dishes rattled in the cabinet. There was a long moment of still silence and then the doctor crawled to the door on his hands and knees, reaching up to turn the knob.

I unbuttoned my pants and let them drop, pulling one foot free to avoid Benton's fate. Millicent glared at me for a moment, her mouth tight in an angry knot, then stood and slapped me. I followed her when she stomped into her bedroom and grabbed her from behind. Our feet slid and we grunted as we struggled, then our balance failed and we fell onto the bed. I scrambled after her and caught her arms as she tried to fight me off with a pillow.

When it was over a flush the shape of a bird was printed across the top of Millicent's chest. "You'll go now that you've had what you came for?" she said.

"I came to tell you the good news," I fibbed. "Marmu has given me the money for a studio. Get dressed and I'll show you."

She snorted in disbelief, but took up her dress from the floor and pulled it on. I searched for my pants for a long drunken moment, then realized I was dragging them behind one leg.

Millicent found a shawl and a hat and stood before a mirror

for a moment. "All right," she said to my reflection, "let me see."

I took her by the elbow and pulled her along Royal and at the corner of Canal took an impulsive right turn. In the middle of the block a window held a For Let sign.

"Here," I told her. "Here is where Marmu and I have decided to open the studio."

Millicent cupped her hands against the glass and peered inside.

"The first floor will be a large gallery with couches and chairs and oil paintings, perhaps there will be a piano—there will be a piano. The second floor will house the studio." The more details I added—a bust of Homer ordered from New York, an assistant hired, newspaper advertisements already placed—the more comfortable I became with the lie. "I would like you to act as hostess, to greet the clients when they enter, to play the piano we have bought. Marmu agrees you are the only one for the job."

Millicent turned away from her view of the empty room and studied my face with the same concentration she'd given the dark space on the other side of the glass. She tested the knob. "Do you have the key?"

"We have not made the final deal," I explained, believing what I said.

Millicent nodded. "I've made plans to go and see my mother in Mobile."

"Your mother in Mobile?" It was the first I had heard of her mother. Fool, I almost believed her water-born, Aphrodite from the Mississippi. In my most rational moments I assumed her mother was a slave.

"When I return from Mobile I'll look for you here."

⁂

The next morning I went to Francis Marmu's office on Canal Street. Tall poles of sugar cane were carved into the blood-and-cream marble fronting the building. Inside I found Marmu in amazing humor. Near Baton Rouge a rebellion of cane cutters had been put down by a small army he'd hired and preparations were under way for a party in honor of the resurrection of his profits. He'd learned of the rout only moments before I crossed his threshold; a magnum had been opened. The dozen clerks he employed had left their desks and drank toasts.

He clapped me on the back and handed me a stout cigar when he saw me. "You must come to my celebration!" he told me.

"I will, I will, but I've come to ask a favor."

Marmu waved his cigar, signaling me to continue.

"I would like to open a studio on Canal. My current address is far from foot traffic and a more central location would boost my business."

"Wise, wise. Very wise," Marmu agreed.

I took a breath and prepared for defeat. "The favor would be a loan so that I could open such a studio."

I had come on the right day, at the right hour. Marmu was flushed with victory. It took all of his composure to keep him from vaulting his desk to get at his cashbox.

I signed a stack of contracts a clerk paused long enough from the party to bring out.

"A partnership," Marmu told me. "Now we have two things to celebrate this evening."

I left with a dispatch case filled with money, a halo of cigar smoke above my head. I went first to the sign painter and paid for a huge banner, then set out to locate the landlord of the address where Millicent would find me when she returned.

⌒P

I paced from the house to the studio wishing someone would come for a portrait, anything to fill the slow sweep of my watch's hands. I boiled coffee and drank cup after cup until I could feel my eyes move dryly in their sockets. I mopped the floors, stood on a chair and knocked down spiders' webs from the corners of rooms with a broom, then emptied the supply cabinet and replaced each and every item in careful place. I was proud of my shining floors and neat rows but startled to find how little time I'd filled with an eternity spent cleaning. I drank a small sip of Armagnac to calm myself, then panicked and filled my mouth with violet lozenges, blowing into my palm and sniffing my breath for signs of the liquor.

I wished for a family in need of a portrait to send grandfather in Berlin.

I considered climbing onto the roof and washing the skylights, then made myself sit when I realized I was being ridiculous. Remembering Benton's views triggered a deep sigh of relief—something to do with my hands. I laughed over the spectacle of him tripping on his own pants. I owed the poor fool ten soliotypes with which he could lure his Susana south, and I intended to give him two extra to make up for his embarrassment.

I finished each slowly, begging my watch to eat minutes. So little light came through the yellow tissue covering the developing room's small window that each view looked the same, all dozen filled with the hard angles of buildings and a jumble of people and mules.

I took the soliotypes into the studio and laid them out on the table in a long row so I could decide which color of case would convince foolish Susana to accept Victor's proposal. Red seemed the obvious answer.

A horse's head appeared in one plate, its rump in another down the row. I put the split nag together and then noticed the same thing happened to letters painted on a rug merchant's windows. I paired the parts of the reversed message and made a triptych—horse, horse and words, words. Other groupings occurred. One set of five was a fragmented panorama of an entire block of Royal Street, the windows of Millicent's apartment visible in the next-to-last plate. The remaining four provided a duo of diptychs: A butcher and a customer who paused in their discussion of a goose were as perfectly recorded as they would have been had they brought the bird to the studio; a gang of children tying a bottle to a dog's tail with a length of twine was reduced to a circle of smears, only the bottle and the string clear. Crowds were thinned. Running boys and horses disappeared, their quickness erasing them.

I pulled the view of Millicent's windows from its row and searched for a face at the glass. There was none. I studied the plate and felt my breath catch the same way it had caught the day Daguerre held the portrait of a sunflower in his trembling hand. The clipped breath startled me, as did my racing heart. In my hand I held a soliotype of the front of a building.

<p

I made one hundred views of New Orleans. My feet ached from the walking and my shoulders burned from the weight of the camera, the tripod, and the bag of holders with their plates inside.

There were so many soliotypes that the small table in the developing room was quickly covered and I had to stack them around my feet. I did not look as I took each from above the heated mer-

cury and washed it. The studio's windows were black when I finished. The weak light of the spirit lamps in the developing room
showed only the outlines of furniture. I pushed a table against the
wall and laid all one hundred and twelve views edge to edge on
the floor, then lit a lamp. Its flame burned in the doorways of
shops and the windows of houses, burned in the hand of a man
imploring a laughing crowd to prepare for the Second Coming,
burned like flaming hair on the figurehead of a ship being filled
with bales of cotton.

The soliotype does not guarantee beauty—ugly things can
find their way before the lens—but it does provide a pause, a
held breath, and sometimes ugliness softens when it pauses and
holds its breath. Frozen for a moment, New Orleans's ugliness
was dimmed. I surveyed the ugly city I'd made myself ignore for
years.

A knock jerked my head up. "You are *late*," a strange voice
told me through the door.

"Late?" I could not look away from the views.

"It's Joseph. Miss Vivian has sent me to fetch you. She is losing faith."

⌀

Marmu's face was blackened with burnt cork and he wore a
twine noose about his neck. "Down with the niggers!" he
hollered. Joseph pushed me forward and Marmu caught me in
a handshake and pulled me along the hall and into a party of
yelling black-faced drunks. Vivian sat in a corner with her mother. Above her thick pale neck Charlotte Marmu wore a mask
the glossy color of coal which was painted with wide red lips.
Vivian was barefaced. She glared at me while I separated myself
from her father and made my way to the corner.

"I'm sorry I am late arriving," I told mother and daughter. "I was at a temperance meeting, and the discussion was so engaging I did not notice the time passing." I turned to Mrs. Marmu. "When will the heathen learn that the answer to their problems is not to be found in a bottle?"

Vivian tried to keep a smirk to herself but could not. Her mother made approving noises from behind her mask and I was sure her hidden smile was as large as the mask's painted grin. "I have heard you spoken of highly, Monsieur Marchand," she told me, her French so poor I was momentarily unable to recognize the words.

"I am glad to hear that," I answered in English.

Spats did not appear to be in the room. "Where is your fiancé?" I asked Vivian.

"William has gone to Boston this morning and abandoned me here."

"He has business to attend to," Mrs. Marmu defended.

"Why have you not sent me any notes?" Vivian asked in rapid French.

"Slowly, dear," her mother begged.

"When do you estimate the heat will return?" Vivian carefully pronounced, her words like tickling fingers.

A roar filled the room and we turned to watch Francis Marmu aim a boot at a servant's rear. A line of men formed and took their turns kicking the man. Mrs. Marmu stood and raised her mask. "You'll excuse me, Mr. Marchand?" I nodded and she set out across the room to berate her husband.

As soon as her mother was out of earshot Vivian asked, "Have you quit loving me?"

"Quit? Loving? You?" I stammered.

"Slowly, dear," Vivian mocked.

She led me to a pantry and had Joseph stand sentry. The

party raged while she and I reminded ourselves in the dark of the other's ears and chin, neck and hips. Marmu's laugh shook the house and was almost hidden by the hiss of fabric under our fingers. I combed her hair with my hand. Vivian's mouth tasted of peach liqueur. Joseph knocked code on the closet door and we froze. A bottle broke on the floor and a man cursed. When Joseph rapped the all-clear, our teeth clicked in the mad rush to resume the kiss. "Slowly, dear," Vivian said when we parted for air. A crackling cloud of raised skirts billowed about my waist. I bent my knees to even our heights. We moved against the wall, the door.

She left me alone in the pantry and ran for her room so she would not be seen with flushed cheeks and mussed hair. I counted to one hundred as she had instructed, and when I opened the door Joseph pulled out his watch and told me the time, grinning at his shoes. He led me back to the party and Mr. Marmu caught me in an embrace. I felt burnt cork rub from his face onto mine.

"Victory!" he yelled in my ear. "Nothing is as sweet!"

Shots rattled in the courtyard. Marmu pushed me to the window and I saw a Roman candle vomiting flame. The courtyard blazed, fireworks hissing and sparking. Red and green suns burned under my lids when I closed my eyes. Marmu cheered and shot his hand up in a toast, tossing his wine on all near him. I slipped from his grip and found the door.

I blinked until the street materialized, the twin suns slowly fading. The taste of Vivian's tongue was still in my mouth. A rocket striped the sky. I watched its orange tail and remembered the lamp's flame flickering in the views.

౪

When I knocked on Victor Benton's door I heard a scramble and the muted noise of objects falling onto a rug. A minute passed silently, then careful steps came nearer and nearer. I knocked again and heard a startled gasp, then Benton asked, "Who's there?"

"Claude Marchand," I told the door.

There was a long silence. "Are we friends, Marchand?"

As far as I knew we were not. "All is forgiven," I assured him.

The doctor threw open the door and embraced me, a startling action—if we were friends we were new friends, not the kind who hugged upon meeting. "You've got soot on your face," he whispered into my ear.

I pulled away and touched the mark Marmu had left on me. "I have the views," I told him.

He nodded and ushered me in, checking the stairwell before he closed the door. "One can never be too careful. Before I left Boston my mother-in-law-to-be told me she was hiring someone to watch me."

The room was barely furnished. Even so, the clutter was amazing. Papers were scattered across the floor, books lay open on chairs and sills, bottles filled with vivid juices were set in a circle on the table.

"I'm sure it was a lie, one intended to keep me honest." The doctor smiled. From beside an open book he lifted a small plate on which rested several lumps of what appeared to be dark green resin pressed into the shapes of nuts. Their odor was strong, a distillation that made me think only of the color—they smelled dark green. "Hashish," the doctor explained. "A decoction of Indian hemp, butter, and a small quantity of opium. You have enjoyed it?"

I shook my head no.

Benton's brows bounced happily. "I'll boil some coffee!" he yelped.

I swallowed my nut of hashish and drank the two cups of coffee the doctor assured me would complete the dose. He ate two lumps and drank so many coffees I lost count.

"There must be silence for a bit," he told me.

We stood looking at each other, the clock's clicking letting us know time was passing. Benton bit his lips as if he could not stand the hush he'd demanded.

"What's inside?" he said after we'd watched ten minutes pass. He toed the valise.

The hashish was already moving in my blood and it took a moment for me to recall that the luggage was filled with views.

"New Orleans," I said when I could remember.

Benton clapped his hands, then rushed to the couch and shouldered it across the room, its feet cutting trails into the floorboards. He pushed it so close to the chimney piece that I feared for its upholstery, then took off his shoes and stuck his feet almost into the fire. "Let's see them," he said.

I opened the valise and took one out. A pair of Negroes lifted a crate onto a wagon. Their heads, hands, arms, torsos, and legs looked as if the men stood under moving water. Only their feet were clearly recorded. Victor dipped his hand into the case and came up with a man feeding his mule a bit of candy.

"They're both very good," he said.

Even though I should not have been amused, I laughed. Victor laughed along with me, then reached into the bag and took out more which he balanced along his legs, the two on his kneecaps tottering like see-saws. "Money well spent," he judged. "The obstinate girl will be convinced."

"There are more," I let him know.

Benton stacked the dozen from his lap beside him and removed plate after plate from the valise. Soon the couch's cushions were covered; the case still held many more. The doctor looked up, wild-eyed. "Do they ever end?"

I held a portrait of a shopkeeper kissing the head of the infant in his arms while behind him a hatchet-faced woman tried to decide between the chicken hanging from her left hand and the one hanging from her right. The ugly thing was taking on a startling, beautiful life of its own.

I upended the valise. Views skittered across the floor and shimmered like spilt mercury. Victor bent and lifted a soliotype of a man in a dirty robe yelling threats of flood and pestilence to the passing crowd. One side of the young doctor's mouth deeply dimpled the cheek. "Susana," he muttered.

ℰ ℰ ℰ

Plate 18—Man Proselytizing before a Crowd, *1845. Half-plate daguerreotype.*

Plate 19—A Butcher's Shop, *1845. Half-plate daguerreotype.*

IN ANY SOUTHERN U.S. city it is not uncommon to come across examples of the local-color cityscapes or "views" that many daguerreians sold in their studios. Often such photographs are discovered far from their point of manufacture, leading to the assumption that they may have served as precursors to the photographic picture postcard. These daguerreotypes, invariably inexpensive sixteenth-, sixth-, or quarter-plates, are usually of recognizable landmarks or monuments. These two plates are oddities. Neither offers anything close to a landmark, and both are the much larger, much more expensive half-plate size. There are mentions later in the century of officially commissioned photographic surveys of New Orleans, and it is possible that Marchand, dean of daguerreians, may have been paid to roam the city making a daguerreotype census.

Pl. 18 is a wonderful work managed in spite of—and with the help of—the technological limitations of the daguerreotype. Because of the long exposure needed to capture an image, the arms of the man preaching to the crowd appear to be wings. He must have been an engaging speaker: many faces in the group paused before him are clear, meaning the men and women whose noses and lips we can make out did not nod or look from side to side while Marchand made the photograph.

Pl. 19 is both a wonderful piece of art and an interesting example of documentary photography: Shot from inside the shop and framed by the store's window, geese and hams hang from hooks, steaks and chops lie in rows, and the black dots of flies mark every piece of meat.

❧

*T*HE COLD SNUCK away in the night—I went to sleep in winter and awoke in spring. The lie I told Millicent became true piece by piece. Furniture upholstered in velvets the colors of fruits cluttered the first-floor salon—mango chairs, a black currant couch. I spent hours changing their arrangement, hoping each new pattern would make the place bearable, then gave up in distress—there is no anodyne to clutter. I dropped hints and painters plagued me with bargains. I bought huge oils and covered the salon's walls, took them down, then hung them again. I had a piano wedged under the graceful curve of the stairs leading up to the studio. I could not stand the place, the cluttered room a mimic of those I hated. I drew the line at caged birds and retreated up the stairs to the studio.

I invited Vivian to come and witness the progress and she sent a polite refusal which stung me. I had expected to see a note about her clipped engagement in the papers in the days after we had shared the closet, but no such notice appeared. Much as I wanted to ignore it, I let the salon's clutter fill my mind.

I bought two backdrops for the studio, one dark, one light. They were hung on a system of rods and pulleys which allowed them to be quickly switched. I brought only some of the props from the small studio on Toulouse—one book from the tall stack, one umbrella, one saber. I wished I could have only the pinecone I'd made all my sitters hold in Natchez. Skylights were cut and sun filled the room. Before the glazier could seal off the sky a cloud opened and soft rain fell through. While workmen yelled to each other and ran up ladders with tarpaulins, I stood in the gentle shower wishing the water would melt away the rooms below.

I quickly found that the only way I could stand the place was to make its portrait. I made a study of carpenters hammering, their arms transformed to blurred arcs, and one of loitering delivery men smoking cheroots and working up the gumption to ease the heavy marble head of Homer down from a wagon. I kept the two plates in my pocket. When the clutter threatened to crush me, I pulled the soliotypes out and noted the tense angle of a carpenter's knee, the loose hang of the deliverymen's shoulders.

The day the rugs arrived Vivian sent a note lambasting me for the closet indiscretion. In it she imposed a set of rules including a two-foot neutral ground between us, and the company of a trustworthy chaperone. *Joseph,* she wrote, *is bewitched by the watch you bought him, and therefore cannot be trusted to alert you to control yourself.* I tucked the note into the wallet filling with her letters.

I hoped Millicent would return from Mobile as a large tapestry was being hung or the bust of Shakespeare was being uncrated, but she did not. I found myself sometimes sure an octoroon I'd seen from the edge of my eye was Millicent, but unfamiliar faces turned to me when I yelled her name.

I hired an assistant named Philip Breson, a tall boy with thin arms, wrists, and ankles. The sapling claimed to be a pupil of Daguerre's, but simple questions proved he'd never seen Paris, let alone Daguerre. He was fibbing in desperation—he toted a case over-full of clothes and looked as if he'd not eaten in week. He convinced a joiner to pause from making some shelves and sit for a portrait. I watched the boy move the bemused man into a flattering pose, then remove the lens cover and keep score of the seconds by blinking his left eye. What he brought from the developing room was impressive. The joiner's bearish head and gnarled hands were well placed and Philip's finishing of the plate was precise—he was someone's pupil.

The rear of the studio was a maze of pantries and aborted staircases with queer closets below them. When I first saw the jumble of odd-sized doors and the steps that led nowhere I deduced that the building had been a carpenter's first attempt. I installed Philip in the largest of the strange rooms, one with an archer's slit window and space for a palette and chest. I gave him a dollar and recommended that he eat a light meal. His thanks agitated me slightly—I thought of Remy while he pledged to do a good job—but I felt generous when later I spied him carefully sipping soup in the window of a café.

Slipped under my door on Toulouse was another agitated note from Vivian, two lines informing me she'd calculated the length of my arm to be between three and three-and-one-half feet, and therefore I needed to add two feet to the last note's two and remain at least four feet from her person. I imagined standing before Millicent with my arms outstretched, laughing and demonstrating my dangerous wingspan.

18 March 1845
Mobile is a room above a shoemaker's shop on Marais and I spend my days reading the newspapers and enjoying the sound of shoes and boots being made below me. It is good not to talk.

22 March 1845
Thrills me to spy on Claude from inside shops opposite. Today there are new curtains, a bust of a bald man, and a purple fainting couch.

1 April 1845
I watched from the small crowd when he opened the studio. Claude made portraits at no charge and I considered sitting before the camera but the stupid fear he would not recognize me sent me running. I went to my rooms on Royal last night to fetch a hat and found much of the furniture gone. Told the landlord to sell it piece by piece to pay the rent but wish I had told him to spare the elephants. Only an orphan remains and I nearly killed myself carrying him to my hideout.

⌐

ONE MORNING, FRESH from a haircut and a shave, I met Vivian in the street. I saw her before she saw me and I followed when she darted into a bookshop. A musty clerk wanted to help me and I had to pretend to have forgotten what I was after. He was happy to try and guess, and only the invention of an author rid me of him. He wandered muttering the made-up name while I hunted the shop for Vivian. I found her in a tiny room in a back corner, before a shelf, intent on the spines. I stood behind and looked where she looked—guides to flowers and plants.

"Planning on taking up gardening?"

She flinched but did not turn. "Yes," she said curtly, then pulled a book from the shelf and opened it. Tissue covered a colored plate of leaves and seeds.

"May I escort you to coffee?" I asked. When I touched her shoulder she took a sudden step to maintain her four feet of safety.

"I am engaged to William Spats." It sounded as if she were simply trying out the sound of the statement.

"At your father's celebration you told me he'd abandoned you." I moved in her direction to watch the retreat.

She skipped away. "He has gone to Boston to buy a house where we will live. He will return for me as soon as he has made necessary arrangements."

"Come with me to coffee," I said.

"No." She looked down at the book in her hands. "Leave me alone."

"You do not want to be alone," I told her.

Our room was dusty with neglect. I slapped down spiders'

webs with a stick. The window had been left open and a small bird had squeezed through the grating and died on the floor. Vivian cried over it until I hid it under the tent of an open book.

I ran my hands up under her skirts and she pushed me away and rushed to the corner and puked into a chamber pot. My first fear was Fever, but when she looked up the beard of vomit was pale and I realized how silly I'd been—summer was far away. "The smell of coffee is so strong," she explained.

I went down to the warehouse and brought back the dipper from the water barrel. "Give me his portrait," I told her while she drank.

Her eyes went wide. She set the dipper on the floor and took the soliotype from her bag. "Do you love me?" she asked, her eyes on the closed case in her hands.

"Of course," I said, and she came to where I stood and passed me the soliotype. I put it into my pocket. She took my hand and put it on her face and I let it drop to her shoulder, then her breast, and soon we were naked. Dust rose from the bed when we rolled; a mouse came from the pillow and I was glad Vivian did not see it.

"You're getting fat," I teased when she stood to dress. Her smile was pained when I poked her belly. "I like it," I promised. "You were too thin."

Joseph brought me Vivian's note that afternoon: *My mother knows there is something afoot, and so you must not speak to me in the street, or send me letters. My heart belongs to one man.* I spent the rest of the day grinning like a fool, the note in my pocket.

⁂

Spring moved toward summer and I did not notice the new heat until my shirt clung to my armpits. I opened the studio on the first day of April. Business was amazing. Newspapers and citizens behaved as if I'd brought them yet another marvel, not simply changed my address, and for two frantic weeks we worked every moment we had sun. Philip and I braced ourselves for more of the same. We discussed hiring another assistant, and such talk jinxed us. The river of customers quickly thinned to a trickle, then went dry.

The studio, hardly old, was a new place without the lines of primped mothers and fathers and children and blushing newlyweds. Crowds gone, I could see the paintings I'd bought. I began to loathe one odious mess of green trees stuck into green hills, flat greenish clouds above. Our footsteps echoed in the empty rooms as if Philip and I paced a church. We treated the rare portrait sitter with absurd enthusiasm—two portraits for the price of one, unceasing praise for the cut of her dress, the part in his hair. Their eyes sparked with unease and they seldom returned. I spent entire days inventorying the supplies I'd laid in when I had been sure unlimited prosperity lay ahead. I calculated the building's width and depth—stacked in neat rows were enough plates to pave the floors, upstairs and down, in mirrored tile.

↩

In the second week of May I turned away the first man bearing the corpse of a Fever victim. I thought he held a child, the tiny hand dyed citrus, but when I came nearer I saw a woman's tired face. My mouth went dry. Victor Benton was with the man. He'd shaved off his beard; the new white of his chin, cheeks, and lip seemed as artificial as his woolly whiskers had been. The doctor's eyes opened wide when I announced in a whisper that I did not make memorial portraits.

"What *do* you allow before your holy camera obscura?" Benton snapped.

Philip stopped plumping the pillows on a chaise.

The husband was not listening. He looked down at the wife in his arms and made a mewling noise like a mother cat trying to wake a dead kitten. He shook her gently.

I worked up enough spit to loose my tongue from the roof of my mouth. "Do you have a portrait of her?" I asked.

The man looked up, his eyes blurred by tears. "There's one we got when Lucy and me were wed in Jackson."

"Would you make a portrait of his dog?" Benton asked.

I ignored him. "Is she smiling in that portrait from Jackson?"

The towhead nodded and I watched as the thought of his grinning bride curled his mouth with a smile.

"What if he'd arrived with a ham? Would you make the ham's portrait?" the doctor demanded.

"I loved her," the man told me.

I reached across the dead woman and rested my hand on his shoulder. "She loved you," I promised.

Benton and I stood at the window and watched the man cross the street. "That was quite a show." He tugged off his jacket and slung it vaguely in Philip's direction. "I hear your business is slow, now I know why: you're turning it away at the door. To compensate you should sell tickets to the melodrama—'She loved you!'" Victor swooned onto the couch Philip had made ready. "Hang that up," he told Philip, pointing to the pile of his coat on the floor.

"Hang it yourself," the boy said.

I laughed and Victor made a face. The doctor crossed his wrists over his chest and closed his eyes. A hummed dirge came from the death mask he faked. "Say the poor man had come to you with a leg of mutton, would you have sent him packing?" Victor's eyes were still closed.

His abuse was better than thinking about dead Lucy, so I walked into his trap. "I'd make soliotypes of a dog, a ham, or a leg of mutton."

Benton's smile was the only change to his corpse's pose.

"What do any of those three have to do with my refusal to make a portrait of a dead woman?"

"Meat," the doctor explained. "It's all meat in the end. A dog, a ham, a sheep's leg, that woman, me, you. There comes a time we're all no more than meat."

"What a happy thought, all of us meat," Millicent said.

I spun. Victor jerked upright, his arms still crossed over his heart.

She pointed over my shoulder. "My piano?"

"Your piano," I agreed. For a moment I was sure she would turn and her profile would prove me once again mistaken, that she would become another of the women in the street I wished were her. Victor and I watched her cross the room. There was no mistake, it was her. She struck a single key, the note loud as a pistol shot in the silent room. Benton embraced himself, a palm on each shoulder. Millicent played a scale, then sat and coaxed a tune from the secondhand piano. We three men listened as if we'd paid to hear Millicent attempt to trick music from the wildly out-of-tune thing. The door opened with a clatter and only Philip turned his eyes away from the crescent moon of skin above Millicent's dress and below the tight knot of her hair.

A hand landed on my shoulder. "I need my money," Marmu hissed into my ear. "I need it now."

Behind him Vivian, like Victor, shielded herself with crossed arms and gaped at Millicent.

"Business has been slow," I told him. "The city is already nearly deserted."

Marmu's brow was hung with beads of sweat. "New Orleans is Hell. Everyone with a brain between their ears has gone away." He closed his eyes. "Gone away to nights requiring a quilt." His eyes clicked open. "You don't need to tell me there's no business in this furnace. If there was I wouldn't need you to pay back your loan."

Millicent struck a chord so sharp my teeth hurt. I ached to look at her. "I don't have the money," I reminded him.

Francis Marmu made a hissing noise through his teeth. "I'll close up this shop if you don't come up with my money."

He gave me a shove for good measure, then spun on his heel and headed for the door. I stumbled toward Vivian and she danced away, then hooked a thumb at Millicent's back. "What is she doing here?" she asked through her teeth.

"It appears she's playing the piano," I snapped.

Vivian set her mouth as if she were about to cry out, then said gently "So nice to see you, Mr. Marchand." Her father stood in the street calling her name and she turned and went to him.

A dim urge to follow rose in me as I watched her leave, but the sound of the piano snuffed the urge. Millicent played one more tune, then stood and announced she needed a nap. She gave each of us a light kiss good-bye on the cheek, Philip reddening when she pulled him up by the chin to give him his.

"Poppa Marmu come to foreclose?" Victor asked when she was gone. "What timing the old man has."

I could still feel Millicent's kiss. A mirror showed no scar burning on my cheek, and this surprised me.

"I hate to speak of money at a time like this," the doctor cooed, "but I have a business offer for you—two, in fact."

Dust danced in a fat beam of sunlight. I wondered if Millicent would disappear as threatened if the studio were to dissolve in the night.

Benton snapped his fingers in front of my eyes. "Hearing messages from on high, Joan?"

"The offer?"

"Make the portrait of every Fever victim I send your way. Charge double—a premium for the special care Marchand must take while doing such delicate business—and give one quarter of that doubled fee to me."

"I don't make memorials. They're tawdry, sacrilegious."

The doctor snorted. "Spare me. The simple facts are that the summer will be long and many people will die. I cannot stop that, no doctor can, this is New Orleans. Just weeks ago you managed Midas's magic for me, everything at which you pointed your holy camera obscura became gold. Gild some corpses." He lifted his jacket from the floor. "The summer will be all the more long should you have to spend it alone."

I kneaded my eyebrows with my thumbs and gave up. "Triple the normal rate."

"Triple it is.

"Offer number two is this," he continued. "The mayor, the City Council, the papers, the grocers, a handful of doctors with their hands out for coins, and what's nearly an army of other assorted fools swear Yellow Fever is not here in New Orleans, that there's proof it'll skip the city this year. They are, as poor Lucy proves, all liars. A group of honest men, most of us doctors and surgeons, are getting ready to face the attack and to tend to those who cannot run away to New England. We need money for medicine, but if the mayor gives us money he'll be admitting that Mister Jack is here."

"Admirable that you and your friends will suffer the summer with the poor," I hissed. I was rattled by Millicent's conjured appearance, by Vivian's chilly exit, by the fact I'd agreed to make portraits of the dead.

Victor sighed an annoyed sigh. "We'll pay you to make views which prove that the Fever is here. The truth, shown in a dozen or so of your soliotypes, will force these liars to admit their lies—and it is Truth that the soliotype shows, is it not?"

"You have me in a corner."

"I do," he agreed. "But I'm offering you a paid escape from it, as well as a chance to do your fellow man a good turn." He shot his cuffs and fiddled with his collar.

"Susana was convinced," he said. "Your many views of this fair necropolis made her believe she was wasting her time in Boston. The dear girl didn't even bother to send a note, she just knocked on my door yesterday. We marry in a week. Be my best man?"

"Me?" I was astounded.

"It's because of you that she's here, Claude. That makes us friends, almost brothers." He left whistling what Millicent had played.

Philip came to me and said, "Do you think he's right?" and at first I could not understand what I was being asked.

"He's not my brother."

The boy shook his head. "Do you think we're no more than meat?" A tin cross hung around his neck on a length of twine. He rubbed the thing with his thumb.

"I think we are much more, but the doctor would soon be a lunatic if he agreed. The butcher has none of the priest's worries."

Philip nodded, still busy with the cross.

<p>

Benton asked me to come and have lunch and make portraits of him and his soon-to-be wife the next day. I took a bottle and stopped at the baker's on my way.

Susana's nose looked as if it had been boiled. "I went out and tried to match the views to the city," she told me. Victor bounced his brows and drowned a chuckle in a glass of my wine. There was no food aside from the cakes I'd brought.

"I didn't realize the sun could do this," she sheepishly admitted while settling into a chair before the camera. Susana looked like an automaton: her every gesture was mechanically precise, her hair was the color of hammered brass, and her eyes looked as if they'd been carved from mahogany.

"The dear girl was upset when she could not find the same darkies. I had to tell her that there are more than a few Africans in New Orleans."

"Some wear such lovely clothes," she said in amazement.

"Where is Millicent?" Victor asked, his brows still jumping.

"The African?" Susana chirped. "Your octoroon lover?"

I turned to Victor. "Did she mention to you if she intended to return to her old rooms on Royal?"

Benton's brows no longer jumped. Susana looked back and forth from him to me, her mouth slightly open. The doctor scowled. "No," he said, then sucked his glass dry.

"Victor was kind enough to help Millicent through a short battle with headaches last year," I told Susana.

One of Victor's brows crept slowly upward.

"It was as if a cannon was firing in her head. She held her ears and begged it to stop," I explained.

"She cried out and damned the Chinese for inventing gunpowder," the doctor added.

"She sang loudly, attempting to cover the booming."

"She clamped her eyes so tightly shut it took her an hour to open them back up."

"She demanded to know what slight, insult, or blood feud engendered the battle in her head."

"She called for surrenders."

"She offered the generals of both armies advice from the Bible—'Love thy neighbor . . . ,' 'Do unto others . . . .'"

The silence begged to be filled with laughter when Victor and I stopped.

"What was the cure?" Susana quietly asked.

Victor shook his head. "Laudanum?" he asked me.

I nodded vigorously and stopped up my mouth with a cake.

"Laudanum," the doctor told Susana. "And rest."

⁓

13 May 1845

Benton and Claude were speechless when three days ago I tired of spying through the studio's windows and walked in and sat before the piano. Every day Claude sits and stares at my back while I play—Small profit for all I have lost. Tonight he followed me when I left the studio and I was happy until I hid in a doorway and after he passed followed him to the Marmu house and watched him stare at the windows.

⁓

MILLICENT ARRIVED EVERY morning at ten o'clock and began with a bright waltz, paused for her luncheon at two, left when the light failed. The sound of her playing the piano was like a string tied around my finger to remind me why I was making memorials though each one sickened me, why I was wooing Vivian even though I was angry with her, why I didn't simply lock the studio's door and let my debt to Marmu become delinquent. The fictions I'd invented demanded I make memorials, woo Vivian, not close the studio.

When there were no customers I sat and watched Millicent's shoulders moving in their sockets as she played. We exchanged few words. She did not return to her rooms on Royal and she did not offer me her new address. When I asked, she told me she was staying with a friend. One night I tried to follow her; she made turn after turn and I found myself in an alleyway which ended at a solid wall. The next night I trailed her around a corner and suddenly I was alone in an empty street which echoed with laughter that rang out from a window. The third time I tried to follow she left me standing on the edge of a canal she seemed to have conjured to block my way. On the other side of the water I watched her become her shadow as she walked away, then disappear into the gloom.

On the way home after one such goose chase I passed the Marmu house. I stood and watched the windows. Those on the second floor were dark, and the first floor's curtains were blank, no shadows painted by the lamp within. I had not heard from Vivian since she and her father had come to the studio.

✑

The first plate I made for the Howards was of a plank running from the second-floor window of a house on Barone to a window of the house which stood close beside. The one on the right had a yellow card nailed to its door, a Fever quarantine notice.

"Why's this worth a soliotype?" I asked. Victor pointed. I looked up to see a man carefully walk from the sill of the quarantined house and step through the open window of the house next door. A moment later he trotted into the street, carefree and smiling.

I watched a woman bribe the man whose job it was to nail yellow cards to doors he had on a list—a pie and a single coin kept the card from hers—then watched the same man threaten to nail a card to the door of the next house, one that had not been the site of a Fever visit. That trick got him a bottle of wine and a fork. He sat on the stairs before the innocent door and ate his pie and drank his wine, the frightened folk he'd swindled watching from their windows.

We walked to the public square and I made a plate of two men kind enough to hold a pose as they loaded a round into a cannon's long throat. Barrels of tar were being eased down from the beds of wagons and arranged into crosses. Victor cajoled two urchins into standing atop a barrel so that I could make their portrait.

We went to a stonecutter's and watched him chip names into gravestones. After much counting of fingers he estimated he'd made nearly a thousand of them in his time. Victor was writing in a little book while he asked the man questions. At one point he handed Benton his hammer and chisel and showed him how to cut a cross into a small scrap of limestone.

Victor had me make soliotypes of the animals dead and bloated in the street. Rats descended from ships and swarmed the city, breeding at an insane rate each summer. Poisoned sausages were left for them, and when they died from eating them the rats lay under the sun until they rotted away, twitching coats of flies covering their fur. Dogs, too dumb to know better, ate the sausages as well, and their carcasses littered alleys and stank. I carried a tin of lavender lozenges in my pocket; when the smell was too much to bear I held the open tin under my nose.

The sun dulled and hid behind clouds late in the afternoon. The doctor bought me a large stein of *weiss bier* and a plate of wurst in a café owned by a German with a walrus's mustache, joking between bites that we'd soon join the rats and dogs. Filled with our meal, we came upon a cursing man pulling a small wagon filled with rags and bottles.

"Is that German?" Victor asked. A single plate of sausages had convinced him New Orleans was filled with folks who spoke a language filled with long, growling *R*s.

I listened to the man complain. "Not German," I told him. "Probably Rum, possibly Whiskey."

We both laughed, even a stupid joke hilarious in its contrast to all the ugliness we'd witnessed, then we turned the corner and discovered why the rummy was pulling his wagon. A great black horse lay slumped in the middle of the street. His skin held close to his bones and his ribs stood out like a xylophone's keys. The sight jerked our laughter away from us.

༄

Benton placed an advertisement in the *Daily Picayune* announcing I was once again willing to make memorial portraits because of a softening of heart prompted by my rediscovered faith in Almighty God. A headline above the advertisement proclaimed New Orleans free of the Fever. Its text explained that most of the city's learned men were of the belief that Mister Jack would not make an appearance in dear New Orleans this year; in fact, we might never see Jacky again.

The dead queued up like nightmare devils and waited for

their turn at me. Victor's customers became mine when their
hearts stopped knocking, and dozens of hearts quit as May
headed toward June. I tried to follow the doctor's advice, but it
was not possible to transform the dead via the soliotype in the
same way a busy street could be transformed. I tried my best.
Little boys I posed with a rubber ball in their hands, little girls
with a doll in their arms. It was no use, no number of favorite
toys could revive a dead child.

Philip was calm while he finished the plates, short with
screaming widows and blubbering orphans. I envied his control
and modeled my face after the flat mouth and the empty eyes of
my assistant. Deep in my skeleton I recoiled at the sight of each
corpse, but I controlled my skin, my muscles. Not a single twitch
gave me away.

One night I met Benton in a saloon and mentioned that even
though the Fever was making my wallet thicker, it seemed nothing could erase my debt to Marmu—in the flush of need I had
agreed to outrageous interest on the loan, and my payments did
little more than keep the numbers static. Victor nodded and
tugged at the air below his chin where his beard had recently
hung. "I think there's an answer," he said, then excused himself
without telling me what this answer was.

Walking up Canal the next morning, I saw a line of men
standing before the studio's door. When I came closer I heard
Victor's voice. "Better than a letter, more true than a drawing.
Want to show Momma what's become of her baby boy? Want
to show your friends back home where you walk? Where you
work?" He held a soliotype in each hand. Squares of reflected
light flashed on the amazed faces of those listening. I opened the
door and the men followed Victor inside. All dozen bought a
view, many took two. When they were gone, Victor turned to

me. "A simple answer: It worked for me, why not let the rest of mankind benefit from your pictures of this fine metropolis?"

There was an advertisement in the *Bee* and the *Daily Picayune*. Victor had a joiner come and install a long shelf at eye level, then populated it with what remained of the hundred-plus views I'd made for him. I made portraits of the dead all morning, then went into the streets and made portraits of the city all afternoon.

The cashbox became heavy and soon I had much of what I owed Francis Marmu. I took him an envelope filled with notes.

"How is Vivian?" I asked, unable to hold the question in.

Marmu's head snapped up. He stared at me as if I had asked him a riddle, then counted the stack of bills three times and wrote me a receipt. "She is well," he said, then handed me the slip of paper.

༄ ༄ ༄

Plates 20, 21, & 22—Nuptial Triptych, Dr. and Mrs. Victor Benton, *1845. Quarter-plate daguerreotypes.*

MARCHAND'S SECOND STUDIO, a two-story affair housed in a building on Canal between Dauphin and Royal, opened with much fanfare in the spring of 1845. Almost every newspaper, French and English, praised the new studio. The *Daily Tropic* described it as "the City's most lavish example of a heliographic arts studio. The salon is as deep as the building and appointed with wonderful examples of the daguerrin [*sic*] art, as well as with pleasing specimens of Classic Greek sculpture, and busts of Shakespeare and other figures from history and literature. . . . It is a wonderful place for the ladies to have a likeness rendered." The *Bee* agreed, adding, "The expense Mr. Marchand has invested in his rooms is evident both in their appointments and in the finest examples of camera obscura art available in New Orleans." The *Picayune* furthered the universal admiration with the simple judgment, "Claude Marchand's studio is near to perfect and his work does credit alike to the operator and the art."

The nuptial triptych was a specialty of the studio, one which Marchand's newspaper advertisements claimed he had invented. In fact, his invention was only a modern turn on an old tradition. The triptych's case housed three portraits—the small individual portraits exchanged by courting couples Monday morning after Sunday night proposals as left and right panels (fiancé on the left, fiancée on the right), and a formal wedding portrait as the middle panel. Marchand's triptych was only different in that it utilized three daguerreotypes, not three oil miniatures.

The subjects of Pls. 20 and 21 are posed as was the fashion: young Doctor Benton holds a volume of Horace, his fingers tangled in the pages; Susana, the soon-to-be Mrs. Benton, chastely clutches the Bible. The props are not unusual. The daguerreotype took from classic portraiture a love and respect for icons: Soldiers held pistols and sabers, mothers their young; schoolteachers leaned against Greek pillars; young lovers clutched flowers and gazed drunkenly. Good daguerreotypists provided trunks of hats, sidearms, musical instruments, and great works of literature from which to choose. Marchand's prop shop is rumored to have rivaled the Opera House's.

Pl. 22, the Bentons' wedding portrait, is unconventional in that the groom's head is turned to gaze upon his bride instead of directly at the camera.

Felix Moissenet reports that Marchand and the doctor,

originally from Boston and educated at Harvard College, became fast friends after meeting at a party. Benton, like most learned men of the day, was interested in all technological advances, including the daguerreotype. Marchand was famous for his volatile temper and lack of social graces—he is said to have slapped a woman during an opera because she would not stop talking. Despite Marchand's hot blood, their friendship bloomed and Benton even experimented with the art. Sadly, a fire consumed the Benton family home in 1901 and no examples of Victor Benton's work are believed to have escaped the blaze.

Plate 23—Greta Dürtmeer, *1845. Sixth-plate daguerreotype.*

Plate 24—Memorial Portrait of Georg Dürtmeer, *1845. Full-plate daguerreotype.*

A NEWS ITEM in the *Daily Picayune* tells the story behind these two daguerreotypes. It reports that Mrs. Dürtmeer went to the Marchand studio one June Sunday to keep a portrait appointment. She was served tea and cakes while the camera and plate were readied, then was seated and arranged—neck positioned in the iron rest so that her head would remain still during the exposure, parasol angled against a knee, background adjusted to catch the late-morning light. Problems then arose. Mrs. Dürtmeer was, as Pl. 23 proves, a homely woman. Despite the crack Emily Hulbert claims he made about her portrait, Marchand was known by many as a photographer who could manipulate the camera kindly.

Mrs. Dürtmeer's face was full and heavy, but her head small. Marchand knew how to compensate. He raised the camera and adjusted the headrest so that Mrs. Dürtmeer's head projected before her shoulders. She was annoyed and insulted by the adjustments and felt the portrait she was presented with was not good enough to warrant such indignities. She screamed at Marchand that he was incompetent, and she refused to pay. Marchand, the article claims, calmly explained that "The soliotype is a mirror, and if the mirror is held before Medusa. . . ." Unamused by the reference to her lamentable hairdo, Mrs. Dürtmeer threw her portrait at Marchand and stormed out.

She hurried home and recounted the entire debacle to her husband, adding, one assumes, insults and attacks on her purity. Georg Dürtmeer was furious. He equipped himself with a set of pistols and his wife led the way back to the studio. According to the article, Marchand was suffering through a portrait session with "a brat of Irish origin" when Dürtmeer crashed in, pushed aside an assistant, and challenged Marchand to a duel. He accepted. The two men exited onto Canal, crossed to the neutral ground, and prepared.

This is the point at which the article's author, the *Picayune*'s Stanley Roberts, became an active part of the fracas. "I was discussing the season's mildness with a drygoods shopkeeper when a man I knew as the heliographic artist Claude Marchand and another man, his shirt front heaving, pulled pistols and began to step off distances." The reporter was pressed into service as Dürtmeer's second; Marchand's studio assistant provided that service for his employer.

Mrs. Dürtmeer and a small crowd watched as the men stood back to back, then paced away from each other—"a pickaninny with a fine voice was paid a penny to count aloud"—then turned and fired. Dürtmeer got off his shot first, but it was wide, striking a horse standing before a milk wagon.

Marchand's shot was perfect. Dürtmeer fell dead and his wife "threw herself ululating upon his corpse." The police arrived and arrested Marchand, his assistant, the child paid to call out numbers, and Stanley Roberts. The assistant, Philip Breson, was charged, for some reason, with loitering, Roberts with the same, the number-calling youth for disturbing the peace. Except for Claude, all were released when Victor Benton paid assorted fines.

Deciding what exactly Marchand's crime was required a day of study. On Monday he faced the judge to plead guilty to the charge of dueling on a Sunday, an offense surely found by a studious clerk in the margin of a document from the century before. Marchand paid a twenty-dollar penalty and was freed.

He hurried to his studio and gathered a camera and some plates, then made his way to the rooms of Herman Lance, the undertaker to whom Georg Dürtmeer's body had been entrusted. The connections between the physicians who tended to the dying, the photographers who took memorial portraits, and the men who prepared bodies for eternal rest is easy to figure. In Pl. 24 Dürtmeer is posed on a plain cooling board much like the ones upon which slain outlaws were posed after Wild West executions.

That evening Marchand rounded up the newspaperman and other witnesses to the duel and paid a visit on the widow Dürtmeer. "He rang the bell and the Widow answered. At the sight of Marchand, she sank into a chair. When he pulled from its wrappings the portrait of her husband, her shrieks were grotesque and the entire party hurried for the relative silence of the street."

S

*S*USANA DEMANDED HER knot-tying be delayed until her burned shoulders were healed enough to support the ornate dress she'd carried from Boston. I witnessed the marriage the morning of June the 1st. Victor's face bore a scratch from eyebrow to jawline which he admitted in a whisper had come of Susana's strong urge to remain chaste until the priest deemed them man and wife. After rings were officially on fingers and the Bible closed, the newlyweds came to the studio with me and I made a portrait of them holding hands and smiling, Victor's face turned to hide the cut Susana had given him.

Directly after they left two men carried in an open coffin, by then no longer a novelty. They put the lidless box on a pair of trestles which stood just inside the door for the purpose and rolled their shoulders to recover from the weight. When Philip peered down at the corpse it yelled my name. Philip skipped backwards, tripped over his own toes, and fell solidly. The coffin bearers sniggered.

The dead man yelled "Marchand!" again.

Halfway to the talking corpse I heard Millicent recognize his voice. "Felix," she muttered. He lay posed in the box with a card lettered *Amor meus febris est* held over his chest.

"I'd wondered where he'd been hiding," I told Millicent. I crossed myself and set my hands to pray.

He slit an eye and hissed, "Quit your jokes. I've been killed by poetry."

I covered my mouth. "And a quarantine has not been ordered?"

Philip giggled as he got to his feet.

Millicent wiped away a phantom tear. "I regret I never told him I loved him," she stammered in mock sobs.

Felix opened his slit eye fully and aimed it at us. "Abused by an artist and his animated merkin. I deserve this?"

"Which poet has slain you?" I asked, humoring foolish Felix.

"Emily," he sighed.

"Emily Hulbert?" Miss Hulbert was a quick wit, and I'd been told her sonnets were as near to perfect as a woman could manage, but she was the kind of plain-faced girl for whom a bounder like Felix would never fall. I checked my watch. She had an appointment to have her portrait made in just fifteen minutes—Felix knew her schedule.

To cover his embarrassment, Philip fetched Millicent a long lily from a nearby vase. She lay it across the placard and told me, "I shall write the Pope—Saint Felix, Patron of Whores and Wine Bottles."

Felix snapped his eye shut and set his face into what he thought would pass for a dead man's expression.

"He looks as if he needs to move his bowels," Millicent observed. "Pity the grave holds no latrine." She turned and so did not see Felix's tongue sprout from his pursed lips.

He sucked it in and explained, "She has spurned me—thus killed me." His voice splintered. "I want you to make my memorial. The murderess must see her victim."

The coffin bearers lifted Felix and carried him up the stairs in his box. Felix held the lily and made his face into a better mask for the camera. He did not open his eyes when I lifted his warm hand and put the portrait under it. They carried him down the stairs and replaced him on the trestles.

Emily passed dead Felix as if he were not there and we climbed to the studio.

A cloud wrapped itself around the sun. While we waited for the light, I asked her if Felix's attentions were new.

"He's been at it for months," she admitted. "A week ago he held a pistol to his ear and asked me to marry him. I refused and he pulled the trigger—it was not loaded. The next day he found me in a café and stood over me reading a long obituary he wrote."

"You're not flattered?"

"Felix doesn't love me, he loves poetry. I don't mean to insult you, but he doesn't love you either. What he loves are soliotypes."

"Better them than my eyes," I joked.

"If only he could love you for your eyes. I don't think he could love anyone for their eyes. Felix loves art, but he's ignored the most important thing about art: He cannot sit at a table and share dinner with it, he cannot trade jokes with it. Neither can we, but as artists we have an option Felix does not: We can make art from the people with whom we share dinner, with whom we trade jokes, and"—she lowered her voice to a whisper—"with whom we share our bed. Felix has confused us with art; at his most lucid he thinks we provide a direct conduit to it."

The sun burned away the clouds and Emily straightened for the camera. I thought about the portraits I'd made of Peter, Millicent, Vivian. I removed the lens cover and in the silence I heard the murmur of Millicent mocking Felix below.

When I came from the developing room Emily held a portrait of a dead woman whose kinfolk, absentminded with grief, had left behind. "Congratulations." She turned the plate so that the dead woman faced me. "I could not write an elegy even if it were for my dearest friend."

"A elegy for a stranger is easy," I said. "That may be the thing Felix does not understand about artists."

Emily nodded and traded the memorial for the portrait I had just made. I looked at the memorial and saw my face reflected on the plate's surface. Emily followed each of her sittings with a salon, so the invitation to the next day's gathering was no surprise. "Vivian Marmu will be there; she wanted me to tell you." Emily winked and pinched my hand. A tickle of excitement made the hairs on my arms stand. Millicent's laugh came up the stairs and made my heart jump.

I walked down with Emily and watched her cross the long room. When she passed Felix the coffin bearers lifted the box and followed her out the door. Philip stepped out after them and watched the procession file down the street.

I shadowed Millicent again when she left the studio that night. The days had lengthened and I was able to keep her in sight at a great distance. Hidden behind the corners of buildings and the bodies of convenient horses, I followed undetected. She went into shops and bought a bottle of wine, a baguette, a half-moon of brie, a box of small cakes filled with custard, a slim candle. Daylight faded as she went about her errands. I was pleased that even in the dusk I did not lose her.

Millicent stopped to listen to a light-skinned black play a fiddle on a corner. I watched from behind a tree, enjoying the tiny twitch the music caused at the base of her spine. When she dropped a coin into his hat and moved on I crossed and added my own coin, then kept up my pursuit. She made a turn to the right, walked a few blocks, went to the left, and at the top of the zed stood before my door on Toulouse. She turned and waved.

We ate in the courtyard. The moon was a watermark on a cloud. Millicent stuck the candle into the dirt of a pot of weeds and its flame was like a flower. I could not stop touching her, her ears, her knees, her hands. When only a crescent rind of cheese remained Millicent said, "The studio is a marvel. I doubted you, but you proved me wrong." She took a pastry from the box and handed it to me. I held her thumb in my fist.

With her free hand Millicent parted the row of buttons down her dressfront, each one coming from its hole with a pop. She opened her dress and drew an X of custard on her belly. "Do you remember the night we met?"

On my knees, I cleaned away the cross with my tongue.

Emily Hulbert met me at the door and would not let me in. "My mother's ill," she tried. "The party has been canceled." For a poet, she was a rotten liar.

I heard laughter and the ringing of spoons in cups. She caught my wrist when I pushed past. I pulled her along while she begged me in a harsh whisper to stop.

"I'm sorry," she said when I stood at the library's threshold. A few dozen people chatted in scattered groups. In a corner, on a small couch the color of blood, Vivian sat with William Spats, her hand folded into his. Conversations stopped one by one, the room growing quieter and quieter until only Vivian and Spats spoke. They looked up when they noticed the silence. Vivian's ears reddened, Spats's high brow shone in the foreign heat.

"I'm sorry," Emily told me again.

I walked down Canal to the studio and stood behind my camera. What else was there to do? A young man with pimples came in and showed me a card that explained I AM MUTE. I made his portrait and after he paid he pulled a card printed with THANK YOU KIND SIR from a deck he took from his pocket. The silence he carried with him calmed me, then a fat woman arrived complaining.

I watched gripes fill her head like air filling a balloon when she had to shut up for the likeness to be made. When I handed her the portrait, her balloon of complaints popped. "You've made me ugly, you son-of-a-whore!"

Rage got the better of me. "It's nature made you ugly, and the only whore's son I know is your son."

Her aim was poor. The portrait missed me by feet. She thundered down the stairs crying more complaints while Philip wailed laughter from the floor. "I've pissed myself," he happily confessed. I laughed with him, so hard I almost pissed my own pants.

An hour later I was waiting for a cranky child to be bribed by his mother to sit still when the fat woman returned, fat husband in tow. He opened a case to reveal a gleaming brace of dueling pistols. "You'll never forget this day," his fat wife said in a voice I'm sure she thought menacing.

I remembered the day when I had gone to kill Daguerre, remembered the sight of Vivian's hand in the hand of Spats. I wished I had the pistol I'd planned to use to murder Daguerre, remembered my stolen coat, then suffered a backward tumble of melancholy thoughts: Peter, Claude, Daguerre, father. I took a pistol from the case.

We crossed to the neutral ground and stood back to back. The fat woman delivered a screed berating me and praising her dear, gelatinous husband. A man came from a store and begged to be the fat man's second. A crowd quickly formed; a man in a derby with a dented crown took bets, yelled odds. I was favored

2 to 1 when Philip gave a little black boy a coin and the child began to recite numbers in a high voice. The fat man and I turned on the agreed count and I watched down my barrel as the fat man's pistol sneezed flame and smoke. My ears rang. Behind me a horse cried out. I pulled my trigger. My ball sank into the soft folds over the husband's heart and a red stain blossomed on his shirtfront. His wife toppled onto him and behind me winners huzzahed and rushed to collect their bets.

⌘

2 June 1845
Benton came to tell me Claude has killed a man dueling, he does not know who, and I fear he has lost his mind over the girl and killed William Spats. Told Benton this and he told me about quicksilver miners who lose their hair and teeth and become violent and insane. He explained that the poison soaks the miner's hands and gets into their blood and that Claude breathes the poison when he boils quicksilver under soliotypes. Benton left to gather money for Claude's fines—I gave him all I had which was little.

⌘

I LEARNED MY victim's name when the judge read it out: Georg Dürtmeer. I was charged with dueling on a Sunday, spent the night in jail, paid a silly fine, and went on my way Monday morning as if no man had yet been shot. In my desk I found the portrait of Spats Vivian had given me and gouged out his eyes with the tines of a fork. My head ached from lack of sleep and lack of coffee. I felt guilty for killing the fat man. The clock showed I had less than an hour of light and I hurried to pack the odds and ends of supplies left in the old studio.

The undertaker who had the corpse of Georg Dürtmeer seemed to expect me. He led me to the dead man, then had an assistant carry him into the street and the sunlight so I could make a soliotype. The skin of Dürtmeer's face had tightened. He appeared to be at the start of a good laugh.

People looked away when they passed. The undertaker grinned and nodded to the pedestrians. "They cannot stand the sight," he told me. "They want me to sew a happy face onto death, then hide death in a box, then hide the box, but at the same time they want you to make a record of the face I've sewn so they can look at it again and again. They do not know their own desires."

"We are a jumble of wants," I agreed.

"'A jumble of wants,'" he repeated. "That's a fancy way of saying it."

It was dark by the time I finished and cased the portrait. On Chartres I passed a group of boys wearing veils like a gang of short brides, a new method for fighting off the Fever's night vapors. I went to the saloon on Esplanade where I knew I'd find Stanley Roberts, the newspaperman who had stood as Dürtmeer's second. I'd read his story about the duel in the *Daily Picayune*—I was an innocent artist menaced by a fat brute in his telling. The bar was well known. Newspapermen gathered there to drink and fight. Often the papers carried reports of their small riots, reporters giving each other something to write about. I was disappointed by the room. I expected a grand hall; it was dirty and small and stank of piss. Roberts was thrilled to see me, as were all the others in the bar. They reacted as if their great god News had assumed human form. I was clapped on the back, offered drinks, plates of half-finished meals, cigars. When it was clear that all I wanted were directions to the widow's house the entire group decided to escort me. We made our way as a mob, the newspapermen yelling and tossing empty bottles so as to hear them shatter.

Dürtmeer's wife would not open the door when I knocked. She surely had heard us coming, and it is impossible to imagine what she thought was on her stoop. Only when I yelled my name over the muddle of noise Roberts and his chums were making did she open up, and then only to make a try at me with a saber. She slapped me with the flat of the blade and dropped the rusted thing, then slammed the door closed. Roberts tried to stick the sword through the keyhole.

♫

I ate my breakfast slowly, then, hands in my pockets, I sulked to the studio. I expected to find it closed, a placard nailed to the door alerting citizens that the proprietor had killed a man and so they'd need to find another portrait maker. Instead a crowd spilled out onto the street. I cupped my hands against the glass and looked in. The gilded corner of a large frame peeked above heads.

I paid my penny and stood in line and soon I filed past a display in which my soliotypes of New Orleans and New Orleanians hung beside those made by others. The point was clear from the first pair: My subjects were sharp-edged where others were blurred, light washed out the faces of those who had not stood before my camera. Further along the wall I saw what filled the tall frame. It was a pastel view of a parade on Canal Street as seen from atop a building's roof, and beside it was a soliotype of the same scene I had not made.

Victor came and stood beside me. "I feared I'd have to buy

you out of a murder charge, and the price of such a purchase is high, I'm told, so I staged this show in order to afford your freedom."

"This is not mine," I told him, pointing to the plate. A man's suspenders marked the view's center with a clean X.

The doctor put his face so close that the cover glass fogged with his breath. "True, but it's a good one, isn't it? One of my first," he admitted in an excited whisper. "Do you think it's good?"

"Move on," a man behind me demanded.

Next on the wall was a soliotype of the Saint Louis Cathedral I had made, and beside it was Peter's painted version. Along the wall my soliotypes replicated nature. Nothing was left to the imagination or to memory. In our heads each of us carries a storeroom of portraits and landscapes, portraits and landscapes we are constantly painting over, adding details we've newly discovered, altering those we realize are inaccurate. The genius of Peter's work, I saw suddenly as I looked from my cathedral to his, was the way in which it caused each individual to look into their mind's gallery of fluid portraits. The cathedral he painted was many things.

My head filled with fragmented images: Peter painting the little landscape Millicent had tucked up her sleeve, the arm in that sleeve, the shoulder it led to and the breast below that shoulder; Vivian standing nude with her opera glasses raised and my face duplicated and made spherical by the twin lenses; Spats's hand resting on the base of Vivian's back while they danced; the mole I knew dotted the knob of her spine below that hand and the dress; Dürtmeer's blood coloring his shirt like a diagram of the heart I'd wrecked. Then Spats took poor Dürtmeer's place, his shirtfront marked with a heart like a playing-card ace; my hand covered the mole low on Vivian's back; Millicent held me in the loose noose of her arms, her breast warm against my face. I stood beside Peter facing the cathedral. His paints were gray and black. When I looked up the color had left the sky and clouds the hue of cigar smoke marked a slate heaven.

"Where did you get this?" I asked Victor.

His brows bounced. "Millicent offered it when I told her my plan."

When I took Peter's landscape from the wall the impatient man behind me demanded his penny back. I left Benton to dole out refunds to a line of dolts who all claimed they'd been cheated.

Everyone in the street looked queer. A fop's bright cravat resembled a wound, a wide-brimmed hat transformed a short woman into a mushroom. Noontime heat slowed pedestrians and the world looked like a soliotype that had been hastily painted over, the edges of some bodies exceeded by brush strokes—a little girl in a yellow dress burned like a fallen sun—others neglected by the brush—an old man with gray hair, gray skin, and gray eyes looked as if he'd stepped through the cover glass and left his family behind in their yearly portrait.

I went into a gun shop and bought a pistol, its barrel gleaming with oil.

I walked a zigzag route from saloon to saloon. In each I drank whiskey and inquired after Spats. The sun fell while every man I asked shook his head. After dark barrooms filled and it took me longer and longer to sort through the crowds. On Gasopet, before a shop which sold pens and paper by day, whiskey and rum out a street-facing window at night, my search ended. "William Spats from New England is dead," the man in the window told me. "I heard someone say so earlier today." We were alone, the street empty, and the man did not start when I grabbed his ears and kissed him.

I was simple from drinking and it seemed logical that the city held only one undertaker. The man who had carried Dürtmeer into the street so I could make his portrait greeted me warmly when I found his door. I was sure that my quest had become known and I was being led to the body of William Spats, but the man with his hands carefully crossed over the hole I'd blasted in him was Dürtmeer.

"That's not William Spats," I observed.

The undertaker's long face squeezed together, the corners of his eyes and those of his mouth moving toward each other in surprise. "This is Georg Dürtmeer, the man you killed dueling," he explained.

"I already knew this man was dead—I've made his portrait. What I need to know is if you have a dead man named Spats." I lifted a sheet from the face of another man who was not Spats and only then realized I was standing in a room of corpses.

The undertaker saw me shudder and his face softened. "The Fever is everywhere, don't believe the papers. Is this Spats a friend?"

"I need to see him about his fiancée."

"Many are dead, others are running. It would not surprise me if your friend had left her behind." He quickly held up his hand in apology. "That is if he isn't dead. There are a dozen here dead from the Fever, a dozen more from birthing, old age, poison, hydrophobia, dueling." He pointed to corpses while he cataloged the causes of their deaths. "People die because of all sorts of things, even during a plague." He covered Dürtmeer.

Whiskey made my footing unsure. "I must find Spats," I explained.

I was standing at the bar closing one eye and then the other, trying to judge if I was truly so drunk that I was unable to read the label of the bottle from which the liquor I sipped had come. A slap on the back opened both my eyes and I saw that the label's ink was smeared, the words running down the bottle's side.

"Dear Claudie, you cannot make soliotypes in the dark."

I turned to find Victor Benton grinning.

"Do let me furnish you with a dram of fun." He gestured at the bartender; the man ignored him. "It's only fair—it was your views that furnished the money."

"Have you seen Spats?"

Victor pursed his lips. "I've heard he's in New Orleans."

"Have you seen him?"

Victor shook his head. He waved frantically to the barman, who glumly came to serve. Victor gave him enough coins for the bottle with the label I could not read. "You are in need of a treatment," he told me as he took my arm and pulled me into the street. "I must advise that you do not dally in getting a treatment."

I thought of the room full of dead men. "Is it the Fever?"

Victor grabbed my head with both hands and pulled my eyelids back with his thumbs. He studied my eyeballs closely. "Worse," he judged, then held the bottle to my lips until I sputtered whiskey.

He dragged me along the avenue, stopping at the end of each block to try and force more liquor into me. We came to a door and he rapped until a dark mulatta came and greeted him. She helped him bring me up a flight of stairs and toss me onto a bed, then she and he began embracing and kissing and shedding their clothes. They fell naked onto the bed beside me and noisily set upon each other. I rolled to the extreme edge of the mattress and clung to the linens, fearing a fall that drink would make fatally long, while Victor and his friend shook the bed. Victor bellowed through his little death while the mulatta laughed, then he laughed as well.

"Claude, this is my best friend Virginia."

Laughing still, she shook my hand formally, then began to unbutton my trousers. Victor held my arms when I tried to fight her off. She pinned my kicking legs with her knees and took me in her mouth. In spite of my wishes to the contrary, my cock rose.

"The best treatment for a broken heart is a best friend, my friend," Victor advised.

"Call her off," I said, causing Virginia to laugh and spit me out when she choked.

Victor let go of one of my arms to clap her on the back, and I reached into my jacket and pulled out the pistol. "Off of me!" I commanded.

Victor pushed my hand to the pillow. Whiskey weakened me, and while I tried to shake loose of him, Virginia resumed her machinations. She felt my release coming and raised her head. My juice striped Victor's thigh and I pulled the pistol's trigger, wounding the wall and silencing their laughter. They let me go and I rolled from the bed's edge and fell. I met the floor headfirst, and the last thing I saw when I looked up were the faces of Victor and Virginia, grinning and frowning.

♄

I woke to Victor's singing. Each flat verse made it feel as if my brain were trying to escape my skull. I unwound myself from the knot I'd formed, my joints grinding and popping. Benton was shaving while he sang. His right hand peeled uniform strips of cream with the razor, his left hung fluttering at his side. When he looked down and saw me watching his twitching fingers, he held his hands out toward me. The left danced its fit, the right was still as stone.

"Behold the surgeon," he sang, his smile huge and real. "No bottle's contents can keep him from his calling."

He turned to the mirror and tipped back his head. I feared for the thick pulse I could see beneath the lather—I was so damaged by whiskey that I could not fathom anyone could not be similarly injured—but he scraped his neck clean of whiskers and soap without a nick.

There was no sign of Virginia. I stood too quickly and the floor tipped like the deck of a ship.

"Spats is dead," Victor told me.

"So I've heard. What's your proof?"

Benton pointed to the floor that'd just quit pitching. "Virginia's neighbor is a novice undertaker, and last night he woke us yelling when one of his clients moaned."

"Spats?"

"Spats." Benton hooked his lip over his teeth and shaved under his nose. "We hiss and rattle even when we're no more. The air in our lungs has no desire to die with us."

"I want to see him."

Victor buttoned his collar. "Of course you do."

⌒℘

A thin line of dried black vomit ran from either corner of Spats's mouth and down over his yellow chin making his jaw look hinged like that of a ventriloquist's dummy.

"Fever," I said aloud.

"You'd think so," Victor said. He looked at a small certificate tied to Spats's thumb with a twist of string. "My colleague claims malaria." Benton smiled and shook his head. "We all do what we can to make history cleaner."

The doctor watched impassively when I drew the pistol from my coat and aimed at Spats's head. The hammer snapped and I looked down the barrel at Spats for several long seconds, enjoying his death.

"The wound she's given you is deep and jagged," Victor said. "Such cuts heal badly, Claudie."

I paid him no attention and braced the camera on a box I set upon Spats's chest. His dummy's face filled the entire frame.

Like a watch well wound and left in a drawer the studio kept its hours even on the days I woke on a floor to the ugly voice of Victor Benton. Millicent and a towheaded girl played a duet on the piano while a larger version of the girl fanned herself in time with the music. Upstairs Philip was arranging a third, even larger version of the towhead before the camera. I hurried past them into the developing room.

Drained of all color by the soliotype, Spats looked even more like a marionette. I cased the portrait in black. When I emerged, my head filled with a vision of Vivian's shocked eyes looking up from the portrait, Philip handed me a note. The seal was big enough to hold the print of a fist surrounding a signet's mark—Marmu's fist. It cracked to bits when I broke the wax. *We must discuss Vivian* was scrawled in hasty script.

"A messenger paid me five dollars to make sure you got that," Philip told me. He tried to give me the bank note.

"Keep it," I happily told him.

A card tacked to Marmu's office door read *Leave Deliveries With Roland* and an arrow pointed to the wine shop next door.

I cupped my hands against the glass to try and peek in and the door opened a tiny bit. The busy clerks and their desks were gone. Dust sparkled in the bands of sun that came through the half-drawn shades. In the darkest corner of the room Vivian and her father sat at opposite ends of a long bench. When Francis Marmu met me in the middle of the empty office he looked like a portrait of himself made when he was young and in poor health: The skin around his eyes was blue as a bruise; his face was unshaven and drawn tight across his cheekbones. He yelled "She—," then a fit of coughing doubled him over. His voice and his coughing filled the empty room and for a moment the noise seemed to hang in the air like the dust in the sunbeams; Vivian's crying took up where his echo ended. He spat, then weakly spoke: "She carries your child." I thought of our last meeting above the coffee warehouse and counted days and weeks, figuring in my head she was three months along. Marmu turned and pointed to Vivian. "You will have to marry her," he announced, and when I tried to tell him I was more than willing, he held up his hand to silence me. "There is no argument you can offer."

I made my face into that of a man ashamed, defeated. "You are right, sir," I agreed. "I will have to take the penalty for my crime." I could barely keep my voice below a happy shout.

Vivian's crying dulled to a thin wail. I moved a step in her direction and Francis Marmu shoved me back.

"I'll find a priest and we'll get this ugliness over with. Now go away."

In the street I danced and laughed. A little girl was selling flowers from a wheelbarrow and I bought her entire store, filling both my arms with daisies, then gave them away one by one as I made my way back to the studio. I still held a large bouquet when I walked in. Millicent rose from the piano and smiled when she saw the flowers and my grin. I handed them to her and said, "Vivian is now my wife and so you will have to go—she does not want you here." Millicent's smile faded and she dropped the flowers. They scattered around my feet. She slammed the door so violently its glass webbed with cracks. Sunlight came through the door and the shadow pattern of the fissures lay atop the flowers.

ℐ

14 June 1845
William Spats has died and Francis Marmu has decided to
hand over his daughter to Claude—This morning there is
notice in every paper that he and the girl will marry.
Yesterday Claude brought me flowers and begged me to for-
give him and I told him Remember that I am the one who
encouraged you to do this so do not beg me to forgive you.
My hands shook and I dropped the flowers. They were daisies
and I wanted them, but my pride would not let me stoop and
gather them, so I left the flowers on the floor. I know that I
made this pain but it hurts me so deeply I want to blame
someone else for it.

ℐ

NOTE I assumed would tell me when and where Vivian and I would marry arrived the next morning, but instead of instructions in Francis Marmu's jagged hand, the message written in Vivian's cramped script told me *My father has been taken by the Fever.* Marmu's hacking cough and yellowed eyes had not been the mark of drink and distress. It was a wonder he had had the power to stand and face me.

I heard the noise of hammering before I saw Joseph perched atop a chair balanced on a stair, tacking black bunting over the threshold. Vivian was supervising and steadying the chair. Joseph saw me first and quit hammering. Vivian followed his eyes, abandoned her duty, rushed me, and girdled me with her arms. The chair tipped off the stair and Joseph fell, tearing the black banner from its tacks as he did.

I made the memorial at noon, then sat with the women for lunch. They glared at their food as if it had killed Francis Marmu. Charlotte Marmu let out occasional gasps, sobs smothered in sighs. I was suddenly ravenous. I ate my portion, then helped myself to Vivian's. A clock started to ring the hour and Mrs. Marmu rushed from the room sobbing. I pulled her plate across the table.

"Did he find a priest before he died?" I wondered.

Vivian sucked in her breath as if I'd hit her. "We cannot be married until a decent period of mourning is over with," she told me.

I nodded and smiled, my mouth full.

Vivian shook her head. "You eat like an animal," she muttered, then looked down at her lap and worried her serviette.

I swallowed and wiped my mouth.

"I am too tired to be good company," she apologized as she stood. She bent and let me kiss her cheek, then left me to my food.

⳼ ⳼ ⳼

Plate 25—Memorial Portrait of Francis Marmu, *1845.*
Half-plate daguerreotype.

Plate 26—Mourning Portrait of Charlotte and Vivian Marmu, *1845. Half-plate daguerreotype.*

Plate 27—Spirit Portrait of Charlotte Marmu Standing Behind Her Daughter Vivian, *1845. Half-plate daguerreotype.*

Plate 28—Memorial Portrait of Charlotte Marmu, *1845. Half-plate daguerreotype.*

Plate 29—Mourning Portrait of Vivian Marmu, *1845. Half-plate daguerreotype.*

FRANCIS MARMU WAS one of the many victims of yellow fever in the summer of 1845, the summer that would host the decade's worst epidemic. In Pl. 25 Mr. Marmu is posed reclining in a chair, a Bible held loosely in his hands. Such "sleep of death" poses are often seen, especially if the subject is very young or very old. Adolescents, teenagers, and young adults are usually posed in sickbeds or in their coffins, a reflection of the fact that their deaths are more startling and sudden. The portrait is in a black morocco memorial case with an engraved silver funerary mat and silvered outlines. Poems, death notices, and letters were often pinned to the velvet facing mats of memorial cases; Mr. Marmu's has a small brooch engraved with his initials and those of his wife and daughter pinned to its plum-colored cloth.

In Pl. 26 Charlotte and Vivian stand hand-in-hand, both in second-stage mourning dress, a clue that dates this plate several months later than Pl. 25. Although the cover glass has been cracked and some deterioration has occurred, careful inspection proves that in Pl. 26 Vivian holds Pl. 25, making the daguerreotype an odd diptych.

Pl. 27 demonstrates how a master like Marchand could transform one of the daguerreotype's shortcomings into a wonderful effect. Vivian's pose and both women's dresses are the same as those in Pl. 26; both portraits were undoubtedly made during the same sitting. In Pl. 27 a ghost image of Charlotte Marmu appears to be standing behind her daughter. While spirit photographs became somewhat common in the late 1860s, this is one of the earliest known examples of the technique. The ghost image was managed by having the "spirit" subject move out of the picture before the exposure fully elapsed. Pl. 27's cover glass has also been broken. Pieces of the glass are missing, and the deterioration is much worse than that suffered by Pl. 26, but the ghost effect is still dramatic.

Charlotte Marmu died in the first week of July, and Pl. 28 is a very typical memorial portrait save for the presence of a cat peeking over the coffin's edge.

It was not rare for entire families to be carried away, common for the older members to be the least able to recover. Each summer orphanages swelled with young survivors. Vivian's resilience can be explained by this passage from Felix Moissenet's pamphlets: "The Marmus were originally from Massachusetts, a fact neither Francis nor Charlotte let be forgotten. A trip to the Marmu home in the summer months would invariably set the stage for a sermon on Devil Summer and his Hell Fires and Demon Mosquitoes. Vivian was born in New Orleans, and when young she suffered and recovered from a bout of the Fever. Such good luck made her, as well as so many other natives to this fine City, impervious to Mister Jack. Her parents, alas, were not so lucky—in short order the poor child was left without father or mother."

In Pl. 29 orphaned Vivian is stunningly posed. She holds a lily and gazes at the memorial portraits of her mother and father which stand on a small table at her elbow. Marchand's use of light and shade is a marvel. The drape behind Vivian is a range of peaks and valleys, the folds of valleys dark with shadow, the peaks snow-capped with well-directed light. The table's legs guide the eye upward from the dark pool of the carpet to the pale line of the lily which leads to Vivian.

⌒

WHEN I MADE my way back to the studio, coffins rested on the sawhorses and a line of portrait sitters and assorted mourners loitered in front of the display which compared my views of the city to the soliotypes made by others. Rumor had it at least two men had closed up shop after Victor's stunt led to their mocking in the papers.

Philip pulled me aside and read to me from a small piece of paper. He told me how much money had been managed in the last few weeks, how many soliotypes had been made, what number had been made of living subjects, what number of dead, what made up the small balance—a beloved cat, a hat made by a milliner who wished to show a woman in Charleston what he was capable of, a sword to be offered in a raffle, a collection of dried hands cut from the small arms of monkeys by a seaman who figured he could sell the lot to some museum somewhere. "He had me make six versions, then could pay for only five." Philip held out the sixth portrait. Tiny fingers curled in remembrance of jungle vines.

"Again, how much?" I asked, not quite able to believe the figure he'd mentioned. He took the soliotype from my hands and replaced it with the paper. His penmanship was delicate, ladylike. The number was absurd. I felt guilty for not being there to help.

"The full attack of the Fever is yet to come," he said gaily.

"We shall be rich," I agreed.

The Marmu house was closed to me. The quarantine demanded by the yellow card nailed to the front door so often ignored in New Orleans was honored not out of reverence for law and medicine, but because the two remaining Marmus cloaked themselves in the black dresses and black moods of true mourning. June aged slowly. The only times I spoke with Vivian were when Joseph fetched me because she wished to whisper from behind the curtains of a street-facing window. I could hear her mother sound sobs deep in the house while Vivian asked me if this or that friend could come to our wedding, if we could take a holiday somewhere on the seashore.

One day she passed me a tiny package wrapped in butcher's paper. I had not seen her skin for a week and I was almost unable to let free her hand to take the package. Her mother called her name and she yanked away. I tore the brown paper and found the soliotype I'd made of her when she and Spats had come to the studio. She'd cut a bride's dress from onionskin, drawn on lace and buttons, and pasted it to herself. I took the portrait to a seamstress and hired her to make the dress Vivian had imagined. When she asked Vivian's size, I formed my hands into remembered waist, hips, shoulders. The old woman grinned and draped smooth satin over my fingers.

I began to live like an anchorite. I quit drinking cognac and coffee, did not replenish my opium when it was gone. One night I found a Bible deep in a drawer and read random verses. On my way to tea and sweet rolls one morning, fresh from a long night of deep sleep, I met Benton on his way home, our schedules now opposites. I'd lost two teeth in as many days and a third was loose as a baby's. I hailed the doctor and asked for his opinion. Victor had me squat, tip my head back, and open my mouth. He ran a finger along the patch of raw gum.

He looked worried, then smiled as if his concern had been a joke. "You need a decent meal," he prescribed. "As do I. Susana will cure us both."

I laughed and tried to leave him to his debauched homecoming, but he hooked his arm in mine and pulled me along.

"The Fever is at full boil," he told me, his voice falling to a secretive tone.

I felt bad for assuming I'd caught him on his way from Virginia's. "Have you been with victims?"

He giggled. "Claudie, we're all victims."

We climbed the stairs. The door was barricaded from inside, a contract tacked to it. It outlined behavior Susana considered acceptable—card games at home, trips to the theater in her company—and behavior that would no longer be tolerated—unexplained nights away, excessive consumption of whiskey, et cetera. Benton read the thing twice. The second time he formed the words with his lips as if he were working a language he did not speak. He set his shoulder against the door and pushed, but it did not budge.

"Sign it," Susana instructed from within.

"I will not," he told her, then took a running try at the door. He caromed off and danced in a circle, holding his injured shoulder and biting his lip. A pen skittered under the door.

"Sign it or you'll rot in that hallway."

The doctor shrugged and looked at me with a sheepish grin. I turned and offered him my back. I felt the pen through the paper and my jacket and my shirt.

℘

Victor proved an excellent domesticated husband. He staged a single rebellion—a night spent not with Virginia, but with the other doctors of the Howard Association—a rebellion that under the terms of the contract he'd agreed to led to his banishment from Susana's bed and a period during which she acted as if he were invisible and inaudible even when he yelled her name over and over while jumping and waving. Victor spent a day apologizing, then sent me to Virginia with a note telling her he could no longer visit her. She read it while yawning and combing her hair. "Tell him I'll miss him," she said matter-of-factly, then asked me to pass her a japanned dish filled with small tortoise combs.

I spent many hours with the Bentons. Susana acclimated to the city quickly. She drank as much wine as her husband and treated me like a respectable fiancé, never once mentioning Millicent. We played dominoes and listened to Victor torture a fiddle he'd been given by a patient in lieu of payment. Susana knew her Latin and Greek, and it took only a few cups and a gentle push for her to pluck the fiddle like a lyre and offer up Seneca. I watched Victor and Susana tease each other, touch each other with unconscious caresses, smile at each other's jokes even if they were poor.

Philip and I made dozens and dozens of portraits a day. The papers promised the Fever was not to be found inside the city's borders, but each week there were more and more dead. Philip devised an apparatus which involved a camera suspended from a scaffold which pointed down at the faces of those snug in coffins. Articles praising the humanity and tenderness of such an invention appeared next to editorials lambasting anyone foolish enough to believe there was an epidemic at work.

Those who could afford to hide in their parlors and court-yards sent their servants on every errand. In the street I saw blacks leisurely appraising the fruit they'd been sent to fetch, shopkeepers nervously covering their mouths with kerchiefs, and workman going about their trades. The only happy men I saw were my fellow suitors. Boys and men, white and black, we offered lovely promises to curtained windows, closed doors, garden pickets, mail slots. I spent so many days speaking to Vivian while she was seated in shadow with the scrim of a curtain between us that when I closed my eyes to think of her I saw her face as if in a soliotype with lace pasted atop.

༄

Two weeks after Francis Marmu died Vivian and her mother walked into the studio. I nearly fell when I jumped from my seat.

"We are here for portraits," Mrs. Marmu announced.

"Yes, yes, of course," I babbled. "You're both so beautiful today."

Vivian grinned and looked at the floor. Mrs. Marmu shuddered as if I'd insulted her.

"I mean to say that it is beautiful to see you recovering so well," I tried.

"We will never recover," Mrs. Marmu promised.

Behind her mother's shoulder Vivian shook her head and silently mouthed "No."

"Recover? Never, of course not," I agreed, "But it is good to see you out."

"The air reeks of filth. I would be better off in my home."

"A beautiful home."

I led the Marmus up the stairs. Vivian sat and her mother stood behind her. Mrs. Marmu could not stay still. Vivian's posture troubled her. She took her daughter's head by the ears and moved it side to side. I was sure she'd made all needed adjustments, but when I removed the lens cover Charlotte Marmu briskly stepped from the portrait's frame. Vivian sat completely still and stared at me while her mother frantically drank a glass of water.

I replaced the botched plate with a new one. Refreshed, Charlotte Marmu managed to stand still for the entire exposure. I took both plates into the developing room and was so flustered that I was unable to remember which was which. The first I finished was the botched one. In it Vivian sat calmly, the ghostly outline of her mother hovering behind her. The other turned out perfectly.

I handed the botched portrait to Mrs. Marmu, the perfect one to Vivian, then realized my mistake and snatched the queered soliotype from Mrs. Marmu before she could open its case.

She pointed at me. "Make your promise," she told Vivian.

Vivian looked at the portrait in her hands. "I promise I'll never marry him." Her voice was calm, but a long tear tracked down the side of her nose.

Mother Marmu turned on me. "My husband"—she paused to cross herself—"told me about how you took advantage of Vivian. I would rather she bore a bastard than marry you." She jerked the portrait from Vivian's hands and threw it at my feet, then grabbed Vivian's arm and pulled her down the stairs.

I looked at the portrait I held, put my finger to the glass over Vivian's face. I heard feet on the stairs and turned, expecting her. Millicent stood at the top of the steps. "Do you truly love her?" She tipped her head back and looked down her nose.

"First I'm abused by an insane woman and now I have to listen to you mock me?"

"I'm not mocking, I'm asking you a question."

I paced a tight circle for a moment, kicked the portrait Mrs. Marmu had thrown at my feet, then took up the water glass Mrs. Marmu had drank from and threw it the length of the studio. When it shattered I felt as if I'd broken my prize possession. "Yes," I admitted.

"And do you love me?"

I looked at the glittering mess I'd made on the other side of the room. "No."

Millicent snapped her fingers and I turned my head. "Say it now," she told me.

I looked into her eyes and could not.

"Good enough," she said, then turned and descended the stairs.

I opened the case and looked at the portrait of Vivian and her ghost mother, then threw it down just as Charlotte Marmu had thrown down its more accomplished twin.

I wanted to line up portraits of my enemies and toss rocks at their faces. I imagined glass shattering and the jagged points of stones putting out eyes, tearing off ears. I walked through the streets hating each thing I saw, then turned and retraced my steps, collecting rocks as I went, keeping only those with dangerous edges.

The plates of Vivian and her mother were not on the floor. My jacket hung on a hook in the developing room, dead Spats in its right pocket, dead Marmu gone from the left. I found Philip sitting on a box, smoking the stub of a cheroot just outside the door. The afternoon heat made the air waver like water; the smoke from Philip's mouth shook as it rose. I watched him watch a pretty girl walk down the empty street and through the liquid air. I admired the way in which his face was undamaged by the world.

"Did you take a portrait from my jacket?" I asked.

He had not heard me coming and jumped up when I spoke. He dropped his cheroot and tried to hide it under his heel. "I'm sorry," he said. "What did you just ask?"

I held up the jacket. "Did you take a portrait of Francis Marmu from my pocket?"

He shook his head and looked frightened by the question. "I would never take anything from your pockets," he swore. "Miss Millicent took those two from the floor, but they were both of women."

I nodded. "Charlotte Marmu and her daughter."

He smiled as if we were in league. "I hope they're well?"

♔

My targets disappeared, I went into the street and threw my best stones at moving dogs and rats, my duds at the dead.

I bought a long wand of bread and a piece of cheese too hard to chew. A storefront hung with skillets reminded me of the night I'd given Victor the views, and that memory made me want hashish. My rocks gone, I threw my cheese at a cur in an alley's mouth. Night was falling and the lamps were being lit. Masks were back in fashion to fight off Fever and a man and a woman passed wearing strips of embroidered silk.

Victor was not at home. Susana named the Fever victim he'd set out to watch die, then all but dragged me over the threshold, offering food, a hand of cards, news of her sister's twin babies. "One's a boy named Leslie, the other a girl named Roberta. Don't you think they got them turned around?" Her mouth was purple from wine and her hair was loose and wild about her shoulders. She wore Victor's robe unbuttoned and beneath it only a light gown.

All I could think of was hashish. "Turned around?" was all I could say.

"Leslie is a girl's name," she explained, then laughed nervously. "We were drinking wine," she furthered. Susana blushed vividly, pulling her robe closed when she realized it was open.

"And Roberta is a boy's with an *a* appended," I said.

She nodded, then tucked her bare feet beneath the robe's hem. We stood in silence, I embarrassed as much as she. I could recall no mention of hashish in Victor's contract with his wife. "May I have some hashish?" I tried.

She smiled, happy to have the subject veer away from her bed, and fetched a small box rattling with hashish-paste nuts. I took one, thanked her, and left too abruptly. I was rude, I knew, but seeing her purple mouth and the honest flush of her cheek and hearing her happy voice made me hate Vivian for the promise she'd sworn, made me despise her mother for pushing her to swear it.

I dissolved my nut in a cup of strong coffee I bought from a shop, drank the potion in three long, sour swallows. The city became more and more lovely as I wandered, the exception being the alleys in which I was sure I saw the low shadows of alligators.

On the corner of Chartres a parade was passing and I stood watching, my mouth open in joy. Soldiers passed on horseback for what seemed like hours, each waving a painted handkerchief. A band in a wagon came after them. The hashish was making me feel as if my arms were floating up away from my body and it took all my strength to hold my elbows to my sides. A steamboat came up the street and for a moment I thought I had not noticed that the crowd had carried me to the river's edge, then I saw that the men on deck were as tall as the smokestacks. The boat was thirty-odd feet long and seemed lit from within, the name *Henry Clay* glowing on the wheelhouse. Horses pulled the Henry Clay past, steam rising from its short chimneys, and behind it was a printing press being worked by a gang in aprons, their hands black with ink. One handed me a broadside and I took his wink as a sign that he was passing me a note from Vivian. I folded the paper and stuffed it into my pocket, then ran from the corner before something even more impossible rolled along.

I had to concentrate mightily to manage to fit my key into its lock, and as I struggled I happily wondered what news was contained in Vivian's note.

The ink had been wet when I folded the paper and the message was a jumble of words atop words. I was turning the broadside around and around in my hands when Joseph opened the unlocked door and walked in.

"She's dead," he told me, and I knew by his calm he was speaking of Charlotte Marmu, not Vivian.

I abandoned the letter and stood to shake his hand. He would not take my hand. I sat and started to put on my boots.

"Her mother's death changes none of the promises she made. She will not be your wife."

One foot shod, I sat holding the second boot, its use suddenly a mystery. "I'll believe that only when I hear Vivian say it."

Joseph pushed me down when I tried to rise. "She does not wish to see you, that's why I'm here, not her."

His hand was on the knob when I hopped to my feet and said, "Pray, what time is it?"

Vanity bested him. He produced his watch and I snatched it from his palm. The chain flashed across his fingers and his grab was late. Joseph lunged at me and I hit him with the boot—its function suddenly clear—splitting his cheek. He fell holding the wound. I skipped two steps back, fearing his response. It looked as if he could not understand the blood filling his palm when he took his hand away from his face.

"My watch," he whimpered.

"Your watch?" I yelled. "Your watch, your watch, your *watch*." I placed it on the desk and threatened to hammer it with my boot heel.

He got to his feet slowly; his hand left a bloody mark on the rug. He made a slight move toward me and I raised the boot, closing one eye to take careful aim.

"Tell her I will arrive for tea tomorrow. Tell her I will not be sent away."

Joseph nodded and backed out the door with his eyes on his precious watch.

Only a moment passed before the idiot knocked on the door he'd just closed. The sound of the watch breaking was like that of a hard-shelled beetle being murdered. It leaked gears and springs when I dangled it from its fob. I jerked open the door and held it in Joseph's face, but it was Philip who stood gaping at the flattened and misshapen watch. I hid it and my boot behind my back. "I assumed you were someone else," I explained.

The hashish intensified like a fit. I stepped away from the door and carefully wrapped what was left of the watch in newspaper, stowed the package in my jacket, then sat and put on my boot. A tiny, sharp cog pierced my foot when I stood, so I sat again, removed the boot, pulled the minuscule bit of watch-works from my heel, stuck my foot back in the boot, and only then remembered Philip in the doorway. He was visibly upset. His tongue darted out and wet his lips again and again. One of his eyes was swollen halfway shut.

"Come in, come in," I said as if the mistake were his.

"I know you were looking for this." He held out the portrait of Francis Marmu that had gone missing from my jacket. "It and these"—he offered the two portraits of Vivian and her mother, the coverglass over both cracked like the watch's crystal—"were bound up in twine and wrapped in oiled paper. I thought they were food until I unwrapped them." From his pocket he fetched the twine and waxed paper. "This was bound up with them." A little pouch of newspaper held a shard of glass. The pouch had been made from Francis Marmu's obituary. Philip rubbed his pressed-tin cross and shifted his weight from foot to foot while I studied all the items. "It is hoodoo," he told me. "Devil magic."

"Mrs. Marmu has died," I said before I could stop myself.

Philip clenched his cross. "You are a slut, Millicent is a slut, Vivian Marmu is a slut, and the lot of you will burn in hell."

With the edge of the crushed watch I cut a shallow notch from Philip's eye socket to his ear. He staggered, then found his voice. Yelled prayers filled the street.

♔

17 July 1845

Went to ask Claude for a small loan and found him yelling at the ceiling—The girl and her mother had just gone and he was upset by something that had been said. I asked him if he loved me and he said No but could not look into my face and when I made him look at me he could not say No when I asked again. Told him to go eat and then to go to sleep and he nodded and went. I went to the developing room to check the pockets of Claude's jackets for coins and found six dimes and

*a bit of cheese wrapped in waxed paper. I was eating the
cheese when Philip found me. The day I first saw him and
kissed him to make Claude jump I saw meanness in the boy's
face and I saw the same meanness in his smile when he closed
the small room's door. I swallowed my cheese and tried to
move past him but the room is very narrow and he grabbed
my neck and said I have heard blackies will lie down with
anything, even a dog. I could not breathe with his hand at my
throat. I tried to pull it off with both my hands and when I
did he put his other hand up under my dress with as much
meanness as he held my neck. Tried to say Stop it but my
voice was gone. When I put my thumb into his eye Philip
yelled and let go of me and I kicked his crotch with all my
strength and when he fell I kicked his throat. Hate made me
unafraid and I took my time downstairs looking for a portrait
I had seen Philip admire often each day. In it he sits holding
an umbrella with the mean smile on his face. I took the soliotype to my room and tied it to the engine from a music box
that I dropped and broke last week and set Philip spinning.
My aunt told me a man whose portrait is fastened to a top
and spun will take to loving both men and women. I hope
Philip's spinning will send him to loving anything, even a dog.*

℘

I SAT HOLDING the nude of Millicent. My fingers closed
around her body, she cocked her head as if puzzled, ear almost
on her shoulder. I peeled back each finger and exposed her bit
by bit until the tilt of her wonderful head was explained—my
hand tipped the couch on which she lay up off its legs and balanced it on end. Millicent's toes were curled like a fist's fingers.

I wanted to go to her, but the hashish convinced me dangers waited in the street—Philip and Joseph and alligators—so I sat and watched Millicent appear from and disappear into my fist. The sky lightened by degrees, layers of night peeled away until an orange light burned behind the uneven teeth of dormers and chimneys. Only then did I believe the streets to be safe.

Before Philip deserted the painted city he cleaned his room deep in the studio's hive of pantries. I found a pair of old shoes I'd given him shining from fresh polish in the middle of the scrubbed floor. He left no note save a scrap of brown paper weighted down by coins its calculations proved he owed me— I'd paid him a week of wages in advance after he mentioned his admiration for an umbrella he'd seen in a shop's window. I filled my pockets with his pay and stared at the gleaming shoes. I was sorry I'd cut his face. How could I blame a boy betrayed by an entire city?

A voice I did not know called my name in the salon. It was a child delivering the summons from Vivian: *Bring camera, &tc.*

$\mathcal{P}$

Charlotte Marmu's coffin was polished so highly I could see the moving reflections of my hands on its surface. The gray cat stood with its paws on the coffin's edge and peered in when I removed the lens cover.

Vivian stroked the box's side. "It was supposed to be my father's. Some petty debt was owed, so he was buried in a rough box." She blew her nose angrily.

"Joseph lied to me," I told her.

Vivian looked at the coffin, studying her mirrored face tattooed with the wood's grain. "No he didn't," she said. "I made promises to my mother, and I intend to keep them."

There was a tap at my shoulder and I looked up into a pistol's eye. Behind it Joseph smiled and pointed to the door. His cheek was laced with tiny knots of gut stitching.

Thunder rolled above me and the breeze was as moist and warm as breath. A wagon almost killed me when I stopped in the middle of the street to slap my pockets as if what I'd just lost might be found in my jacket. An old man in a high hat was kind enough to yank me clear, the wagon driver abusing us both as he passed. When I tried to thank the man a tooth fell from my mouth. He backed away violently shaking his hand, then stuck his arm up to the elbow in a horse trough, soaking his sleeve. My tooth cracked under my foot when I stepped toward him to explain. I felt as if it were only the first bit of my skeleton to abandon me. The man jogged down the street, a line drawn behind him by the water leaking from his cuff.

My joints were loose, my knees useless. I sat on a stair and held my head in my hands. A tongued survey of my teeth turned up another one wobbling. Blood filled my mouth and I spat it almost onto the tops of Victor Benton's shoes. He carried a gift wrapped in a long, narrow box. A flower of ribbon was bright as a poppy. He dropped into a squat in front of me, the box across his lap like a rifle. "She'll not have you," he observed.

I was horrified. "Is it written across my face?" I imagined words inked on my brow and covered it with my hands.

He hooked his arm with mine and jerked me to my feet. "Your face is clean," he promised. "The Marmus' servant boy boasted the news last night while I was mending the rip you gave him."

People were staring. I buttoned my jacket and leveled my hat. "She has no reason to refuse me. Once I saw her mother in a box I expected kisses and thanks. Keeping promises to the dead is idiotic."

Victor urged me along the street. "She's new to the job of orphan, Claudie, give her time. You think you look like a savior, but she sees a wolf."

"I'm no wolf."

We stood before his door. "True," he agreed. "You're a man in love."

"Is that some sort of riddle?"

Victor sighed. "It's not a riddle, you're not a wolf. Come inside. It's Susana's birthday." He shook the package and it rattled.

I looked at Victor and saw my last ally. I smiled to show him we were friends and was relieved to have him smile back at me. "How old?"

His smile grew. "Twenty. I saved her from a spinster's woes."

The sky opened up as we stepped in the door. Rain crescendoed on the roof while Susana carefully tore the wrapping. The package held a short piece of blond wood and some nails. Pine in one hand, nails in the other, she blinked and held a grin on a confused face. "I don't understand this," she admitted.

"A house," Victor told her, his voice breaking with the happy news. "A house in the American Quarter."

She held him and kissed his mouth and laughed at herself while he described the place. I touched one of the nails in the box, its square head shining. I turned my pockets out onto the table: a scatter of coins; the two portraits of Vivian and her mother, one good and one ruined; the waxed paper, string, shattered glass, and scrap of newspaper Philip had brought me; Francis Marmu's memorial portrait; Joseph's flat watch.

"It's all I have," I told them.

Victor looked as puzzled as his wife had when she opened her box of wood and nails. Susana skipped to me and kissed my cheek with a laugh, rattling nails in her palm like dice. Victor picked up one of the soliotypes and I watched his face lose all color.

"What is this?" He held the portrait in which Charlotte Marmu was no more than smoke.

"The mother darted away while the lens was uncovered. Vivian remained still," I explained.

Victor let go a long breath. "Of course, yes, like moving horses." He shook his head and smiled. "For a moment I feared you'd managed to catch a picture of dead Momma Marmu back from beyond, whispering advice into her daughter's ear."

I took the soliotype from him and traced my finger along one of the cracks which crossed the cover glass.

"Claude," Susana chided, "these are your things. If you want to give me a gift, make my portrait, make our portrait."

It was only then I remembered I'd left my camera behind. It sat beneath Mrs. Marmu, its dark wood so close in hue casket and camera may have been cut from the same tree. Charlotte Marmu's portrait was inside it, a corpse in miniature inside a tiny coffin.

♓

I stomped through puddles and ruined the wet silence which follows rain. Vivian answered my knock and before she could speak I held the queered picture before her eyes. "Your mother has sent a sign that she wishes you to marry me at once."

Vivian welcomed the pitiful trick, I could see it in her eyes, in the way her jaw loosened in relief. She knew I was lying, but the lie saved her from loyalties she had never wanted and so she allowed it. She took the portrait and looked at the phantom. She asked after the dress I'd had made to match the one she'd drawn on onion skin, and I assured her it hung in what would soon be her chifforobe. Afraid to touch her, odd after all the hours we'd spent twined about each other, I wrung my hands behind my back while she looked from the soliotype, to me, to the soliotype. I ventured a hand to her hair. Vivian looked up from the portrait.

"I'm glad there is no one here to see me fat," she said. "The dress will have to be altered."

⚘ ⚘ ⚘

Plates 30 & 31—Wedding Diptych of Vivian Marchand, *1845. Half-plate daguerreotypes.*

VIVIAN AND CLAUDE were wed two weeks after her mother passed away. The *Bee* wedding announcement of July 28th mistakenly states that Marchand hailed from Boston, but does manage to spell *soliotype* correctly. The couple honeymooned in Natchez, Mississippi. After their return, the Marchands and the Bentons passed many hours together. The ever-present Felix Moissenet reports in his August 12th column that Vivian and Susana spent their time talking about infants and impending motherhood while Victor and Claude discussed photography and medicine.

In Pl. 30 Vivian smiles happily, her mourning dress replaced by a light frock pinned with the always-present grosgrain. In Pl. 31 she stands in her wedding dress. The pair of daguerreotypes is in a kidskin case once white that has aged to the color of butter. The mats are engraved with the names of the bride and the groom and the cover is embossed with the wedding date. In both pictures Vivian appears happy—in Pl. 31 her face is contorted with joy.

This groomless diptych is odd in light of Marchand's special nuptial triptychs. Also odd is the mysterious lack of any photograph of a man who spent nearly every day around cameras. The only known photograph in which even a bit of Marchand appears is Pl. 1, and only his hand and his slim wrist are visible.

Plates 32–42—Vivian Marchand, 1845. Full-, half-, and quarter-plate daguerreotypes.

BETWEEN JULY AND September of 1845 Marchand made at least these eleven daguerreotypes of Vivian. She appears in an assortment of poses and settings. Most are simple and seem unplanned. The Canal Street studio closed late in July, and in the second week of August the original Toulouse Street studio reopened. The Marchands lived in a shotgun-style home behind which the small studio was housed in what Felix Moissenet describes as "an outbuilding more suited to horses or slaves than to an artist of Marchand's talents," and it is easy to imagine Claude playfully luring his wife back to the studio, or bringing a camera into the house and making the equivalent of a snapshot. In Pl. 32 Vivian holds out a cake as if she's brought it to show her husband. In Pl. 33 Vivian is dressed for the theater, opera glasses dangling from her wrist. In Pl. 34 she brushes her hair. Pl. 35 is a beautiful study of Vivian looking out a window, her elbow, shoulder, and chin forming a triangle through which sunlight gently pours. In Pl. 36 she sits on a blanket with a picnic lunch. The fruits, breads, and even the flatware seem carefully placed. The sun is reflected in miniature on the surface of a dish, apples and pears around it like planets, Vivian in a loose white dress reclining above the assortment like a constellation. In Pl. 37 she stands in her nightclothes, her eyes bleary with sleep, her mouth a groggy smile.

Vivian appears nude in five of the plates. In four of them

her face is in shadow, masked, or covered by her hands, but in Pl. 38 she stands before a potted tree smiling happily. In these five portraits one interesting fact is clear: Vivian was very pregnant when she and Claude wed in July, a point of reference that proves the woman sprawled on the settee in Pl. 39 and the woman bathing in Pl. 40 and the woman supine on the rug in Pl. 41 and the masked woman reflected in the mirror in Pl. 42 are all Vivian Marchand.

ℐ

I TOOK THE nude of Millicent from my desk and went hunting for her. I had not seen her since she left me fuming in the studio after Vivian had sworn not to marry me. Only her head emerging from my fist, I asked after her in shops I knew she frequented. A cobbler on Marais smiled at the face on the plate and pointed to the ceiling while I stood surrounded by my past—lasts and laces, soles and tongues. I climbed two steep flights and stood on a miniature landing looking into her bright eyes. "I do not love you," I promised the portrait.

There was no answer when I knocked; the door opened when I tried the knob. Millicent was asleep across a narrow bed that all but filled the room. She was nude and colored with light filtered by thin curtains, her head tilted on her pillow so that the portrait was nearly replicated before me.

"I do not love you," I said from the foot of her bed.

She woke and rose to her elbows. A pearl of sweat dropped from her temple and hung at the edge of her eye like a tear. She grinned and the sight of her covered in sunlight animated by the moving curtains weakened me. The pale undersides of her feet lured my mouth.

"I do not love you," I told her again. "I've come to look you in the eyes and tell you that I do not love you."

Millicent eased herself down and smiled at the ceiling. "Pity you couldn't have waited to tell me until after I'd had my nap." She yawned and slowly stretched, hummed while she scratched her belly, lay with her eyes closed and a smirk on her lips.

"I'm going to marry Vivian."

One eye opened. "That's not news." She rolled onto her side and plumped her pillow, laughed into her pillowslip.

I threw the nude at the wall above her. It cracked off the wainscoting and fell by her face. She picked it up and looked, then aped the smile and the pose and pointed behind me. A rectangle of mirror no bigger than a man's two hands hung on the back of the door and showed a reflection of Millicent mimicking her portrait.

"I do not love you," I assured the reflection. "Tell me to leave, to never come here again. Tell me not to bother you."

She shrugged her shoulders. "Stay if you like. Come whenever the fancy strikes you. There's no lock on the door, as you know."

I turned back to her. "I do not love you," I said through clenched teeth.

"You've now told me that five times," she calculated. "And yet there you stand, staring at what's between my legs as if you've never seen a woman out of her clothes. So if it's not love holding you here, is it what hangs between your legs? If that's it, if you're here telling me this and hoping that I'll spread my thighs and listen to you moan *Vivian*, then I will ask you to go and never come back."

I fixed my eyes on hers. "I do not love you."

"Six. Then why can't you turn and leave?"

Desperate to hear her tell me to go, I fumbled with my belt and dropped my trousers. My foreskin puckered at the end of my unexcited cock. Millicent sighed and shook her head. I remembered the mirror behind me and felt foolish to know my bare rump filled it. "I do not love you," I told her again.

"Seven," Millicent said, then stood and squatted above a chamber pot, ignoring me so fully that allowing me to witness the hissing stripe of her urine was not an immodest act.

༂

25 July 1845
Claude said again and again he did not love me. He threw the nude at me and when I think of the look he wore when he threw it I cannot look at either face the soliotype shows.

28 July 1845
I heard them in the street and watched Claude and the girl pass below my gallery, the girl weeping, Benton and his lovely copper-haired wife behind them. I could still hear the girl when they were out of sight.

31 July 1845
Wanted the silly comfort of sitting in a kitchen with a pot of tea so I dressed and found my old key. Raining so violently when I walked to the house on Toulouse that I was quickly soaked to the skin. Had my key in the lock when I heard the girl's voice. The jalousies were closed but I remembered a broken louver I had always feared allowed a view of the front room. When I stood on a rock and looked in I saw Claude and the girl stand-ing naked and arguing. She had her back to the window and

stood before Claude but she is so small that I could see him as if he were alone in the room. His ribs stand out as if he is starving. Held onto the sill and watched them pass a soliotype back and forth while their voices became louder. The noise of the rain on the glass made their argument a mystery until she turned and I saw the swell of the girl's stomach.

THE BOX WAS wooden, open on its top. Vivian stood on a chair and fetched it from a high closet shelf. Two rows of miniature pews flanked an aisle leading to a pulpit behind which a tiny figure of Jesus Christ hung from a cross that'd been taken from a charm bracelet. A flat groom with a golden helmet of foil hair held the hand of a flat bride shawled in a scrap of good lace. Both cut from the same sheet of heavy, cream-hued paper, their joined hands were actually one hand. "I've had this since I was seven," she told me. The priest had fallen onto the groom. Vivian righted him. "My father made it for me."

She plucked tiny guests from the pews and quickly explained each one's removal. "Rebecca Dunn is in Boston for the summer, Mr. Durnby is in Rome, the Smittsons are in London, the Redmons in Savannah." Soon the chapel was empty.

I put a pair of dolls into the church. "Victor and Susana will come."

Vivian took the dolls from where I'd set them. "This is Samantha Redmon and this is her brother Basil," she told me, then tore them slowly in half.

She filled trunks and boxes with gewgaws, her mother's store of clutter. No negotiation was allowed. All that lined sideboards and shelves was carefully wrapped in tissue paper and packed to be moved to the house we'd soon share. I followed her from room to room, amazed by the volume of the junk: little painted plates on stands, dogs made of porcelain, statuettes in all shapes and sizes, badly cut silhouettes of Vivian, badly etched bits of scrimshaw, miniatures in oil so poorly executed it was unclear if the subject was man, woman, horse, tree. Dusty silk flowers faded in knockoff vases; a set of lead soldiers in red coats battled a tribe of lead savages. No curio shop between New Orleans and Boston had escaped Charlotte Marmu's looting.

In the studio behind the house I found a bottle which held buttons, pins, a blue crayon, and a string I'd once tied around Vivian's finger as a joke when she'd demanded I give her a ring. I had a plain gold band made to the string's size. The baker recognized his good fortune as soon as I asked after wedding cakes. Based only on a line drawing I was sold a pricey one. I spent my last night as a bachelor watching the night sky fill with tar smoke and orange cinders and listening to the cannons fire the first dud rounds of summer.

The ring was too small. I had to screw it onto Vivian's finger. The cake's ornate butter-and-sugar icing melted and pooled on the platter by the time we emerged from the labyrinth of vows into which we were led by a gibbering old priest who could not remember our names. Vivian drew a finger through the sweet puddle, then burst into tears so violent the priest nearly annulled the marriage.

We walked through the streets with Victor and Susana behind us, the ruined cake in Victor's arms. Vivian wept loudly, almost screaming. Women came to the doors of shops. Children stopped playing and watched her pass. A mule was startled by the noise and began to toss his head and shift in his harnesses. We reached the door on Toulouse, and between sobs Vivian begged Susana and Victor to go away and take the cake with them.

I hung my coat and hat, Vivian's crying even louder when trapped by walls. A trail of clothes led across the room when I turned. Two stockings curled like commas. Vivian's ankle and foot, just free from the silk, flashed in the bedroom doorway. Her weeping stopped and the sudden silence was unsettling. A bird chirped outside the window and I clutched my heart. I stepped around the shoes and skirts and hose, waiting for Vivian to resume sobbing, but she did not.

She stood calmly on the bed, bed linen pulled over her shoulders, fist a button at her throat. Vivian studied me for a moment. "You're all I have," she said.

When she let the sheet fall from her shoulders her belly was huge. "A giant," I blurted, unable to control myself.

Vivian grabbed up the sheet and covered herself. "You think I'm a monster?"

"No, no, not you. The child, the child. What child is that large at four months?"

"Four months?"

I held up my hand and counted them off. "April, May, June, July." I dropped a finger for each and held my fist in the air.

She put up both her hands, the sheet falling when she did. "January, February, March, April, May, June, July."

I thought backwards through the calendar. "January?"

"We were in the pantry."

I remembered, suddenly, the taste of her tongue that night, sweet with apricot liqueur. I clambered onto the bed, grabbed an ankle, and pulled her down.

Her mouth left a necklace of bruises. We exhausted the daylight and in the dark we had to kick free of the sheets that'd wrapped around us when we rolled and pitched. I held her against me while she dozed. I was stunned with happiness each time she shifted in sleep and reminded me of things I'd forgotten—the sharp points of her elbows, the downy base of her skull, the cool, hard coil of her ear, the moist back of her knee. I reached over her hip, put my hand on the rise of her belly, and held my breath.

I'd planned a honeymoon trip to Natchez but Vivian refused to leave the bed when she woke. "I cannot imagine a trip in this heat would bring me any pleasure," she explained as she lay hugging a pillow.

I felt a tickle of anger, then realized I was acting as if I too had a little wedding in a box. "It's far too hot to travel," I agreed. "You can sleep and read and I can attend to the studio."

Vivian shook her head in quick jerks. "I'll look like a fool if it's found out we didn't go on a honeymoon."

I was confused. "So we go to Natchez?"

"No," she said. "We hide here and act as if we've gone to Natchez."

"You're joking."

She knotted the sheet at her neck and walked from the room dragging its train. "We'll need flour and eggs and butter," she told me.

I followed her to the kitchen. "Shall I make a fake set of whiskers and wear them when I go out? I would hate it if someone recognized me."

"You're being cruel. I'm asking for a handful of days. You're unwilling to give me something that small?"

The first day of our captivity the rain fell without ceasing. The streets below us became muddy lakes. A leak developed in the kitchen and I positioned a pan to catch its drops. I put a pitcher on the back steps. Vivian stood in the tub and I poured rainwater over her head. After her bath Vivian walked nude through the house. I stripped and did the same, chills of pleasure tickling me. I felt our rings had made us new people. She spent the morning unpacking her boxes of gimcracks. Soon every flat surface hosted at least a dozen pieces. The redskins routed the British on a windowsill; little plates made a side table look like a doll's china shop. It unnerved me to have the effluvium of the Marmu house suddenly appear in my house. I stepped carefully and kept my elbows pressed to my sides.

The sun fought through the clouds for an hour in the afternoon and I had Vivian sit in a puddle of light on the bedroom carpet. I'd fetched a camera from the studio when I'd gone for food. She followed me into the kitchen pantry and watched me heat mercury below the plate. When I handed it to her she took it into the light and considered it.

"You'd have to kill a fish to make its portrait."

"What? A portrait of a fish?"

"You have me sit just so and smile just so and hold still just so. If I were a fish you'd have to kill me to get me that still. I feel like a fish when you make my portrait, like a killed fish."

"You're blaming me for a fault that is not mine, a fault of the camera."

"It's not the camera's fault. I don't see myself in any portrait you make of me. You kill me and cut a paper doll to my shape, but even when the doll is just the right shape it is still dead. A dead fish."

I took the portrait from her hand. Her legs were crossed, her hair hung loosely around her shoulders. Her eyes were closed. The ball of one foot shone. "You don't see yourself?" I handed the soliotype back to her.

She studied it. "I see you looking at me. I see a dead fish."

"You're confused. You're mistaking stillness for death. Your portrait will live on long after you have died."

"You don't find that disturbing?"

"Do you?"

"Yes. You want to skin the living and preserve the hides, but empty hides are dead, like the empty balloon of a fish when it is dead."

"I'm not skinning anyone," I snapped, then took the portrait from her hands and left her to putter in her mother's mess.

⁊

I made a portrait of her each of the dozen days we spent in hiding. I had her hold a cake she'd baked to replace the ruined one, convinced her to risk being seen from the street when she sat in a sunny window wearing a toga fashioned from a sheet. She laughed at a portrait I made of her in the tub, a soap bubble crown on her head, but I could not make her recant her claim that the soliotype showed no more than a vacant suit of skin.

Vivian spent much of her time peeking through a tilted louver at a family who lived across Toulouse. Their windows faced ours and they left their shutters open always. A yellow card nailed to their door explained why they never left their rooms—some did obey. Through her opera glasses Vivian watched Father, Mother, Daughter, and Baby for hours on end, gleefully and painstakingly describing to me their meals and card games. She was delighted when one night she could see the hand held by Mother.

Once when Vivian was napping I took up her position. I

expected four beauties, so diligent was Vivian in her observation of them. They were painfully plain, Daughter no more than a shorter version of rail-thin, whey-faced Mother, Baby star-shaped, its fat limbs all no longer than the stump of its head. I watched them eat their noon meal, three jaws working in unison at hard biscuit, Baby circling the room now walking two steps, now on all fours, now walking another two steps. I could not understand their allure for my wife. "Wife," I said aloud, the word feeling Greek in my mouth. I watched Father read the newspaper while Mother and Daughter egged Baby on to walk some more. The street was quiet and I could hear their voices, but not their words, two chirped songs sung at almost the same pitch. They exhausted me with boredom, but I watched, sure the dull people held some secret that would explain Vivian to me. I wanted to throw open the shutter and demand they tell me what the secret was.

I had to shake Vivian's foot to wake her. "They're plain," I accused. "Nothing goes on over there."

She creased her brow. "Who? Nothing goes on where?"

"The dolts across the street. There's not a single remarkable thing about them."

Vivian looked dazed. "They're not remarkable."

"Then why do you watch them?"

She thought for a moment. "I like to watch that plump baby fall down and make the face he makes." She puckered her lips into a clown's frown.

"Tomorrow we return from Natchez," I told her.

The homecoming put us both in good moods. When we woke she agreed quickly to put on the wedding dress for the last portrait of our faked honeymoon. Her smile was large and real.

Afterward she shifted uncomfortably for a few minutes, then shed the dress.

"Have you become such a savage you can no longer bear the weight of clothes on your shoulders?" I joked, poking her in the belly with my thumb.

"I wish I were a savage deep in the jungle." She ducked behind a tree in a pot I'd dragged in from the courtyard for her to sit under for a portrait. "Try it," she challenged.

I stripped save for my boots and stomped around the room. Vivian roared laughter from behind her tree. "Look at yourself in the mirror."

Boots alone made me appear even more naked. I laughed too, then chased her from her tiny forest and into bed. She would not let me take off the boots.

Victor's invitation to tea came almost the moment we opened the jalousies to show off a sham collection of empty trunks and bags Vivian carefully arranged. We rode the car the many blocks to the new Benton home on Circus Street. We were pink from the sun by the time we reached the slim house flanked by two others of identical construction. Susana was in the scrap of yard fighting with a thick weed, the only thing growing from the raked soil. Victor hailed us from the porch just as the weed's grip failed and Susana fell. She held the thing above her head like a trophy while Victor brayed from the porch.

The sitting room was filled with new furniture. A tall clock in the corner found the hour and let loose a booming trio of rings. A mirror big as a pond covered a wall. While Victor and Susana prepared the tea, their happy talk ringing in the kitchen, we fidgeted in our hot clothes. Vivian had filled a wardrobe with her mother's things when she'd finished filling trunks with gewgaws. I'd been against it at the time, but now the blue silk she'd chosen fit well, the child inside her helping her fill the dress. I touched her sleeve and her face smiled at me in the mirror. "I hardly recognize you in your clothes," she told me.

"Do you sew?" Susana asked Vivian as she entered carrying a tray of cakes. Susana could not look away from Vivian's stomach.

"No," Vivian said, then took up a book and held it where Susana's eyes rested.

Susana blushed, then stood motionless until Victor nudged her with the teapot's spout.

"Riley Richmond is our salvation," Victor told us as he poured.

Susana passed me a stale scrap of cake, gave the same to Vivian. "It's your cake. I saved two pieces of it," she told us.

Vivian set the plate aside. Susana looked heartbroken even when I filled my mouth with tough cake.

"Do you cook?" Susana tried.

"If Richmond were mayor, New Orleans would be healthy," Victor explained while he passed me a cup.

"Cook?" Vivian said as if confused by the question. "I would like to learn how to make pies?" she tried, as if unsure what she should be saying.

"Richmond is smart enough to understand what Orion Wagasuc cannot: No city can be free of Yellow Fever while quarantines are bought and sold, animals are left rotting where they die, and people are not stopped from dumping their shit into the streets."

Susana hurried from the room with her hand over her mouth. We could hear her retching in the kitchen. Vivian's face filled with fear. I kicked her foot.

"Is Susana ill?" I asked.

"She's pregnant," Victor explained.

"That's wonderful," I said.

Vivian made a noise somewhere between a cough and a gasp.

Victor sipped his tea and tried not to look at my wife. "I'm hoping you'll come with me tomorrow to make some soliotypes at the Charity Hospital. Wagasuc claims there are three or four Fever victims when an entire ward is filled with them. The Howards will pay you."

"I'll do it for nothing," I told him.

"I'd like to go home," Vivian announced.

Susana's face was green when she came in. "We have tickets to see a show tonight, but I don't think I'll be well enough to go. Will you use them?" She held the tickets out to Vivian.

Vivian looked as if she could not understand what Susana was saying.

"Thank you, Susana," I said, taking the tickets and passing them to Vivian. "Our trip from Natchez was very tiring," I explained.

Vivian started to nod her head again and again. "The heat has made me short," she said. "I'm sorry if I've been rude."

Susana nodded and smiled understandingly.

Vivian walked out while I was saying my good-byes. I had to run to catch her as she marched down Circus. Her eyes were wet with tears. "I hate sewing and cooking and babies," she yelled. She thrust the tickets at me; she'd crushed them in her fist. I let go of her arm and followed her down Circus. I did not know what to say. On Canal I handed her one of the creased tickets. "I need to go to the studio; I'll meet you at the theater." Vivian nodded. I watched the blue silk rectangle of her back shrink and then disappear as she walked along Rampart and turned onto Toulouse.

♂

A trio of men stood chatting before the studio's door. I put on a smile and hailed them while I shook my ring of keys. None of them returned my grin.

These three—Norman, Moellhausen, and Pinistri—had come to let me know that many debts were owed them by Francis Marmu—God rest his soul—and they'd banded together to reclaim their losses. They carried cases filled with agreements ending in his signature, a cramped snarl of lines choking an ornate *M*, the only legible letter. My mark was beside each of his, and I thought of the tall stack of promises I'd blindly signed when Marmu had agreed to loan me money. Mr. Marmu had borrowed from Norman to pay Moellhausen, from Moellhausen to pay Pinistri, and from Pinistri to pay Norman.

"The man was a fraud," said Norman.

"A charlatan," Moellhausen agreed. "He never made a living from sugar."

"When will you be able to pay us?" Pinistri needed to know. He tapped an absurd number written on the back of a *carte-de-visite*.

♂

The ticket was for the showing of a panorama titled "The Length of the Mississippi." The painting was ten feet high and mounted on two huge spools, one to take up the river as the other let it out. Vivian was not in her seat when the show started. The painter, John Banvard, stood to the side and narrated from behind a podium. I listened to him speak, but I hardly heard a word. I had to look at the figure on the *carte-de-visite* again and again to assure myself I had not imagined the fantastic number. Vivian arrived just as the view crossing the stage opened onto flat yellow prairie filled with long blades of grass which were supposed to appear to be swaying in a breeze. She sat and aimed her opera glasses at the moving river.

I bent and spoke into her ear. "Your father has ruined us."

When she turned to me my face's reflection warped on each lens. "How could my dead father do anything to you?"

I held up the card and saw the figure's distorted reflection on the surface of the lenses. Vivian took the glasses from her eyes and blinked at the number.

"This is how much money your father borrowed from three men, three men who feel I should pay them, and it looks like they can make me. Your beloved father cursed us."

"I hate my father," she yelled, so loudly Banvard was startled. Every face in the audience turned to us and miles of river rolled past before Banvard regained himself and took up his speech at St. Louis.

"Do you want to know why?" she hissed through her teeth. "Do you?" A vein stood out on her forehead. I nodded reflexively.

"He caught me *in media res* with William." Vivian raised her glasses. "I was his first," she told me in a whisper so low it was almost lost below Banvard's narration. "He was clumsy and embarrassed, and I loved him for that. He came back for me even when my father told me he would not. That made me love him even more. How can a number on the back of a dirty card mean anything to me?"

I turned to the stage and watched the Ohio join the Mississippi. "When?" I asked stupidly.

"The morning before you took advantage of me in the closet." Vivian put her opera glasses into their case and laid her hands across her stomach. "It could be his, it could be yours."

I thought of our two liquids mixing inside her. She stood and left as Natchez flashed into view, crossed the stage, and then disappeared. Green stick-trees backed the brown stripe of the river. I thought of the party, Marmu in blackface, the entire scene playing out inside my head like the painted river played out on stage. Banvard reached New Orleans and the crowd applauded a landscape which bore only small resemblance to the city. I held my seat while the crowd filed out merrily chattering. Banvard's assistants came from the wings and started cranking the panorama backwards, preparing it for the next showing. I watched the river run north.

I ate a long meal in a café near the theater and lingered through several cognacs and a cigar. My table was near a window and I watched people pass. Vivian's admission of love for another man made the world too large, too filled with secrets and mystery. I eyed a mule drinking from a trough and found myself unable to concentrate on just his slapping tongue. The windows of the building the mule stood before drew my eyes and I strained to make out the dim shapes behind their glass. I stared at two prostitutes walking arm-in-arm, at a rag picker hunting an alley for treasures. I had to cover my eyes with my hands.

The bedroom door was locked when I came home. I found the portrait of Spats I had made months before, the one I had blinded with a fork, and set to abusing it, first tossing stones at it and enjoying the ring of rock off metal, then carefully scraping every trace of the man from the plate until only a silhouette of brass remained on a background of nicked-up silver. I spent the night trying to doze in a chair, starting from sleep each time Vivian sighed or whimpered in her sleep.

꽃

The Charity Hospital's Fever ward was filled with Mister Jack's victims. Each bed was shared, some held three. Those who lay with their heads at the same end of the bed were married or related by blood, Victor told me. Those who lay looking at each other's feet were strangers. Nuns in long habits wiped brows and held a water ladle to set after set of lips.

Dr. Swan, a round man with a wet red face, greeted Victor and shook my hand when I was introduced. "The mayor must have been asleep when he was taught his arithmetic," the Howard jeered. "If we're to buy his bill of goods, these people are all well, not a trace of the Fever making their lungs fill with blood." Victor took off his jacket and joined the doctor at the bedside of a boy who would soon die. His face was yellow and his eyes were open and unfocused. Beside his head the feet of a stranger shook as if the sweltering ward were chilly.

I saw skinned knees through torn pants and shirts dyed with patterns of sweat, heard coughs like ripping paper and the low gasping of those too weak to cough. I begged a nun to let me carry the ladle. I poured water into mouths which formed gracious Os when they saw me coming. I helped newcomers find a place to lie down, held a man who wept when his wife died beside him, translated as best I could the last words of a German who wished to be taken out to sea and fed to the silver fishes.

The sleepless night finally caught me. I lay exhausted on a bed which had been made vacant by the almost simultaneous deaths of a mother and daughter. When I woke and slit my eyes I saw Victor aiming my camera along the long aisle running between the rows of beds. I closed my eyes and listened to him pose the nuns and Dr. Swan. Even those who lay coughing were told to turn their faces to the camera if they had the strength.

I dreamt of the moving trees from Banvard's panorama until

the heel of a newly arrived victim knocked me in the ear. Victor was at my bedside writing in his small journal. He grinned when I stirred.

"I worried for a moment that I'd lost you to Jack," he said. "Your snores are louder than his coughs."

I looked down at the man who shared my bed. His pants were tied with a bit of worn rope.

"Where does it come from?"

Benton closed his little book and set it on his knee. "No one knows for sure. Some speculate it is a vapor that hangs in the air. They're the ones sure the cannons disrupt the plague, that the tar smothers it, that a mask can filter the poison. Others feel it must come from food or water, and there are even those who assume it is a curse some African spun. I have heard that one physician makes a case for trees being to blame." He shook his head at the foolishness.

"Why trees?"

"There are thick forests around the cities which suffer the most—Mobile, New Orleans, Biloxi—but my feeling is that water must be the answer. In cities where rainwater does not stand stagnant in the streets there are few Fever deaths. I think it may be the mosquitoes that breed in puddles, and there are many who agree with me."

"What would Richmond pay me if I managed to destroy Wagasuc's chances?" I asked.

Victor looked confused by the change of subject. "I assume you could name your price."

I took his journal and pencil and copied the number I'd memorized from the card's back. "If he can give me that, I can make Wagasuc look like such a fool not even a dunce would vote for him."

cP

Redgrave, my fictional British surgeon, was back in New Orleans. In the same harsh way he'd warned of the dangers posed by mirrors and soliotypes and argued against the making of memorials, he now made his opinions about the Fever known. He had viewed the sick wards, toured the city and its outlying areas, and come to the conclusion that the yellow pestilence came from the forest of cypress and pine which stood between the city and the lake. I held my pen and closed my eyes and watched Banvard's green lollipops march from right to left. The only answer, wrote Redgrave, was to cut and burn every tree. I folded his letter into an envelope and took his opinion to the office of the *Daily Picayune*. Stanley Roberts was pleased to see me.

"Been dueling lately?" he joked. He made his hand into a pistol.

I handed him Redgrave's letter. He dropped his smile and hid his hand behind his back. His lips moved when he read.

"Publish that on the front page, then follow it every day with articles demanding Mayor Wagasuc do as it says."

Roberts looked up. "You believe this nonsense?"

"It's a lie," I assured him. "Does that matter?"

He shook his head. "Lies are better than truth in this city." He took a copy of the *Daily Tropic* from his desk and read to me. "'It is with happy amazement that this reporter finds himself standing at the start of an August that has yet to witness Mister Jack's yellow stamp mark a single brow aside from a spare handful of those who had the ill luck—and ill manners!— to bring him to the city in their luggage.'" Roberts shook his head. "It is with happy amazement that *this* reporter"—he stabbed his thumb into his chest—"finds himself not covered by ten feet of snow, so mild is New Orleans in August."

Redgrave's opinion appeared next to a boxed column which held a list compiled by the Howards of all those known to have died from the Fever, a list in type tiny enough to allow all 787 to appear—a nice blend of truth and falsehood. The *Tropic* countered with the huge late edition headline *LIES!* below which a letter from Wagasuc proclaimed almost incoherently that the Howards and the *Daily Picayune* were in league against him. Each day following the *Picayune* posted the new number on a board mounted to the side of their offices and printed the same tally as their headline.

Moellhausen, Pinistri, and Norman came looking for money on the eighteenth day of August. The *Picayune*'s banner read *803* and an unsigned editorial demanded that Wagasuc follow Redgrave's advice and do away with the Fever trees. That afternoon I sold the busts and other movables from the studio to a man planning to open a hotel and gave Norman, Pinistri, and Moellhausen the profits and the deed to the Marmu house and all it held. They gave me a new card with a new number on its back.

I hired a wagon and moved cameras, bottles of chemicals, stacks of plates, and boxes of cases to the old studio behind the house. A sign in the window of the Canal Street address sent a crowd to Toulouse before I managed to do more than sweep the floor and open the shutters. One desperate woman cradling the wizened corpse of her infant told me why: All other portraitists had either fled the city when the *Daily Picayune* began its grim scorekeeping, or they were counted in that score. "You're the last one," she promised. I made portraits until there was no more light; I turned away dozens.

ᕲ ᕲ ᕲ

The Yellow Jack *Plates:*

Plate 43—The Howard Association, *1845. Half-plate daguerreotype.*

Plate 44—The Charity Hospital Fever Ward, *1845. Half-plate daguerreotype.*

Plate 45—Trees Being Felled Near Lake Pontchartrain to Combat the Yellow Fever, *1845. Half-plate daguerreotype.*

Plate 46—Jason Meyers, A Stone Cutter, *1845. Half-plate daguerreotype.*

VICTOR BENTON WAS a member of the Howard Association, a group of doctors and other citizens who cared for the sick during the yearly yellow fever outbreaks. Pl. 43 shows the thirty members of the association gathered to discuss the epidemic. The City Council annually granted the Howards absurdly small amounts of money to be used to help the city's poor, while at the same time most newspapers ridiculed the selfless men as doomsayers and panics. Both the council and the papers wanted to keep the outbreak as hushed as possible. Even though the summer of 1845 was so filled with fever deaths that newspapers across the nation took to calling New Orleans "The Necropolis of the South," as late as August 19th the *Daily Tropic* was denying the existence of yellow fever in the city. It is easy to understand why—a deserted city holds neither consumers nor advertisers.

In the summer of 1845 Benton and the Howard Association enlisted Marchand to chronicle in daguerreotypes what would be one of the worst yellow fever epidemics ever to strike the Crescent City. New Orleans's population at the time was

108,699, and that summer the fever carried away almost 3,000 victims, close to one of every thirty inhabitants. These numbers are even more shocking when it's taken into account that as many of the 108,699 fled the city for the summer as could afford to do so. They left to escape not only "Mister Jack," but also the oppressive heat and the annoying clouds of mosquitoes not yet recognized as the means of the fever's transmission. Doctor Benton published a small volume of observations entitled *Yellow Jack*, which accompanied a group of Marchand's daguerreotypes displayed late in August of 1845. Few of these photographs remain. Many may have been in the doctor's possession and were possibly destroyed by the fire that ravaged the Benton home in 1901.

The beds in Charity Hospital's fever ward were filled by mid-May of 1845 and remained filled until the end of October. New immigrants, often the poorest residents of the city, were least immune to yellow fever. Many lived in shantytowns in the swamps north of the city, areas filled with mosquitoes. The large percentage of fever deaths among the poor was constantly offered as proof that they were to blame. Every fall and winter featured numerous calls for bans on immigration—the Irish were a favorite scapegoat.

None of the fifty beds visible in Pl. 44's view of the fever ward is vacant, and most of the narrow cots are shared. Marchand has posed the subjects oddly in comparison to the more impromptu style of the other *Yellow Jack* plates. A dozen nuns stand in a careful line at the end of the aisle separating the double row of beds; several patients prop themselves on elbows to face the camera. Careful scrutiny of the daguerreotype finds at least three beds hold dead men—the first bed of the left row, two beds in the middle of the right row.

Pl. 45 is one of the few surviving examples of Marchand's

landscape work, and the story that accompanies it is fascinating. In the heat of late August, then-mayor Orion Wagasuc took to heart the advice of an English surgeon, John Redgrave, who in a letter published in the *Daily Picayune* hypothesized that the fever which attacked the city each summer had its root in "some type of insect or organism or flora that inhabits the trees and foliage near the city." He was close. The fever was being transmitted by mosquitoes, but they were just as prevalent, if not more, in the open sewers of New Orleans than among the trees that stood between the city and Lake Pontchartrain. The mayor, pressured by a string of *Picayune* editorials, eventually agreed with Redgrave's theory, hired work crews, and sent them on a mission: Cut down each and every tree. Marchand was employed to record the attempt at salvation of the city's populace. As Pl. 45 shows, the daguerreotype process was far from the stop-action now possible with a brief shutter opening and fast film. The trees fall in arcs across the horizon, thirteen falling at once, the entirety of their descents recorded. The yellow fever went undaunted even after this massive effort, and Wagasuc was not re-elected, even though he ran on a platform that stressed the fact that his family too had fallen victim to the pestilence—his daughter, three-year-old Dorcas, died in September of 1845. (Her *Daily Picayune* obituary mentions that Marchand made her memorial portrait.)

A total of seventeen plates of these blurred trees appeared in the *Yellow Jack* exhibit. After the exhibit failed to rally the city to fight what were correctly recognized as some of the true causes of yellow fever—open sewers, inadequate quarantines—many of the plates were sold, among them this daguerreotype. Pl. 45 was purchased by mayoral candidate Riley Wilson Richmond for use in his victorious campaign and has been preserved as a family heirloom. (My thanks to the Richmonds for its use.)

Pl. 46 is the last daguerreotype discussed in *Yellow Jack*. The subject's head is obscured by a cloud of marble chips and his arm is a blur of white cloth as he cuts a name into one of 1845's many grave markers. Benton writes, "Mister Meyers tried to laugh when he judged that the Fever was the best thing for the Undertaker, the Priest and the Stone Cutter, but his mirth gave way to tears. His son James and his wife Roberta both died earlier in the summer, victims of Yellow Jack, and Mister Meyers cut their names into stones."

$\wp$

VIVIAN AND I ignored each other. We could not play our new roles well—orphan, husband, wife, cuckold—so we played none. I spent every daylight hour making soliotypes, most memorials. The *Picayune*'s count grew by at least a dozen a day, and many of the day's dozen found their way to my door in the arms of survivors. Dozens more came coughing but alive. The yellow cards meant nothing. There was no one left in the city to enforce them, and every other door would have needed a placard if there had been men to nail them up. Better to paint a river-facing roof yellow to spook off ships. The parade of sickness was astounding, but even more astounding were the healthy few who stood in line as if nothing were awry, a plague not enough to squash their vanity.

The employment left me so exhausted and blue that after the sun quit, and after I handed numbered cards guaranteeing a portrait the next day to those waiting, I fell onto the bed in my clothes and lay unconscious and undreaming until the cannons sounded the ten o'clock hour. Wagasuc still refused to admit the truth, but he had the tar burning and the guns firing. I surrendered the bed to Vivian when the window glass buzzed with the racket. We had not shared it in weeks; I had not seen my wife out of her clothes since the last day of our honeymoon, and I watched her grow too large for her mother's dresses. My dinner waited in a dish. I ate the cold meal while I listened to the mattress shift under Vivian, then grow still. When I was sure she was asleep—her breath a high whistle followed by a hiss—I took up her opera glasses and watched the family across Toulouse.

They were only three by then. I watched star-shaped Baby die while Mother was in the other room frantically boiling a cure. Her sobs brought Vivian from bed, but one look at me standing with the glasses sent her back without a word. I waited for Mother to come across the street and have a memorial made, but she didn't. The coffin was tiny. Father nailed down the lid, then set out alone with the box on his shoulder while Mother and Daughter sat beside each other and stared at a blank wall. When Father returned he too sat and stared. They were so transfixed I was sure they were witnessing a vision projected onto the empty plaster. They were a remarkable little puppet show. I watched them every night, watched them pet Daughter's head when she walked from room to room holding an empty shirt Baby had worn.

When their lights went out I fetched the dozen portraits of Vivian I'd made during the days we'd pretended to be in Mississippi. I looked at the soliotypes one by one, then made a long row across the tabletop.

❧

Wagasuc came the day the *Picayune*'s headline rose above nine hundred. I didn't notice him waiting until he was at the head of the line. The mayor's eyes were underhung with dark hammocks and his tie was knotted like a bootlace—he looked like a man plotted against. He jerked his thumb at the queue behind him. "It comes from the trees." Redgrave's letter and the *Picayune*'s running tally had convinced the fool. Gangs with axes and saws, he informed, were massing at the forest's edge. "How much will it cost to have you come and make magic pictures of my men cutting down these demon trees?"

I named a silly price for each soliotype, less than what I charged for a studio sitting. What did it matter? Richmond's triumph would follow and my debt would be paid. I walked down the long line handing out numbered cards. No one complained. A few stared blankly at the cards which bore the prints and creases of the hands that'd held them on previous days, others tucked the cards in their pockets and sat down on the crushed-shell path as if they planned to wait there until their numbers were honored.

The first portrait I made was of the mayor standing before the hundred-odd men he'd paid to cut down the enemy trees. Wagasuc combed his hair with his hands, then puffed out his chest. Behind him two men knelt holding either end of an enormous crosscut saw and behind them the rest shouldered their axes and small saws.

A square of bark was shaved from a pine's trunk and a man with a pot of ink and a brush drew the date in sloppy script across the blond spot. Wagasuc borrowed an ax and struck the dated tree its first blow, then held the pose.

Bright birds flew from the crowns of trees when the cutting began in earnest. I made plates I knew would hold no more than blurred shapes—trees falling, the moving blades of saws.

The noise of many axes at work was thrilling. I felt stupid pride in tricking Wagasuc.

Victor arrived several hours after the work had begun, one of a crowd, Stanley Roberts among them, lured by the vague promise offered by the *Tropic*'s late-edition headline: *Mister Jack To Be Killed Tonight*. Roberts winked at me and approached the mayor licking his pencil. "Richmond sends his thanks," the doctor said. He passed me an envelope filled with bank notes. "That's the first bit of the number you gave me."

I used every plate I'd brought. Trees, workmen resting, the mayor urinating while standing atop a fresh stump—each soliotype, no matter how flawed motion might make it, negated a bit of my debt. The light failed and Victor and I sat on a felled cypress's fat trunk. He'd brought a jar of beer with a piece of waxed paper tied over its mouth. The sunset burned in the high limbs of the trees the mayor's men had not yet reached. I felt at peace for the first time since Vivian had told me she loved Spats. We passed the warm beer back and forth. Victor wrote in his little book. I laughed.

"What's the joke?" Victor asked.

I shook my head. "No joke. I'm just happy."

Two trees fell in loud unison. Saws snored and workmen yelled at each other and skipped away from falling limbs. Impatient from lack of forward motion, Wagasuc directed men in from the fringes to form a wedge. It looked as though he aimed to cut a path to the lake.

"This"—Benton pointed to the mess of stumps and scattered limbs—"makes me happy."

<p

He came back to the studio with me to see how the soliotypes would turn out. I held little hope for any but the posed portraits, but it didn't matter. I'd made Wagasuc into a fool and Richmond would pay me for the service. Beer filled my belly and I sang along with Benton as we walked along Toulouse.

Of the three dozen soliotypes more than I had guessed held clear images. The mayor's presence seemed to guarantee a good portrait. Even the picture of him urinating came out well. He looked as if he were a magician, an arc of sparkling water coming from his fist.

"This certainly will get him votes," I told Victor.

The doctor laughed and sorted through the other plates. Most were ruined by motion. Falling trees looked like opened fans, men swinging axes were no more than ghosts above their waists. I put the seven decent views in a row—Wagasuc before his troops, Wagasuc beside the tree upon which the date was written, Wagasuc urinating, and four plates of Wagasuc and various men standing atop horizontal trees wearing the happy grins of giant-killers.

"I'll need to give him at least these three to keep him happy." I took the first two and the last from the line. "I'm sorry the rest are botched, but he clearly is a dullard in these four."

Victor looked confused. He held up a soliotype in which two trees fell toward each other, twin triangles of motion. "Botched? This is amazing."

I returned his confused look. "That's ruined by the trees' movement."

Victor studied the plate. "The movement doesn't ruin it. Quite the opposite, I think. The motion you've recorded goes on forever in the mind of whoever looks at the trees falling."

I took the plate from his hand. "The soliotype is a success only when a moment is preserved in a motionless frame."

Victor picked up another view of falling trees. "What you're describing is an ant in amber, but this is better. This is an ant in a glass-sided box filled with dirt—this is alive."

"An ant in amber is much more beautiful."

"To be sealed in sap is no blessing, Claudie. I think these are beautiful." The doctor waved his hand above the ruined plates like a winner gloating over his cards.

To punish Victor for mocking me, I sent him to deliver Wagasuc's three plates. He also took Richmond the four portraits of the mayor as well a dozen of the ruined views filled with trees.

I paced the room and mimicked Benton. "Beautiful," I snorted at my reflection in the window glass. My reflection sneered in agreement of Victor's ignorance. I looked over the falling trees to assure myself that I was right and Benton was indeed wrong. A portrait of a tree, if framed correctly—alone, the trees behind it so vague they appear to be a solid backdrop—leads the mind to picture a seed, rain, the yellow disk of the sun, the timid green finger poking from the dirt, a pliant sapling, branches painting stripes of shade which lengthen each year, the song of a saw, the concentric circles from which age can be determined. The portrait does all this without motion; the lack of motion puts the mind in motion. Soliotypes which show trees falling and men swinging axes stop the brain's workings. All you can think of are falling trees, men with axes. Victor was wrong—motion kills imagination.

I left the trees forever falling, walked up the path to the house, and found the doors locked, bolts thrown. Two back teeth came loose from their sockets when I squeezed my jaw with my hand. I went to the front room's window and looked in. The lead savages and Redcoats grinned down from their shelf.

The crushed-shell path was so luminous below the full moon

that it drew clouds of insects which rose before me. I searched for Remy's bedding and found it stuffed under a corner cabinet in the developing room. His blanket was patterned with mildew. The rot made me realize with a start how long ago it had been that he and Madeleine and Millicent and I had acted out Shakespeare. I tried to sleep on a rug spread across the studio's floor, but the room was like an oven. I covered the courtyard's cobbles with the rug and lay watching the fire-flecked exhaust from the tar barrels stripe the sky. Cannons boomed like big drums. Below them I heard the long ringing of ten, then eleven, then midnight, then the single stroke of one.

I walked to Marais. Millicent's bed was empty. I lit the lamp and the lime-washed walls gleamed. Save the nude which smiled from the windowsill, no keepsakes cluttered the small, bright cell. My neck loosened on its pivot. I took the portrait from the sill and looked at Millicent trapped in amber.

♏

Sunlight woke me and for a moment I did not know where I was. The glare washed the color from everything in the room. Shadows had edges like knives, my wedding ring was a loop of fire around my finger, then objects came into focus.

I found Vivian stabbing at a needlepoint in the front room, striped by light coming through half-closed shutters. "I have to make your portrait," I told her. She shook her head. I yanked her from her chair and she jabbed her finger with the needle. She tried to squirm away and I did not realize how rough I was being until later when I saw the bruise encircling her arm in the portrait I forced her to stand for.

Vivian gave up and I pulled her down the hall and out onto the crushed-shell walk. A short line was waiting before the studio door. Two men sat atop a coffin.

"There will be no portraits today," I announced.

One woman tried to flag me with the numbered card I'd given her the day before, but I pushed past and slammed the studio's door in her face. Vivian stood in her nightgown and rubbed her arm and sucked the finger she'd pricked, her eyes on her feet while I opened the shutters. The men had moved the coffin into the courtyard's shade and were eating bright wedges of watermelon. The rest of the line had disappeared. I took a card and wrote the date on its back.

"Raise your dress and hold this before your stomach," I instructed.

She pulled up her skirts and I filled the frame with the stretched skin of her round belly. The ample light made the exposure short and Vivian left as soon as I let go of my breath.

The soliotype made her belly look like a piece of fruit, the knob of her navel a clipped stem. I turned the portrait on its side hoping to make it look more like a plum, a pear, anything but a child which might not be mine growing inside of my wife.

Someone knocked. "I'm not making portraits today," I said, trying to see a mango.

"But I am oh so pretty," Victor chirped in falsetto, then giggled in the same register.

I couldn't smile. The doctor, embarrassed, coughed. "I've two invitations to deliver, one silly, one serious: Richmond has rented a vacant shop on Canal and next week he aims to open a show of the soliotypes you made of the trees."

I nodded. "The other?"

Benton seemed perturbed by my lack of interest in the show. "Felix is to be buried tomorrow at noon."

My heart sank. "Felix is dead?"

"No, no. This is the silly one," he explained. "He longs for a woman—"

"Emily Hulbert."

"His claim has always been that she's killed him by refusing him. He's had every doctor in New Orleans certify his death—I've done so twice—but this method of courting seems to have done little to persuade Miss Hulbert. So he's down to his last trick. A grave has been cut in the Jewish burying ground—I can't imagine what was required to get such a thing done—and he claims he'll be buried in it tomorrow. Emily is the only one who can stop the fool. You are to record the event and I'm to be on hand in case a true certification of death is needed."

Victor grinned and shook his head. "Women drive men insane."

I heard a calliope hoot from the river while I stood unable to find a single word.

♪

When I arrived at the cemetery, Felix, two gravediggers, and a small crowd of Felix's friends were sitting on the edges of the hole, their feet dangling. Water pooled in the bottom of the grave and stank of the seeping rot of neighboring graves. Felix was flushed from drink. He climbed into his coffin when he saw the camera. Through clenched lips he commanded I make his memorial.

Benton ambled down the avenue of sepulchers, reading inscriptions with a smile. He bent to yank a weed, then hailed the group as if surprised to find us there. There were birds in the trees, a bottle was passed, the sun bleached the funerary marble until it was hard to feel glum. I replaced the plate holder while the doctor put his ear to Felix's chest and pronounced giggling Felix dead.

Emily's buggy was the first in a row of buggies filled with ladies wearing gay hats. Vivian sat beside Emily, both of them frowning. The drunks quieted and stood aside to allow the women to pass.

"This is stupid," Emily told Felix. "I will not marry a fool, and this is a fool's performance."

Felix moved a single finger and on the cue one of the gravediggers stepped to the box and covered it with the lid. He hammered the first nail, then Emily yelled "Quit." She bent and hissed at the coffin, "You'll die—truly die—if you don't give this up."

No noise came from within and the digger took up where he'd left off. Once the lid was secure, he and his partner lowered the coffin into the grave. It settled in the putrid mud with a wet kiss. The women stood below the small shade of their parasols on one side of the hole, the men held their hats on the other.

Stanley Roberts was the only man in a black coat, so he unknotted his tie and turned his shirt collar backward. "Cupid's arrow nicked a wee deep." Snorts and chuckles came from both sides of the grave. The fake priest tossed a clod of dirt which hit the box with a bang that silenced them all. Emily tipped toward the hole and Vivian pulled her back. "Don't," I heard my wife tell her.

I expected to hear someone quickly call Felix's bluff, expected to hear the noise of his fists pounding on the lid. I heard neither. The two diggers had been leaning on their shovels, bored by the theater, but they came to life when that first handful was thrown and set to filling the grave with vigor. "He must have paid them well. They're doing a good job," Benton observed, then laughed nervously.

Smiles faded slowly, the men's first, as the pine box began to disappear. Emily looked as if she were going to swoon. Vivian held her arm and chanted "Don't." The diggers' progress was quick. Women closed their parasols and cut glances at each other. Men licked their lips, put their hats on, rubbed their palms on the fronts of their trouser legs. Benton stood beside me at the grave's foot and watched as the last blond mote of coffin wood was covered. "Fool," I said through my teeth.

Emily yelled "Stop," and the men did. Victor and I jumped down and dug with our hands. The diggers followed us into the grave and reversed their work with a fury that showed the fear they must have felt while they buried a living man, good pay or not. Miss Hulbert wept at the grave's edge. Vivian stood scowling down at us. Victor hit wood first, and soon we cleared the lid. One of the gravediggers prized it up with the edge of his shovel and Felix was revealed, dirty and pale, but sputtering and alive. He looked up, and we followed his stare. The powder on Emily's face was furrowed by tears. Beside her Vivian shook her head.

"She agreed?" Felix asked in a weak whisper.

The doctor climbed into the box and again put his ear to Felix's breast, heard the heart's knock, and went against his original opinion.

The crowd faded as soon as it was clear that Felix was alive. Only the two gravediggers, Stanley Roberts with his collar still backward, myself, Victor, Vivian, Emily, and the risen corpse remained. Felix demanded a portrait be made. His smile was so huge he looked mad. Stripes of dirt that had fallen between the cheap box's boards ran across his shirt. The back of his trousers, jacket, and hair were slick and dark with the grave's nasty water. He put his arm around Emily; she looked as if she'd been assaulted. Felix pulled her to the buggy and took up the reins, grinning like he'd won the horse, the buggy, and Emily by guessing where a wheel of fortune would stop.

Vivian stood on the grave's lip and looked down at the empty coffin. "Why do you do this?" she asked us all. The gravediggers and the pretend priest traded a guilty look. Roberts turned his collar and knotted his tie. "What's to be gained by making a woman miserable?" None of us had an answer. She kicked dirt down into the open casket.

✑

August's sun boiled the wet air until it shuddered. September took up where August left off and it seemed summer would never end. A line of coughing Fever victims and silent survivors carrying their dead formed before the studio's door well before dawn. The *Picayune*'s headline rose to an even 1,000, then continued to grow. Work filled my days. After the light failed and I sent home the line's tail I spied on Vivian while she ate, wrote letters, read books. Through a knothole I watched her bathe and was always startled by the growing sphere of her belly.

I saw less and less of Victor Benton. Susana was growing larger as well, and between her care and the needs of the poor coughing up black vomit our time together was limited to quick, chance meetings in coffeehouses. What we spoke of was dull and safe—a trained dog said to be able to count to fifty was a favorite subject. I never mentioned the child inside my wife or the fact that my hands had begun to shake gently.

The heat broke records. I slept so little I began to see phantoms in the corners of my eyes. Men stepped from behind trees in the courtyard, but they were not there when I turned to greet them. One fork seemed to be three until I looked at the three and distilled them to one. I heard my name called out when I was alone in the street. Often I worried I'd said something non-sensical to a portrait sitter, a calm face no assurance I hadn't. I began to speak slowly, listening to each word, English sounding new again, sounding to me like it had when I'd recited Milton to Mrs. Smithe. I lost another tooth. Only the foremost dozen remained. One day I thought I saw Millicent leave the house.

7 September 1845
I went today to spy on Claude and when I looked into the frontroom window I thought I saw the reflection of my eyes in the window glass until the eyes blinked and I realized the sash was up. Before I could step down the girl grabbed my collar. I expected her to yell but instead she whispered I am afraid of him. I slapped her hand away and she said He hears voices when it is silent and sees things that are not there. The blue circles of pregnancy rounded the girl's eyes. I told the girl You have brought this upon yourself and she nodded and turned from the window. She is so large with the child that she walks clumsily. I could not find Claude in any window.

11 September 1845
It was too hot for sleep so I went to a café that stays open all night where there is a man who will buy me cakes and beer if I sit with him in the courtyard and let him feel my legs under the table. Claude was asleep in my bed when I returned. His shirt was soaked with sweat and he smelled as if he had not bathed for days. The backs of his hands and his wrists were covered with numbers written in blue ink and sores he had torn with his fingernails. Pinched his nose with the fingers of one hand

and covered his mouth with the palm of the other. He did not struggle and the sucking against my palm grew weaker and weaker but when his eyes opened and he looked up at me I jumped back and watched his chest fill with a shuddering breath. Claude was light as a child and I did not stop to rest as I carried him. The girl opened the door so quickly I am sure she was waiting behind it. Carried Claude through the house and dropped him onto the bed and told her I will come tomorrow and stay with you until the baby is born. She took my hand and kissed it and I patted her head like she was a dog. Claude curled and snored.

♔

$\widetilde{T}$HE PICAYUNE'S TALLY headline added only one or two a day, and one morning it was replaced by much calmer news of foreign assassinations and a slave rebellion in the Indies. The announcement of Richmond's show of my soliotypes was offered in larger type than the number of dead.

He'd rented an empty shop two doors down from where my big studio had once been. A pair of ladies with prim mouths stood at the entrance distributing a pamphlet Victor had written. The little books offered a comment for each of my soliotypes. A single long shelf ran along the left wall, followed the back wall, then turned and came back along the right. Views I'd made for the Howards were mixed in with the blurred views of falling trees and a few of the views I'd made for Victor to use to lure Susana south. Midway along was the portrait I'd made of Felix in his coffin; the pamphlet identified him as yet another innocent victim of Mister Jack. I laughed when I saw him and received angry looks from those around me. I moved

with the crowd and read Victor's hysterical prose. Ladies blot-
ted tears, men huffed behind their mustaches. Those unable to
read the tract were confused. The ugliness of the soliotypes
did not move them, it was the same ugliness they'd walked
through to get to the show. When Victor noticed the illiter-
ates' puzzled faces, he began to read aloud from his pamphlet.

Riley Richmond stood at the end of the horseshoe of my
views shaking all hands and agreeing that something must be
done. He did not recognize me. "The artist!" he yelled when I
introduced myself. Heads turned to us. Victor quit his recitation. Richmond would not let go of my hand. He raised it inside
his as if I'd just won an election and told the room, "This is the
man who made these pictures, the man we have to thank for
bringing us the truth in these pictures." There was polite
applause. "Bow," Richmond demanded from the side of his
mouth. I bent slightly at the waist; Richmond put his hand
between my shoulders and pushed my bow deeper.

"I need my money now," I told him when he let me up.

He smiled. "Your money?"

"Benton told you the figure I required to make Wagasuc look
like a fool. Wagasuc has been made a fool. I want my pay."

"A letter from a surgeon named Redgrave convinced the
mayor to cut down those trees. You made some pictures of that
asinine act. I paid more than a fair price for those pictures. The
price you sent with Victor was absurd. Why would I pay that
for *pictures?*"

Victor saw me opening and closing my fists and crossed the
room.

"Your savior refuses to pay me," I told the doctor.

"You've been paid. Victor, did you give him the money for
the pictures of the trees?"

The doctor nodded. "There is the balance," he reminded Richmond. "I gave you a note with the amount—"

Richmond held up his hand. "I would never do such a thing." He spoke so that he could be clearly heard. People turned from the soliotypes. "If you two men have conspired to hurt my dear friend Orion Wagasuc in any way, then I'll see you punished, and I certainly won't pay your blackmail."

Two toadies stepped up. In unison one pushed Victor and one pushed me. We staggered backward in lockstep. After each shove they raised their fists like pugilists. Faces crowded the window hoping to see a fight. "Come on, woman," the toady shoving Victor said. He cocked his hands and shuffled his feet, gave the air a weak punch. The doctor giggled at him, then shot out his left fist and sent the fool to his arse. His partner hit my mouth in revenge. When I skipped back to dodge the next punch Victor stepped where I had been and broke the second man's nose. I heard the bone's wet snap and felt a sympathetic pain. I thought I tasted the blood pouring from his flattened face, but it was my own blood—he'd knocked loose one of my few remaining teeth.

Victor grabbed my hand and we ran until our laughter knocked the wind from our lungs. We ended up at the river, and we sat on bales of cotton. Victor shook his head while we wound down like toys. "The cheat," he said when he could speak. "The filthy cheat."

I thought of the number on the back of the card Norman, Moellhausen, and Pinistri had given me. Richmond's betrayal made that number seem even more unreal, no more than a wish the three men hoped would come true. How could I take a wish seriously? I stood and kicked the cotton. "I'd like to see them take me before a judge and demand I grant them a wish." I gave the bale two more kicks, one for each creditor.

Victor roared laughter so loudly it brought stevedores and sailors to witness. I laughed too, and then the men who'd come to see what was so humorous joined us, a chorus of laughing men, a dozen of us lost in laughing.

<p>

The perpetual queue of people waiting to have their portraits made had again formed before the studio's door. They'd waited while the doctor and I sat by the river and laughed and I became more and more sure the number on the card was a joke.

First in line was a pretty girl carrying a toy-sized coffin. A loop of rope had been nailed to each side and she held the coffin by these handles. The girl looked far too young to be a mother, far too calm to be the mother of a child now dead. I wondered if this too was a joke until she opened the box and I saw the infant. It was no bigger than the doll its dress must have come from. The girl looked out the window while I made the portrait.

"This is your child?" I asked when I handed her the soliotype.

She nodded. "I need to send this picture to the mother of him what gave me it. He lit out when he found out he gave me it, and his mother's to give me one hundred dollars to make up for him, but I need to show her a picture before she will." She tipped the portrait so the plate's surface showed her face and she fixed a stray twist of hair. I slapped the girl's face. Her mouth made an O from which no noise came.

"Filth," I said to her.

She calmly picked up her boxed baby and turned to go. I shoved her from behind and she fell into the man standing at the top of the line. "You're all filth," I told them. I bent and filled my fist with crushed shell, then flung it at their faces. The line scattered.

Norman, Moellhausen, and Pinistri stood picking bits of shell from each other like monkeys grooming. "Our money," Moellhausen said. "We've waited too long." Norman and Pinistri nodded agreement.

"Where am I supposed to get this money?" I couldn't restrain a giggle.

Norman cut a look at Pinistri, Pinistri cut a look at Moellhausen, Moellhausen cut a look at Norman. "You said you'd have it," Pinistri explained.

"Do you want to know what I have for you?" I asked, taunting them with the surprise. Three heads nodded, three mouths curled with nervous smiles. I opened my mouth and jerked out a tooth, then another, then a third. Three jaws dropped. "Hold out your hands," I demanded. Only Pinistri offered his palm. I dropped the teeth into it, then spat blood. "My flesh, my blood— it's all I have to offer, kind sirs." Norman looked as if he were about to be ill. Pinistri shook the teeth from his hand and vigorously wiped his palm with a kerchief. Moellhausen led his partners to the street.

I took a saber from the umbrella stand and cut the air. The camera's lens flashed like a blinking eye. In that Cyclops eye I watched myself advance. I cut a wound from what would have been cheek to what would have been chin, then held the blade's tip before the glassy eye. I could not do it.

I wondered how fast news of my insanity would travel. Not fast enough to ruin me as well as I wished to be ruined, I feared. I took a piece of chalk and wrote OUT OF BUSINESS across the studio's door in large letters.

⌒

I found Felix before a platter of oysters. He tipped one over his teeth, then smiled and took a pearl from his mouth. He held it in his palm and offered it to me. "For you, madman, a replacement tooth."

"Already you've heard?"

He nodded and sucked another oyster from its shell. "Walls, keyholes, men owed money, women who've been insulted." He raised another shell to his lips.

"Ruin me," I told him.

Felix downed his beer in three long swallows, then looked at me as if he believed the rumors of my madness.

"I've done my best to ruin myself, but I need you to finish me. Report I'm insane, dangerously insane. Tell all that I hit a woman who came to me for a memorial of her dead infant. I want to be thoroughly ruined."

Felix's mouth opened and closed, but no words came out. It was the first time I'd seen him unable to speak. "Ruin you?" he finally managed.

It was not friendship, I knew. He'd ruined his friends before. What he could not fathom was being asked for such a curse.

"Why do you want to be ruined?"

"I'm weak. Today I know without a doubt that I should never make a likeness of any simpleton able to find my door and pay my rate. Tomorrow some fool will come begging for a portrait to give to the girl who will not marry him and my resolve will fail."

Felix's cheeks went red with embarrassment, the second novelty of the conversation. "I'll do it," he agreed.

℘ ℘ ℘

Plate 47—Pregnancy Portrait of Vivian Marchand, September 12th, 1845. Half-plate daguerreotype.

Plate 48—Memorial Portrait of Vivian Marchand, *September 20th, 1845. Sixth-plate daguerreotype.*

PL. 47 CONTINUES CLAUDE'S loving record of his wife's short life. This portrait, the last of what must have been a series documenting her pregnancy, is simple: the entire frame filled with Vivian's bare stomach, a hand-lettered card recording the date held just below the navel, the backdrop unpatterned and dark to provide striking definition to her light belly.

While he was documenting the coming of his child, Marchand was also involved in recording the yellow fever epidemic. It must have been heartening for Claude to return to vital life after a day photographing death, crushing for him to lose Vivian. She died in childbirth; Victor Benton was unable to save her. Vivian's obituary notice and the engraving on her tomb are the same: "A Loving Mother Who Sacrificed Herself for Her Child."

Pl. 48 is out of character for Marchand. It is a sixth-plate, the smallest and cheapest he offered, a size he almost never used for memorials. The lighting is bad, the angle odd. Unlike the usual careful posings in which an attempt is made to make the dead look as if they are napping, Vivian's face still retains the pain of her passing.

SUSANA BENTON DIED giving birth prematurely to a daughter who did not live long enough to be named. A woman I did not recognize brought the news along with a summons to come and make Susana's memorial. I left empty-handed and found Victor surrounded by books, the floor of his small library covered with open volumes. He pulled more from the shelves while talking to himself, writing notes alongside columns of text he quickly located. The doctor returned again and again to a thick folio on his desk. Its vividly colored plates showed a dozen perspectives of a woman with a child inside. Mother and baby were flayed, their ivory bones, bright ribbons of muscles, the red shapes of their hearts and lungs and livers, and the sewers of their bowels there for Victor to study. He circled a small illustration in a pamphlet, made a sketch on the blank back of the paper-bound booklet. "There was nothing I could have done," he told his figuring, then looked up at me. "There was nothing I could have done," he repeated. "Where's your camera?"

His face tightened like a hand closing into a fist when I told him I could not make Susana's memorial.

"You've returned to that stupidity?" He tugged his wallet from a pocket and fanned a handful of notes. "How much for a portrait of my dead wife?" His voice was pulled thin by anger.

"This is not about money, not about the dead. I would not make her portrait if she were alive."

Victor grabbed my throat. His surgeon's hands were long-fingered and delicate-looking, but the thumbs which pressed into my windpipe were strong and sharp and quickly stopped my breath. I was ready to let him kill me. I kept my arms at my sides and did not struggle. The doctor pulled me close and put his mouth to my ear. "Remember," he hissed, "remember that when you needed money to buy a wife you dropped this nonsense and made hundreds, maybe thousands of portraits of the dead, but when your friend asked for a single of your precious soliotypes, you refused."

I fell sputtering to the rug when he let me go.

$\wp$

I drank whiskey until I could feel the brown fluid push out my blood and fill my heart. The lids of my eyes had a picture painted on their backs, a picture of Susana Benton skinned, and I sat in the developing room trying to keep them open, the sight so awful I retched each time the whiskey pulled an eyelid down. I drank myself to blindness and slept with my face pressed to the floor's cool stones. Their texture was embossed on my skin when I woke.

Peter, when he left with my coat, had taken the hammer with which I'd smashed Daguerre's things. The one I held was from the bottom of my prop box, a relic from a short craze of businessmen posing like carpenters—building the future, they claimed. The prop hammer felt inappropriate until its head cut a clean hole through the side of the first of the three cameras I lined up to destroy.

I heard the high cries of the kittens before I heard steps on the shell gravel. Vivian came through the studio's door holding a black one before her big belly, its pink mouth open wide. Millicent followed holding the same cat. The two women stood side by side, the identical mewling kittens twisting in their hands. Millicent wore a yellow frock Vivian had worn before she'd started dressing in her mother's clothes. Vivian's kitten clawed its way up her dress front and perched on her shoulder. She lifted the cat down and stroked under its chin, then looked up and stared at me silently for a long moment. "Make our portrait."

My entire life was before me. If Vivian had not asked me to make a portrait, I would have demanded they sit and let me make one. I put the hammer back in the box of hats and books, set up an undamaged camera, watched them pose, and removed the lens cover. In moments I held a likeness of my two wives holding kittens, the little cats silhouettes against their light laps.

Millicent plucked the portrait from my hand when I came from the developing room, and she and Vivian walked up the path and into the house.

℘

Through a rip in the kitchen's curtain I watched them eat dinner; I watched them play cards by pushing aside a statuette of Athena and setting my nose on the front room's windowsill. A row of portraits stood on the mantle: Vivian and Millicent and the kittens, Millicent's nude, the memorials of Mr. and Mrs. Marmu. Vivian trumped and Millicent dealt a new hand, the little cats fighting a ball of paper under the table.

I put my eye to a knothole that provided a view of the tub-room and watched Millicent heat the kettle and pour water into Vivian's bath, then drop her dress and join her in the tub. They slept in the same bed like sisters, their arms around each other.

I fell asleep on the shell path below the bedroom window and dreamt of the flaming fish I'd seen swimming in the middle of the Atlantic so many years before. My arm was absurdly long, I reached over the rail and my fingers dragged in the water. The burning fish took them like bait and Vivian's yelling woke me. Millicent pulled aside the curtain and looked down on me. "Get Benton," she said, then turned when Vivian called her name.

Susana's coffin was where the couch had been the day before. Benton sat beside it looking at his reflection in the polished wood, his hands one atop the other in his lap. Curls of steam came from a cup of tea on the floor by his foot. I saw my face float beside his. "Vivian is giving birth and we need you to come and help," I told him.

Victor did not turn. He spoke to my reflected face. "Yesterday my wife dies in childbirth and when I ask you to make a portrait of her you refuse. Today you come to tell me your wife is giving birth and you need my help." When he looked up I saw the odd curls of his reappearing beard. "Where's the joke, Claudie?"

"It might be Spats's child."

Millicent met us in the hall, her hands and dress covered with gore. "It's turned inside her and it's stuck," she told Benton. Vivian shrieked. "It's your son causing her that pain," Millicent said to me.

I took the nude and the portrait of the two women and the cats from the mantel while Millicent and the doctor headed toward the noise.

Vivian's hair stuck to her head, her face red as a drunk's. She looked at me and said, "It cannot be called Francis, William, or Claude." Then her head snapped back and she loosed a yell that rang in my ears even after she stopped. Victor's hands were between her legs. He talked to himself, reciting from freshly memorized texts. "Guide gently," he said, and my son slipped from Vivian slick as a fish. Victor cut the cord and handed him to Millicent. I watched her carry the baby from the room.

"Oh no, oh no, oh no," Benton said behind me. I turned to see him put his mouth to Vivian's and blow wind into her lungs. She did not stir. He put his ear to her chest. "Damn it," he swore, then covered his face with his bloody hands. The blood on the sheet was dark as spilled wine and though I knew she was dead I stared at her hands, waiting for one to move.

"Do something more," I told Benton. I touched her foot.

He held his hands over his ears and shook his head.

"Do *something*," I pleaded.

Millicent came back with the clean baby, laid him down beside Vivian and took a step back, then saw the doctor's paint-ed face and snatched the child from the bed and put him in my arms. He was as limp and soft as a big cat. I feared I would drop him and pulled him against my chest.

"Pick a name," Millicent said.

"Victor," I tried.

"Please no," the doctor begged.

The baby in my hands was as transparent as the baby in Victor's book, his bones visible like a paper lantern's delicate framework. Fearing the child would die before I could think of another I called out the next name I could bring to mind and named my son for Daguerre. His mouth opened and closed, but he did not make a sound until I let out a wail and he joined me in keening.

ℐ

Victor washed his face and stammered the last rights, then bolted, coughing to obscure his crying. I did not move Vivian's head from where it had twisted to the side, did not jerk the pillow from her fingers and place her hands in a neat pile across her heart, did not pull her mouth with my thumbs until she smiled. Millicent covered her with a clean sheet and I made the portrait. I yanked the plate holder free, then kicked the stand out from under the camera. The box hit the floor with a bang but did not break. I kicked it against the wall and kept kicking it until it splintered and collapsed. The lens rolled across the room and under the bed. I got down on my hands and knees and fetched it, then hammered it with a brass elephant until it shattered.

Millicent knelt beside me and wiped the sweat from my face with the hem of her dress. "Now make a portrait of your son," she told me.

"I can't," I told her. "I shouldn't have made the one I just made. I promised myself."

The baby whimpered and Millicent peeked at Vivian's corpse,

then quickly looked away. "Your promise is foolish—make his portrait."

I looked at the baby in her arms and said again, "I can't."

"Foolish," she told me, then turned and left the room.

The baby was on the couch when I made my way back to the studio and Millicent was at work. She put a box on a chair and a top hat on the box, set the last of my cameras on its tripod, slid in the ground glass, made adjustments. From the developing room she got a plate in a holder. She took the hat from the box and put it on, lifted the baby from the couch and put him where the hat had been.

"Hold him," she told me.

"I can't." I started to back toward the door.

"You can't, you can't, you can't. Claude, stop being a fool and come and hold this baby."

I had expected him to be cool, he was so white and smooth, but the head which filled my palm was hot. I knew the pulse I felt in my fingertips was my own, but I let myself believe it was both of ours, our blood synchronized. "His eyes," she said, "Pull open his eyes." With my first and ring fingers I gently peeled back his lids and held them until she stepped away from the camera.

Millicent lifted my son and took him into the developing room. I stood watching the narrow door. To stop their motion I put my hands under my arms and held my elbows close to my sides. When she came out I held out my shuddering hands for the portraits and she gave me the baby. She looked at the solio-types, then closed their cases and laid them on the table. The goathide covers were glossy, one black, one red, and I longed to open them and see the portraits inside. The baby fussed, threw weak punches.

"Please take him," I begged.

"He's not mine to take." She said.

Suddenly I felt like I was holding an anvil. "He's too heavy," I told her.

Millicent sighed and let me pass him to her.

Vivian's face was far more dead in the bloodless colors of the soliotype than it had been on her deathbed and the same grays made the baby dead as his mother. I looked up to make sure he still took air. On the other side of the room Millicent stood beneath the top hat watching me, my son sucking her finger.

I set the two portraits on the table, remembered the two in my pockets, then went to my chest and fetched others to add to the queue. The uncased nudes of Peter and Millicent were smaller than the rest. I added Vivian—Vivian with her tongue out, Vivian among the Natchez flowers, the many Vivians I'd made while we pretended to be in Mississippi, the portrait of her spherical stomach. I put Vivian, Millicent, and the cats in line.

Millicent crossed the room and looked.

"These aren't right," I told her.

"True," she agreed.

She turned the two nudes face down and then gently, one by one, she closed the other portraits' covers.

∽

21 September 1845

Dressed the girl in a yellow dress she told me was her favorite and put a cloth over her face to keep away the flies and felt a kindness to her I never felt while she lived and so at the same time I felt this kindness I felt low and mean though I am the one who closed her eyes and dressed her. I tied a sling around my neck and put the baby in it and went looking for Claude though I was not sure I wanted to find him. The baby grew heavy and hungry and I gave up looking.

⌣ℙ

WHILE DUSK LURED strollers into the streets, I walked looking at the portrait of Vivian with her tongue stuck out. Sunset erased the plate. Below a lamp beside a canal I paused and the portrait dropped from my shaking hand and split the water.